FIGHTING

GREEN

Green Family Saga

Book 3

Kate Foley

ISBN 978-1-913224-36-3

Cover design by Jared Shear

Discover other titles by PJ Skinner

The Green Family Saga

Rebel Green (Book 1)

Africa Green (Book 2)

The Sam Harris Adventure Series

written as PJ Skinner

Fool's Gold (Book 1)

Hitler's Finger (Book 2)

The Star of Simbako (Book 3)

The Pink Elephants (Book 4)

The Bonita Protocol (Book 5)

Digging Deeper (Book 6)

Concrete Jungle (Book 7)

Mortal Mission

Written as Pip Skinner

Go to the PJ Skinner website for more info:
https://www.pjskinner.com

Dedicated to my readers.
Without whom there are no books

Chapter 1

Liz Green glared at the podgy hand which had been slapped on the table beside her in the boardroom. For a moment she considered stabbing it with her ballpoint pen. Instead, she rolled her eyes and groaned inwardly as the plump bottom of the dot-com company chairman wobbled uncomfortably close to her face. Oblivious to her exasperation, he flapped his arms around, colouring with exertion as he extolled the virtues of his project. His face lit up with the zeal of a fanatic as he pointed to the slides showing exponential growth projections valuing his company at hundreds of millions of dollars.

She winced as he let slip the billion number. Just one of a long line of hopefuls queuing for finance. *These people have a cheek. This company is worth ten thousand pounds tops, and that's only because their non-executive directors have some skin in the game.*

Outside in the City of London, the sun had slid down the sky and now negotiated with the horizon. The grey buildings surrounding her office block had turned a shade darker and their ugly fluorescent lights were lighting their windows. Flocks of pigeons flapped their fat way through the dirty air. Liz sneaked a look at her watch. *Seven o'clock. It will soon be dark outside. At least I don't have any more meetings today. Maybe I'll slope off home*. A cough made her glance up. *Damn*. Her boss gesticulated at her to meet him after the presentation. She gave him a pleading look, but he held his thumb and forefinger a centimetre apart and drew his eyebrows together. *Short meeting, my foot. Bernie Sternberg wouldn't recognise a short meeting if it sat on his lap and called him Daddy.*

She nodded at him and returned to making caustic notes on the company's presentation, trying to recall the date when the first dot-com company had come to them for funding. Until then she had enjoyed her job, despite the drawbacks of being the only female on a testosterone fuelled trading floor. *February 1998. That was the first dotcom they funded.* Mike Morton, an entrepreneur with an idea for a pet food website – Food4Pets. His business partner, an old Etonian called Edward Beckett, had left him in the lurch, and he had come to them for backing. For some reason, her boss, Bernie, had been entranced by the Cockney entrepreneur's line of patter, and, ignoring Liz's advice, they had floated the enterprise which exploded onto a rabid market.

Mike soon sold his holding for a fortune and left the business in the hands of new management. Pretty good timing considering the fact Food4Pets had entered deep financial trouble after blowing most of their funding on expensive offices and Lamborghinis for the directors. Bernie had refused to raise further cash from his investors and the company had gone to the wall, to be replaced by the next latest thing.

Liz's bonuses increased in size, and champagne replaced milk in the office fridge, but she struggled to enjoy the bonanza. Her skills were not required after greed began to govern all decisions taken on the select of projects for funding. At first, she had objected to the financial spreadsheets with no assets other than hopes and dreams. But the men on her trading floor realised they were missing out on lucrative pay days, and her objections were ignored.

'So, what did you think of the presentation?' said Bernie, offering her a glass of whisky in his office. She held up her hand to refuse.

'You don't want to know what I think,' she said, smiling.

He took a swig of his drink.

'Probably true,' he said. 'But it will make us a fortune.'

He put his drink down and started to draw a game of noughts and crosses in the condensation on the glass table top.

'Listen,' he said. 'I know you hate all this dot-com stuff, but it won't last for ever. We have to make hay while the sun shines. Look at Food4Pets. They sank without a trace, and might soon take most of their friends down with them. Proper research will come back into fashion after the crash.'

'Let's hope so,' said Liz.

She took a taxi home through the rainy streets gazing out at the grimy pavements and the rubbish bins surrounded by their soggy overflow of coffee cups and sandwich wrappers. She resisted the temptation to call Sean on her mobile phone, a brick-sized entity that filled her handbag. *What if he was drunk again?* She desperately needed his advice and support, but lately he hadn't been in a fit state to give it. *Maybe a hot bath and a glass of Blue Nun will calm me down. It's not like anything horrible has happened. It's just life.*

Liz let herself into the apartment and found Sean watching the news with a glass of wine in his hand. He gazed at her as she came in and his face lit up.

'Great, you're home. Any chance of something to eat?' he said.

'I haven't managed to get to the supermarket this week. Do you want to order a takeaway?'

'No, I'm not that hungry. I'll just have some crisps.'

He took a handful from a bag and crunched on them. Liz poured herself a glass of wine.

'These are too salty. I wish we could buy Taytos here,' she said, helping herself to a crisp. 'I still miss them, and Conran's cider. Sometimes I think I'd like to go back to live in Ireland.'

Sean snorted.

'We escaped from the priests and the hypocrisy years and years ago. Why would you want to go back? You're not even Irish.'

'It's not the place we left. Things change. I'm so tired.'

And you're not the man I left with either. She sipped the sweet wine and swallowed a sigh.

'We're all tired. Work's a total slog. Maybe we should go away for the weekend?'

'Not that sort of tired.'

'I don't understand. You have a great job, a fantastic flat, money to burn. What's wrong with that?'

'I'm burned out. I can't take it anymore. Since the dot-com boom started it's all got worse; the long hours, the misogyny, the pointlessness.'

'And me?'

You're a drunken pain in the arse. Why can't I say it out loud?

'Forget it. I'm just tired. I'll feel differently tomorrow.'

'Let's go to bed then.'

'Can you go home tonight? I need some time alone,' said Liz, putting a placating arm around his waist. 'Please don't get annoyed.'

Sean sighed.

'Women,' he said, grabbing his coat. 'See you tomorrow.'

'You're going now?'

'The bars are still open.'

Sean slammed the door on his way out, something he had started to do more frequently. It brought back long forgotten memories of Sean's father, Brian O'Connor, a violent drunk. She went over to the window and watched Sean weave his way towards the tube station in the lemon-coloured street lighting. He walked straight through a large puddle and shook his shoes in bemusement. Liz sighed and looked into a mirror on the wall, putting her hair up in a scruffy bun. It needed cutting into a regulation city bob with sharp edges, signalling the no-nonsense content of its owner's head. Fine lines had started to radiate from her blue eyes and her formerly radiant skin had become a shade of opaque grey with pallid cheeks. She pinched the skin to bring a blush to her face, but only succeeded in making herself look cross.

Why can't I tell him the truth? She had reached the end of her tether with his drinking which he always brushed off with a dismissive 'I'm in control, not the drink'. But worse than that, a looming sense of the inevitable had begun to haunt her whenever he came to see her after a visit to the pub. Lately, she had begun to tiptoe around him as he became more volatile and unpredictable. Even Isabella, her sister, who adored Sean like an extra brother, had noticed the change in both of them.

'You used to be so happy,' she said. 'It's like one of you is having an affair.'

'One of us is,' said Liz. 'The other woman is called booze.'

'Can't you ask him to stop? Or at least slowdown?'

'If you had any idea how many times we've had that conversation, you wouldn't suggest it. Sometimes, he even stops for a while, but then he falls off the wagon and starts where he let off.'

'Maybe you should take a break? It's not healthy for you either.'

'Oh, I gave up trying to drink with him years ago. I don't even like most alcohol.'

'I meant a break from Sean.'

'I know you did. It's tricky, sis. I still love him despite everything.'

And how could I leave him after so many years together? How would I find someone else, when I work a sixty-hour week? Sean has been my comfort blanket for so many years and now it has started to unravel. I don't know what I'm going to do.

Chapter 2

A butterfly landed on Michael Green's knee as he sat outside on the wooden steps which had already been warmed by the sun. He inhaled the aroma from his coffee before taking a cautious sip, and mourned his morning cigarette as he had done every day since giving up smoking. A vulture sat atop the telegraph pole on the dirt road which ran from their small hotel to the main tarred road. The bird fixed its gaze on Michael as he relaxed on the step. Michael looked up and noticed its vigil.

'You'll be waiting a long time,' said Michael, but the bird continued to stare at him as if willing him to drop dead.

The shrill notes of the safari lodge's telephone broke the silence in the lobby. Michael got up, brushing the splinters from his khaki shorts and sloshing coffee on the steps. His heart leapt at the thought of a booking after the much publicised election violence had put tourists off from coming for the last six months. Maybe he would have good news for Blessing when she returned from town with the groceries.

'Hello, Green Safaris, Michael speaking. How can I help you?'

'Ah, Mr Green, at last. You're a hard man to track down.'

'I hope not,' said Michael. 'I spend a fortune on advertising.'

The woman laughed, more of a strangled cough, like someone unused to such frivolity.

'Oh, no, it's not about a booking, although I've always promised myself a visit to Africa before I die. I'm a solicitor. My name's Hilda Manning. I'm acting for the late George Kennedy.'

Michael sighed. *George dead. It didn't seem possible. He had been so full of life, despite being in his eighties.* Tom Green, Michael's father, had called him out of the blue a month ago, his voice hoarse with emotion, and told him that their beloved family friend, surrogate father to Tom, and beloved adoptive grandfather of Liz, Michael, and Isabella Green, had passed away from a stroke. He had dropped dead in his kitchen while washing up, and no doubt listening to the birds squabbling in the apple tree. The carer had found him lying in front of the sink, washing up brush still in his hand, with a surprised look on his face.

'George, yes, of course. I couldn't go to the funeral, finances being what they are…'

He trailed off, ashamed. George's son, Ben, had offered to pay for his ticket, but Blessing wouldn't hear of it.

'It's not like that's the only expense involved with going to England. We just can't afford it, what with the children's new school fees and everything. Anyway, I need you to paint the sheds.'

She had been right, but George's value to the Green family had far surpassed his monetary support. *How many times had he pulled them back from the brink in the early days in Ireland?* Without George, Michael would never have escaped from his ordeals at school in Ireland, and never met Blessing. Michael had sat by himself in the office on the day of the funeral and read the order of service faxed to him by his sister Liz. Blessing had made sure the children didn't disturb him as he mourned his mentor. *So why was the solicitor calling?* George had been well off, but he had a son, Ben, and he had long stopped subsidising the Green family.

'Ben Kennedy told me about your money woes,' said the solicitor. 'He couldn't find your number, so I had to search out your parents in Ireland. Anyway, I'm glad to get hold of you. Do you have a fax number by any chance? I'd like to send you a copy of the will.'

'The will? I'm not sure I understand.'

'George left you a house. Didn't he tell you?'

'A house? Where?'

'In Ireland, I believe. County Kilkenny.'

'Are you sure he didn't leave it to my father?'

'Quite sure. Look, why don't I send you the relevant page of the will, and the codicil with the instructions.'

'Okay, have you got a pen?'

Shortly afterwards, the fax jerked into life, spitting out a few blurred pages which fell to the floor of the lobby coiled into a roll. Michael flattened them out onto the dining table, separating the pages by splitting them with the letter opener. He read them slowly, his excitement increasing. *Holy shit. This isn't a house, it's a mansion.* Blessing drove up in a cloud of dust, and Michael ran outside to help her unload the car. He carried the food through to the kitchen and stacked the perishables into the fridge.

'What's this?' said Blessing, picking up the pages. 'I thought we had a booking, but this is from a lawyer. Please don't tell me we are being sued by a client.'

Michael walked back into the dining room, a spring in his step. He put his arms around Blessing, his hands crossed over her belly.

'It's from a lawyer, but she's more like a fairy godmother than a wicked witch.'

Blessing turned around and narrowed her eyes at him.

'Make sense, husband,' she said.

'George Kennedy left us a house.'

Blessing's eyes opened wide.

'Don't joke with me.'

'I'm not. He did. Honest. Read the fax.'

Michael handed her the relevant page, and Blessing sat on the bench in the window, her legs folded under her. A wave of emotion flooded through him as he gazed at her beautiful profile with its halo of afro hair. He watched her lips move as she read the page with deliberation. Her education had been slip-shod at best, but she had a razor-sharp intellect on which Michael relied. Luckily, their children had inherited both Blessing's brains and her beauty, and were both showing signs of heading for successful careers. She let the page rest in her lap and gave him a shrewd glance. He waited.

'Do you need to decide what to do now?' she said.

'Hilda, the lawyer, told me she'd call for instructions in a day or two.'

'Okay. The place sounds enormous. I'm not sure what I think yet.'

'Neither am I. Let's talk this evening when the children have gone to bed.'

'By the way, I'm meeting Nancy for a coffee this afternoon. Do you need me?' said Blessing.

'No, we don't have any bookings. Go and have fun. I've got to sort out my thoughts anyway.'

After Blessing had left, Michael took out an old box of photographs George had given him when he attended the public school down the road from George's house. He blew the dust from the lid and prised it off. Taking the faded photographs out one by one, he examined them for clues, but he couldn't spot a property in any of them that he hadn't seen before. He lingered over the photographs of George's trips to Ireland, especially the one where George had found out about Michael's appalling treatment in the Christian Brothers' school in Kilkenny. There was one of the whole family on the beach with George and Mrs O'Reilly. Blue stood among them, her long pink tongue lolling out of her laughing mouth. He noticed his pinched face as he sat between Liz and Isabella who were both smiling. His t-shirt hid a multitude of sins that day, but not for long.

He put the lid back on the box and had lifted it into the alcove when the telephone rang again.

'Hello, Green Safaris, Michael Green speaking.'

The line buzzed and clicked.

'Ah, Mick, this is, erm, Dermot Gallagher speaking. I'm calling from Ireland. Can you hear me?'

'Yes, I can, but I have no idea who you are.'

'Oh, right, of course, I'm the solicitor, for the house, you know.'

'The house?'

'Yes, the big house. Up on the hill.'

'Do you mean George Kennedy's property?'

'Yes, that's the one. It's in a desperate state.'

'Is it? I haven't ever seen it.'

'Oh, I wouldn't be bothered with that old place. It's falling down.'

'So why are you calling me exactly?'

'I have an offer for the land, from a local man. He wants to knock down the house and graze cattle there instead.'

Michael smiled to himself.

'Oh, I had no idea the house was in such a parlous state. I nearly wasted my time going to look at it,' he said.

'Well, I just saved you the bother. I can send the papers to you by fax and you can sign it over to me.'

To him? Not to the farmer? Now, that was a slip of the tongue right there. As if I'd sign the house over to someone without even seeing it.

'How much does he want to pay for the land?' said Michael.

'Three hundred pounds. That's the going rate for pasture around here. He'll have to pay to knock down the house himself though so it's a great deal for you.'

'And what's your cut?'

The lawyer cleared his throat.

'Sorry, the lines terrible, I didn't get that.'

Michael smirked to himself.

'How much will you get from this transaction? I doubt it would even cover a phone call to Kenya.'

'That's between me and the client.'

'You'll have to do a lot better than that. I intend to come and see the house myself shortly. I won't be making any decisions before then. So, thanks for the call—'

The line went dead. Michael shook his head. Maybe it got cut off. That would be par for the course in their area. Or maybe the lawyer had realised Michael was on to him. *What was his name anyway? Damn, I should have written it down.*

Chapter 3

As she emerged from the lift, weighed down with her food shopping, Liz heard the telephone ringing inside her flat. She struggled to the door, swearing under her breath as one of the bags split and several carrots rolled out along the hallway. She dumped the bags on the floor and forced the key into the lock. Despite the delay, the phone still rang as she entered and grabbed the receiver from the cradle.

'Hallo?'

'Liz, it's me, Michael. Have you been out jogging or… Oh God don't tell me you were—'

'Don't say it. And no, I wasn't. We don't bother with that anymore.'

'Only on a Saturday night then?'

'Not even that. I'm just back from work, and now my vegetables are scattered across the hall.'

'Do you want me to call you back?'

'No, don't bother. You talk, and I'll round up the miscreants. What's up?'

'George left me a house.'

Liz dropped the carrot she had picked up. It bounced through the grating and down the lift shaft. She heard it hit the sides as it fell to the bottom. She straightened up and leaned against the wall, frowning.

'Our George? Why did he do that?'

'I don't know. I'm as surprised as you; but the solicitor sent me a copy of the will, so I'm pretty sure.'

'But that's wonderful, isn't it? Where is the house?'

'In Ireland.'

'Ireland? I didn't know George had a house there. Why didn't he mention it?'

'I don't know. I believe the property belonged to Lee's parents. He never went back to Ireland after she died. Maybe the memories were too painful. Anyway, Lee's parents left the house to him, and he has left it to me.'

'You don't sound very pleased. I'd be ecstatic.'

'Blessing is far from ecstatic.'

'Oh. But isn't this just what you need? Surely, you can sell the house and raise money for your business?'

'Actually, I wondered if we should sell the business instead. We could move back to Ireland and start again.'

'Are you sure that's wise?'

'Blessing doesn't think so. But I'd like to see the house before we make any decisions.'

'Are you coming over from Kenya?'

'We're considering a trip, but the ticket prices are astronomical.'

'Why don't you let me pay for them? I just got paid a bonus from our last deal. Call it a loan if you like.'

'I couldn't accept your money. Blessing would kill me.'

'You can pay me back when you sell the house, or your business.'

'It certainly is tempting. I haven't seen Mum and Dad for years. We could leave the children with their auntie for a few days.'

'Or longer.'

Michael laughed.

'Or longer. How's our intrepid sister?'

'Oh, you know Isabella. If she isn't in trouble, she goes looking for it. The BBC have sent her to Brazil to make a documentary about spider monkeys.'

'This is all Max's fault. She would never have been so intrepid if he hadn't forced her to go to Sierra Leone to keep her job. Her old boss wouldn't sent her farther than the corner shop.'

'Or Pete's,' said Liz. 'That man was a liability. His influence can't be underestimated.'

Michael laughed.

'She's always been a bit wild. Maybe she'd have escaped from normal life even if she hadn't met him.' He cleared his throat. 'Will you please take some time off and come to inspect the house with me?'

'I don't know. We're so busy at work just now.'

'You're always busy. The firm won't collapse if you take a few days holiday. Bring Sean and we'll have some fun together, like the old days. I'm sure Maeve O'Connor can't remember what her son looks like.'

'She calls him sometimes, but it's true he should make the effort and go home to see her and his sister.'

'And how is Nuala these days?'

'As wild as the hedgerows.'

Michael laughed.

'Somethings never change. The youngest sibling is always the spoilt, wild one. Sean's got Nuala, and we've got Isabella. Listen, I've got to go, but I'll take up your offer of the tickets. Just give me a couple of days to sweet talk Blessing and I'll let you have our plans. I know Sean's still not keen to go home, but you can persuade him.'

Liz sighed.

'That maybe even trickier than persuading Blessing. Anyway, I'll have a go. Keep safe, little brother.'

'Love you, sis.'

Liz stood in the door way holding the receiver, contemplating her split shopping bag before shoving the telephone into her pocket and bending down to herd the carrots into another bag. Back in her flat, she peeled and topped them ready for insertion into her slow cooker with a piece of beef skirt and a couple of onions for the next day's supper. She pulled a frozen pre-prepared meal out of the freezer and shoved it in the oven, setting the timer to ensure she didn't forget it. Then she poured herself a glass of Chardonnay and put her feet up while she watched the news. Soon the smell of fish pie made her wrinkle her nose and hope it wasn't too old to eat. She cooked some frozen peas and squeezed out some ketchup to make the meal more palatable.

Before long, she heard the rattle of a key in the lock and she tensed herself in anticipation. Sean's face appeared around the edge of the door. It lit up when he spotted her on the sofa.

'Ah, there she is. The prettiest girl in London, and she's all mine.'

He strode across the room and crouched in front of her, taking her face in his meaty hands. He gazed into her eyes and sighed. The smell of beer almost knocked her out and she tried not to flinch.

'I still can't believe it, after all these years,' he said, oblivious to her rolled eyes. 'How ever did I persuade you to hang around with me?'

'Must have been magic,' said Liz. 'I always thought Mickey was a leprechaun.'

'Good Irish blarney, more like,' said Sean, burping. 'I've always had the gift of the gab.'

'For God's sake,' said Liz, averting her face. 'You stink like a brewery.'

Sean swivelled to plonk himself beside her on the sofa, a petulant line to his lips.

'Now is that any way to speak to a man who's after declaring his love for you?' he said.

'I'm sorry, but you reek of alcohol. How many pints have you drunk?'

Sean stiffened and turned to her; his eyes narrow.

'Six, not that it's any of your business. Who made you my mother?'

Liz wilted under his glare. *Not another argument about the same thing.*

'I got some news today,' she said.

'Oh, and what was that? Yet another bonus? That's hardly news at this stage, is it?'

It would be, if you got one for a change. Liz swallowed her reply. She had earned more than him for years, but it had never been an issue. Lately he had been spending more of her money than his, from their joint account, which they set up as a prelude to getting married, something that hadn't happened either. Sean did their tax returns and Liz found it easier to let him have access, so she didn't have to think about it. She had her own separate account too, but she hadn't told him about that one. Her rainy-day fund; just in case.

'Michael has inherited a house in Kilkenny.'

Sean's eyebrows flew up.

'You're kidding me.'

Liz shook her head, glad to have distracted him from the usual path of their arguments.

'George Kennedy left a property to him in his will.'

'Stop the lights! Are you serious? Will he keep it?'

'I don't know, but he wants me to come to Ireland and look over the house with him. Blessing will come too.'

'And how will they afford the tickets. I thought they were skint…'

He stared her down. Liz coloured.

'They'll pay me back. Eventually. Anyway, Michael wants you to come too,' she said.

'Me? Why?'

'He wants to see you. Maybe we could visit your mother too. I thought—'

Sean stuck his hand out.

'You thought wrong. I've no intention of going to bogland. My mother can come over here if she wants to see me.'

Liz frowned. Sean was the spitting image of his mother, with his sandy hair and freckles, and piercing blue eyes. His every gesture betrayed him. What a pity he had inherited his father's taste for drink and resentment.

'Well, I told Michael I'd go. And I'm not changing my mind.'

'Fair enough. Give him my regards. I can't believe how times have changed. He used to hate Ireland.'

'But he got over it, and it didn't take him nearly thirty years. Can't you?'

'I said no, and I'm not changing my mind. Have you got something to eat?'

Chapter 4

Liz stood on her tip toes, biting her lip with anticipation as she watched the passengers disgorging from customs into the arrivals lobby of Dublin airport. She hadn't seen her brother Michael for three years, and she had found it hard to deal with his absence from her life. His visits to the British Isles had become infrequent since setting up his safari business with Blessing, mostly due to a shortage of money, and she missed her partner in crime. He was the keeper of many of her childhood secrets and worries, and she of his.

Liz had arrived in Dublin only an hour before, also from London, and her small suitcase sat on the floor beside her. Sean had refused point blank to come, despite last minute appeals by Liz and his mother. He had instead planned a trip to watch Liverpool play Manchester United with his drinking buddies, and he had turned off his mobile phone. She rolled her eyes as she replayed the scene he made when voicing his indignation that she should go to Ireland without him. *He could be so childish sometimes.*

Michael and Blessing Green were due to transfer flights at Heathrow, and Liz crossed her fingers there had been no delays. She shifted from foot to foot, peering at the throng emerging from the bottleneck, searching the crowd for their familiar faces. Finally, they appeared, trailing their suitcases behind them, Blessing wrapped up in a long down jacket and wearing dark glasses. As always, she looked like a film star, and Liz felt dowdy in comparison. She tugged at her old-fashioned tweed coat and mohair scarf, her black hair straightened in its recent bob making her look severe and tired. Michael's eyes widened as he saw her and an affectionate smile creased his features.

'You made it,' he said. 'We're so glad you could come. Aren't we, darling?'

Blessing beamed and gave Liz a warm hug.

'Hello my sister. Habari gani?' she said.

'Nzuri. Habari ya safari?' Liz replied.

Blessing laughed.

'You have not forgotten your Swahili,' she said.

'I don't know any other words,' said Liz, smiling.

'How is Sean?' said Michael, looking around. 'Didn't he come?'

Liz frowned.

'Oh, you know, too busy as usual. He doesn't like going home to Ireland at the best of times.'

'It's funny how we ended up loving Ireland while he hates it,' said Michael.

'It holds only bad memories for him. There's no convincing him otherwise,' said Liz.

'Well, you're here, and we're happy to see you. Let's find the hire car and get going.'

Soon they were driving south to Thomastown through a constant drizzle blurring the familiar emerald landscapes of low hills and hedgerows.

'Ireland should be called Greenland,' said Liz.

'Or Rainland,' said Blessing. 'Doesn't the sun shine in this country?'

'In Ireland. there are three types of weather. It's raining, it has just rained, or it's about to rain, as Mrs O'Reilly used to say,' said Michael.

'Which one was she again?' said Blessing.

'Dear Mrs O,' said Liz. 'Our surrogate grandmother, landlady of Dunbell, our first home here, and scourge of the feckless.'

'It's weird how you ended up with Mrs O'Reilly and George Kennedy, as your adopted grandparents. Were your real grandparents dead already?' said Blessing.

'No, they were still living. They just had Victorian upbringings and stiff upper lips. They weren't cold on purpose,' said Michael.

'I think I preferred George and Mrs O anyway,' said Liz. 'I can't get over George leaving you the house. I didn't know he had another one.'

'Ben Kennedy told me it belonged to his mother's parents, and has been empty for years since they died. George had asked Ben if he wanted the house, but he has no interest in living in Ireland.'

'Neither do I,' said Blessing.

'You haven't seen the place yet,' said Michael. 'You might change your mind.'

The atmosphere in the car chilled a few degrees, so Liz changed the subject.

'Are you sure you can find it? You know what the signposts in Ireland are like.'

'The locals should know,' said Michael.

They arrived in a damp Thomastown after a couple of hours on the road and had a coffee and a piece of barm brack in a local café. The owner's eyebrows shot up when Michael asked her for directions.

'Kilanon Glebe? Are they selling it? We used to play there as children, and when they left the house empty, we… well, you know teenagers.'

Her eyes glistened with malice as she looked them over, dwelling on Blessing's dark skin. *The gossip will be all over town in five minutes.*

'My father knew George and Lee Kennedy as a young man,' said Liz, elbowing Michael. 'We decided to pop in on our way south to see Lee's childhood home.'

'My mother went to school with Lee Kennedy. She always speaks highly of her,' said the woman, her tone softening.

'Maybe we could talk to her about Lee?' said Liz.

'You'd have to go to Kilkenny. Mammy moved there years ago.'

'First things first,' said Michael. 'Can you tell us how to get there?'

'It's easy to find. Just take the road to Kilkenny and it's on the left before you get to Kilanon Church.'

For once the directions were accurate, and soon they turned down a driveway past a small gate lodge almost swallowed by rhododendron bushes.

'Oh, isn't that a beautiful cottage?' said Blessing. 'Do you think it belongs to the house?'

'I'm not sure, but we can ask the solicitor,' said Michael. 'The horse chestnut trees are amazing. Can you imagine the conkers in the autumn?'

As they rounded the corner, the driveway opened out and a stone fountain sat in the middle of it. Behind the fountain, a large house sat on the brow of the hill, its walls covered in creepers. Michael whistled.

'What a house,' he said. 'I never imagined—'

'It's a wreck,' said Blessing. 'Look at the windows. Most of the glass has been smashed.'

Liz stepped out of the car and stood speechless in the drizzle, her hair gleaming as the drops caught the weak sunlight breaking through the clouds. A feeling suspiciously like home wrapped her in seductive tendrils and she shut her eyes to luxuriate in the novel sensation. Behind her, Michael helped Blessing out of the car, ignoring her mutinous muttering, and making encouraging noises.

The house had a classic Georgian, two-storey design built over a raised basement. Sash windows stretched almost floor to ceiling and many of the panes of glass had been smashed. *Teenagers? Vandals.* The walls were straight, except for the western corner which had bow windows on the side to catch the evening sunlight. To the left of the main house a stone archway linked it to an out-building. Through the archway, Liz could see a courtyard surrounded by more single-storey out-buildings. They had peeling yellow-painted arched doors and small glass-paned windows. She could visualise the cobwebs that lurked inside their wooden frames.

Behind her, Liz could hear Blessing grumbling about the state of the house and Michael's gentle replies. He had taken her hand and he brushed a raindrop off her face. Liz turned back to the house. It seemed to reach out to her with ghostly hands pulling her to the front door. She mounted the wide stone steps that swept up to the fan-lit entrance and pushed at the panelled door which opened with a creak. Michael, who had been fumbling with the key, put it back in his pocket.

They stood in the hallway and Liz entered the first room on the right, a large, dual-aspect room with a bay window and a fireplace. She could almost imagine the logs burning and hear the hissing of the resin. The bare boards were stained with glue and treatment against insects but they looked sound. The room on the other side of the hall was of a similar size, without a bay window. At the end of the hall a large kitchen looked out over the same lawn as the dual aspect room, and a utility room made up the ground floor. All of the rooms had recessed shutters, some of which hung off their hinges or had fallen to the floor. The floors were littered with glass shards from the broken windows and several rocks whose purpose was self-evident sat on the boards.

Upstairs, the group found four bedrooms of similar sizes arranged around a small landing. Liz noticed that although several of the upstairs windows were broken too, there was no glass on the floors. *Someone has been up here and broken them from inside; maybe the same someone who opened the front door.* The glass could easily be replaced but the jagged edges looked like wounds. A single bathroom had been tacked onto the back of the house at mezzanine level. It had an old-fashioned cast-iron bath with lion's feet and a decrepit toilet. The tiled floor had lifted and a smell of mould permeated the room.

'Yuck,' said Blessing.

'Nice bath,' said Liz. 'People in London love those.'

'It needs a shower,' said Michael.

'It already has one, from the look of the damp patches on the ceiling,' said Blessing. 'This house has more leaks than my colander.'

Liz didn't comment. The house seemed so familiar to her, as if she had lived there before. She felt jealous of Michael, and his close relationship with George. After all, George had paid for Michael's boarding school in England, while Liz, and their sister Isabella had stayed in the convent in Kilkenny under the rule of the nuns. She had never complained, working day and night to succeed in her Leaving Certificate, counting the days until her schooling finished. Her grades had helped her escape from the suffocating grip of Catholic Ireland in the seventies and ensured she got noticed when she started work at the brokers in London as a temporary secretary.

She returned downstairs and wandered out of the back door into the courtyard. The outbuildings had stone walls with slate roofs. Inside they were dry, with old straw and patches of motor oil on the floors. Liz grunted as she pulled open the door of one of them and then her mouth fell open with astonishment. The front half of a beautiful vintage car lurked in the gloom, balanced on some breeze blocks.

'Wow,' said Michael, coming up behind her. 'It's a De Dion-Bouton. What on earth is it doing here?'

'A what?'

'A De Dion-Bouton with a V8 engine. A type of vintage car.'

'What's it doing in here?'

'From the look of things, they were using the engine on a pulley to saw logs. It's a crime against beauty.'

'It's certainly tragic looking without its back-end.'

'Have you seen the walled garden?' said Michael. 'It's completely overgrown, but I think I spotted some apple and plum trees in there.'

'Where's that?' said Liz.

'If you go out through the archway and turn right, you'll see the entrance.'

Liz ducked under the archway even though there was no danger of hitting it with her head. She approached the walled garden where the grasses had grown waist-high, obscuring the cobbled pathways. The rain had stopped and watery sunshine penetrated the light clouds to shine on the garden. Several fruit trees poked out of the swarth, their jagged-edged leaves and white blossoms forming halos above the grass. Bees hummed their way from flower to flower and birds defended their territories in the bushes. Liz longed for a wooden bench with warm laths to sit on, so she could absorb the atmosphere in the garden.

Blessing appeared at her side.

'We need to get going soon, if we're going to arrive at your parents' house before supper.'

Liz sighed, but she followed Blessing to the car without comment. Michael had a spring in his step, and Liz recognised the signs of a grand plan. *Blessing will never agree to it. He's living in cloud cuckoo land.*

'Isn't it a fabulous house?' said Michael.

'Amazing,' said Liz. 'So full of character.'

'If by character you mean leaks and rodents,' said Blessing.

Michael rolled his eyes at Liz and gave her a thumbs up.

Never in a million years she thought, shaking her head at him.

Chapter 5

The rain fell heavily on the dark limestone pavements of Kilkenny, running down the gutters towards the River Nore, where it joined the rushing water flowing south. Saint Canice's Cathedral's famous round tower loomed tall in the inky night sky as Tom Green welcomed Michael, Blessing and Liz through the front door of their townhouse. Tom took their coats and shook the water from their sopping umbrellas out into the street. He shooed them through to the cosy kitchen where Bea Green hovered between saucepans full of vegetables, monitoring their contents for rebellion as they came to the boil. The saliva inducing aroma of a joint roasting in the oven filled the air, increasing the family's anticipation of a delicious feast for dinner.

'It's so lovely to see you all,' said Bea. 'Christmas has come late this year.'

'So says the woman who decorates in November,' said Tom.

Liz smiled. Their mother loved Christmas, and Tom liked to tease her, but he would still capture the moon for Bea if she asked for it.

Bea had cooked a piece of beef, Yorkshire puddings and roast potatoes in the oven. Michael got his wrist slapped for pinching one of the crunchy roast potatoes before supper.

'Honestly, where did you learn those manners?' she said, before slipping him another.

Silence reigned as they ate, broken only by appreciative noises and the scraping of metal on bone china plates. Tom filled and refilled their glasses with a delicious Italian Chianti 'bought at a bargain price from the local wine merchant'. After a dessert of homemade strawberry ice cream with crisp wafers, they talked for hours about George and Lee, and the early days in Ireland. Blessing soon declared herself tired from the journey and retired to bed, but not before giving Michael a look that Liz interpreted as a command for him to join her. He lasted a couple of minutes longer before he too disappeared upstairs. Tom watched them go with an air of scarcely disguised impatience.

'What did you think of the house?' he said, as soon as they had both left. 'I didn't want to ask after Blessing made it clear she wanted nothing to do with it.'

Liz took a sip of her wine.

'I fell in love with it,' she said. 'It's a square Georgian shell with broken windows and a leaky roof, but I felt as if I had been there before. It's a tragedy Blessing hates it. I suppose Michael will have to sell it now.'

'Maybe he'll persuade her to give it a go?' said Bea.

'I doubt it. She only came to Ireland to see you and Daddy.'

'It does seem like a pity. I had forgotten all about the house until George left it to Michael. Lee mentioned the place to me a few times in passing. I would have loved us to keep it on. I believe she planned to move back to live there with George, but after she died, George gave up on the idea,' said Tom.

'Maybe someone will buy it and do it up,' said Liz.

'I doubt it. People prefer new builds these days. Those old country piles are just too much work,' said Tom.

'How's Sean?' said Bea. 'We're sorry he couldn't come.'

'Oh, you know Sean,' said Liz. 'Still nursing his grudge about Ireland.'

'What about the Good Friday agreement?' said Tom.

'He says the IRA haven't decommissioned all their weapons yet and he'll believe it when he sees it.'

'He lost his brother because of the Troubles. It's natural for him to be sceptical,' said Bea.

'Sometimes it's a bit much,' said Liz, sighing.

'Is there something you're not telling us?' said Bea, knitting her eyebrows together.

'Nothing I can't fix,' said Liz. 'I'm off to bed.'

Liz kissed her parents and mounted the narrow staircase, passing Michael and Blessing's room on her way. As she had suspected, they were still awake and having a heated discussion in loud whispers. Blessing's urgent tone told Liz all she needed to know about the subject. She shut her bedroom door and sat on the bed with her eyes closed. Kilanon Glebe materialised in her thoughts and she imagined herself in the walled garden on a sunny day with the insects buzzing in the flower beds. Fat plums hung from the branches of the fruit trees and bees sucked greedily on their escaping juices. She pulled the covers over herself and dreamed about the orchard.

The next morning, Liz woke early, a habit from many years of working at the brokers. She liked to be the first in the office so no one could get a jump on her with the early news or trades. The cold floor made her rummage for her woolly socks and she threw her coat over her pyjamas. She crept down the stairs to the kitchen, hoping to have a quiet cup of tea in the sleeping household, but Michael had beaten her to it. An air of gloom cloaked him as he hunched over his cup.

'The early bird gets the worm,' said Liz. 'But you don't look too pleased with yours.'

'Blessing wants me to sell the house,' said Michael. 'She can't see its potential.'

'That's not true,' said Blessing, appearing at the door. 'I can see how wonderful we could make it, but we just don't have the time or the money. And then there's the other thing.'

'The other thing?' said Liz.

Blessing avoided her eyes.

'I can't live here. Did you see the way the woman in the café looked at me as if I had dropped in from outer space?'

'She stared at all of us. She's probably the local busybody,' said Michael.

'That's not what I meant. How many black people have you seen since we got to Ireland?'

'I saw one or two in Dublin, I think, but I take your point,' said Liz.

'The children have had enough problems in Kenya because of their father, Liz, I don't want to make it worse by subjecting them to racism here as well.'

Blessing gave Michael a pleading look.

'Just imagine how the money from the sale of this house could help us, darling. We could do up the hotel and buy a second jeep for the safaris. We could finally compete on an even playing field with the other companies.'

Michael sighed.

'I know it would be the right thing to do, but just because I should sell it, doesn't mean I want to. Let's see what the solicitor says this morning. It might be impossible to sell the house as it stands.'

'It didn't look that bad,' said Liz. 'Nothing that a few slates and some new window glass can't fix.'

'Don't forget a new kitchen, bathroom and a central heating system. It probably needs rewiring too,' said Michael.

'A man called from Ireland and offered us three hundred pounds for the house and land,' said Blessing. 'I hope it's worth more than that.'

'Someone rang you from Ireland? When was that?'

'I think he rang the same day the solicitor told me I had inherited the house.'

'Whoa, that's quick work. They've got some cheek offering you so little,' said Liz.

'He said the farmer wanted to knock down the house and use the land for farming.'

'I hope you told him to get lost,' said Liz.

'I didn't get the chance,' said Michael. 'The line cut off, or he put down the phone, when I told him I wanted to see the house before making any decisions.'

'The cheek of him,' said Liz. 'Let's make some breakfast. Who wants bacon and egg?'

Chapter 6

After breakfast, Liz, Michael and Blessing left the Green parents' house and struck out along Kilkenny High Street towards the lawyer's office. For once the sun broke through the clouds and shone on the gloss painted wooden doors and window frames of the traditional shop fronts. Through the butcher's window, a plump man in a striped apron could be seen, wielding his cleaver with gusto over a fresh carcass. Spotting them gazing through the glass, he gave them a cheery wave and shouted a greeting. Liz waved back, getting a kiss blown at her for her enthusiasm.

They crossed the road at the end of the High Street and headed up The Parade towards Kilkenny Castle. The right-hand side of The Parade had a terrace of typical Georgian houses covered in red ivy. The offices of Flaherty, Gallaher and O'Brien occupied the first floor of the house nearest the Kilkenny Design Centre, itself opposite the Castle. Newly painted black railings lined the worn limestone steps leading to a bright green door crowned by an exquisite fanlight. A smiley, middle aged woman swung open the door when Michael knocked, and they were shown into a large reception area. The sun streamed into the windows illuminating the expensive antique furniture in the waiting room. A wooden staircase followed the walls up onto the next floor. Several doors led off the reception area into the private offices of the solicitors who worked there.

A short time later, Niall Flaherty, the lead solicitor, beckoned them into his opulent quarters.

'Welcome to Ireland,' he said, and directed them to sit on some handsome, George II, mahogany armchairs.

'It's not exactly our first visit,' said Liz. 'We were brought up here.'

'You were?' said Flaherty.

'I attended the Christian Brothers in Kilkenny for a year. Did I go to school with you?' said Michael.

'I don't think so,' said Flaherty, with an air of condescension. 'I went to a private school in Dublin.'

'That's funny. I thought I recognised you. It's probably just my imagination,' said Michael, refusing to rise to the bait.

Liz wondered if Flaherty would have been so rude if he had known that Michael went to a well-known English public school. Flaherty sat himself behind his oak desk and peered at them through his cloudy glasses, wrinkling his nose to stop them slipping off. Despite the seniority of his position, he didn't appear to be out of his thirties yet. He had a shock of black hair which had been plastered down onto his square skull. His flat nose showed the wear and tear of several unattended breaks. Liz took in his stocky body and battered face, and guessed he had played rugby. The combination of brains and brawn interested her more than she like to admit to herself.

'You're here about Kilanon Glebe, I suppose?' said Flaherty. 'I have the papers ready, Mr Green. I hope you weren't expecting to take possession today. There are some formalities that must be gone through before we can register the house in your name.'

'Formalities? I brought a copy of the will and my birth certificate and passport for you to verify,' said Michael. 'Is there something else I need? We have travelled here from Kenya so I hoped to deal with all the paperwork today.'

Flaherty examined him over the top of his glasses.

'It's a pretty straight forward process, but we won't be completing all the paperwork today. First, we need to commission a valuation of the house, and once we get that, I'll need a banker's draft in pounds for the taxes,' he said.

'Taxes?' said Blessing.

'Inheritance taxes,' he said. 'You must pay thirty-three percent of the value of the house in tax before you can register it in your name.'

'That won't be a problem. I heard that it's only worth three hundred pounds,' said Michael. 'I can give you cash if you like.'

Flaherty coloured.

'Three hundred pounds? Where on earth did you get that figure?' he stuttered.

'Someone called me at home in Kenya and offered to take the house of my hands.'

'They were codding you. It's worth a hundred times that figure. I think the last assessment came out at three hundred and fifty thousand, including the thirty acres. I imagine its worth more now. You'll need to pay someone to value it.'

'But that's over one hundred thousand pounds in taxes,' said Liz.

'Correct,' said Flaherty. 'You need to arrange for three different estate agents to estimate the value of the house and give you a written assessment. We'll use the average price in order to calculate the amount of tax you owe, and then inform the tax office of the valuation. If they accept it, you pay the agreed amount into the government account, and bring me the receipt at registration.'

'Oh,' said Michael. 'That's more complicated than I imagined.'

'And far more expensive,' said Liz.

Blessing put her hand on Michael's knee to get his attention.

'Be realistic,' she said. 'There's simply no way we can afford to keep the house. We'll have to sell it.'

'You can grant someone power of attorney to deal with these matters,' said Niall. 'Do you know anyone you can trust over here? Of course, if you want, I can deal with matters for a fee.'

'I'll do it if you like,' said Liz, before she could stop herself.

'But do you have the time, Sis? It may not be as simple as it looks. I certainly don't have the money to pay the taxes right now,' said Michael.

Flaherty coughed.

'As I am after saying, I can pay the death duties and act for you in the sale. We'll forward you the balance once all fees are paid,' he said.

'That sounds sensible,' said Michael. 'It would certainly be a weight off my mind.'

Liz squirmed in her chair and kicked his ankle.

'Please let me do it,' she said. 'Sean will know all about this sort of thing, and I'm a qualified accountant. If you decide to sell once you take possession, I can arrange some time off and show people around the house. It would be great to take a break from my job for a while.'

'If you're sure,' said Michael.

'I'm sure. I have my passport with me, if that is sufficient for you to draw up a power of attorney, Mr Flaherty? We can sign the document today if you manage to get it ready,' said Liz.

Niall Flaherty frowned as his commission disappeared.

'I suppose so, but I don't recommend it. Things can go wrong quickly around here.'

'Then I'll have you to help me out of a pickle, won't I?' said Liz, receiving a grimace in return.

'Are you sure?' said Michael.

'Quite sure. If Mr Flaherty can have his clerk draw up the document, we can go and have lunch with Mum and Dad, and come back later to sign it.'

'Is that what you want, Mr Green?' said Niall. 'I don't recommend leaving this matter to an amateur.'

Liz bit her lip. *He may be handsome but he's got some cheek.* Michael shrugged.

'She's the eldest sibling,' he said. 'She can be quite bossy when she wants to, and I'm not going to look a gift horse in the mouth.'

'I think we have a deal,' said Liz. 'What time should we come back, Mr Flaherty?'

'The name's Niall, and the document will be ready at four o'clock,' said Flaherty. 'You can always change your mind if you need my help.'

Liz picked up the doubt in his voice, but Michael and Blessing shook his hand, all smiles. *This is going to be a lot more challenging than I imagined.* She gave the solicitor one of her famous hard stares when she shook his hand, and his double take gave her the gratification she craved. *Don't mess with me, mister solicitor, I'm not sugar and spice.*

When they got outside, she tugged the sleeve of Michael's coat.

'What was the name of the guy who said the house was worth three hundred pounds?' said Liz.

'I can't remember. He's just some chancer trying to fleece the unwary.'

'He's got some cheek,' said Blessing. 'But even I was surprised by their valuation.'

'Maybe you should keep an eye out for any farmers casting covetous glances at our fields,' said Michael.

Liz laughed.

'I don't think anyone has cast any sort of a glance at my land for years.'

'What about Sean?' said Blessing.

'Except for him,' said Liz, looking at the ground.

'Anyway, I doubt you'll hear from that bloke again,' said Michael. 'He guessed I rumbled him. He won't fool us a second time.'

Chapter 7

Niall Flaherty gritted his teeth as he waved off the Greens and shut the door of the office. He watched them discussing the meeting outside on the pavement. Liz's face showed surprise at something Michael said, and then they all roared with laughter. He couldn't help noticing how animated she seemed and how the joy brightened up her face. She might be no spring chicken, but his mother always told him that old chickens made the best soup. Liz radiated sex appeal and feisty humour. She would be formidable to get to grips with, whatever the context. *How frustrating to get a spanner in the works when the fiddle had seemed so straightforward at first!*

He blamed the Kennedy family for taking the house from under his parents' noses. The house was rightfully his through inheritance, but his grandfather had gambled it away. He had kept it on his radar ever since, determined to get it back. His cousin, Dermot, his partner in crime, found his obsession annoying. He kept telling Niall about much easier pickings in the county. People were gullible. They always believed everything their lawyer told them. But Niall stuck to his guns. Kilanon Glebe belonged to him. And now he had to deal with the Greens instead. He'd never let some stuck-up English bitch prevent him from getting his hands on it. Maybe he shouldn't have rung her brother in Kenya, but it was worth a shot. He'd have to pay more now but there were ways of reducing the price.

He ran his hands through his hair which sprung up as he released it from the coating of gel that kept it more or less controlled.

'Make me a mug of tea, Siobhan,' he said to the receptionist.

'How strong?' she said.

'Strong enough to trot a mouse across the top of it. Don't you know by now?'

She nodded and kept her head down, unwilling to engage as she recognised the signs that he was looking for a fight. Defeated by her stubborn refusal to engage, Niall wandered back into his office and ran his hand over the still warm back of Liz's chair. He frowned. *Just what I didn't need right now. Joan of bleeding Arc poking her nose where it's not wanted.* He sat down behind his desk and shuffled the papers before shoving them back into the folder. *Patience.* Someone knocked on the door, and before he could react, or refuse entry, Dermot Gallaher strolled in, his arms flapping, and beamed at his cousin like a demented lighthouse.

'I wish you wouldn't do that,' said Niall.

'Do what?' said Dermot, pulling up one of the armchairs and sitting in it so his knees touched the desk.

'Burst in uninvited.'

'I knocked, didn't I? Why are you all bent out of shape this morning? Weren't you due to sew up the deal with the Brits today?'

Niall pursed his lips.

'There's a complication,' he said.

'Ah, that explains it. The great Niall Flaherty has been bested. Was it that gorgeous girl with the dark hair and the violet eyes I saw outside on the pavement?' said Dermot. 'Now there's a ride if I ever saw one.'

'She's hardly a girl. I'd say she's touching forty, and you'd never get a ride off her. She's a ball breaker.'

'No one can resist my blarney. It's a pity I won't get to prove it.'

'You might. She's threatening to help sell the house.'

'You mean in person? It might be hard to pretend we're not interested.'

'It might.' Niall rubbed his chin. 'But I'm sure that between us we could provide a distraction.'

'She doesn't strike me as your type.'

'I didn't say I liked her, but when has that ever stopped me?'

'Do you fancy a bet on the outcome?'

'Save your money. You don't stand a chance against me. Brains always trump beauty.'

'I'm a lawyer too, in case you haven't noticed.'

'Don't kid yourself, the cream always rises to the top.'

Dermot swallowed his reply. Niall always got what he wanted, by fair means or foul.

'So, what did they say about the house?' he said.

'I told them about the inheritance taxes and Michael Green's wife nearly had a conniption. She insisted that he sell it.'

'But isn't that exactly what we wanted?'

'Ah, but then, Miss Bossy Boots said she'd deal with it instead. I couldn't dissuade her.'

'So much for your fatal charm.'

'It wasn't that sort of conversation.'

'The bet's on then?'

'Let's see what happens when they go home. Maybe she'll change her mind and leave me to it. There's money to be made here. We just have to hold our nerve. Anyway, we have that other thing up our sleeve, in case of unexpected outcomes.'

Dermot raised an eyebrow.

'How did you pull it off?' he said.

'How do you think? The usual. A bit of blarney and baksheesh.'

'Where is it?'

'In the safe. Not that we'll need it.'

'It's better to cover all the exits. If she's as smart as you say she is, we'll need our wits about us.'

'This could be fun. She's not our usual prey, but we need a worthy opponent for once. The others were like putty in our hands.'

'Who doubts the word of their lawyer? It's like taking candy off a baby.'

Chapter 8

On her return to London, Liz found that she had become obsessed with the house in Ireland. She daydreamed about sitting in the orchard surrounded by the humming of bees and the smell of honeysuckle. She haunted its rooms in her sleep, opening the ancient shutters and waxing its wooden floors. Bernie caught her gazing out of the office window several times and wondered if she had a new lover, such was the look of rapture on her face. He didn't dare ask her for the reason. Liz could be sharp tongued and he didn't want to suffer her wrath.

Liz took her obsession to several hardware shops and emerged with an armful of catalogues about boilers and radiators, catalogues which she hid from Sean so he wouldn't guess her intentions. She shoved them under her mattress. Heating porn, she thought, and sniggered to herself. She chose colours for the walls and rugs for the floors, and even went to a kitchen supplier to play house in their display section. When she caught herself frying an imaginary egg on the hob, she knew it had gone too far, but how to forget the love of your life? *Would it be the one that got away?*

Despite her dreams, she did not neglect her promise to Michael. Niall Flaherty suggested several estate agents to her for the task of evaluating the property, but her instincts told her that they were likely to be friends or relatives of his, and she felt disinclined to give them commissions. His superior nature had got up her nose and she wanted to show him just who he was dealing with. Her inquiries to the main estate agents in Ireland led to the selection of three senior agents more likely to be independent assessors. They visited Kilanon Glebe and provided the three estimates of its value necessary for the calculation of the amount owing in inheritance tax to the Inland Revenue in Ireland.

Their estimates were all in the same ball park as other similar houses for sale in the area, which gave her comfort as to their veracity. She sent their estimates to Niall Flaherty who elaborated the petition of payment for the inland revenue. Within weeks she received confirmation that the government would accept the amount proffered. The alacrity with which the Revenue services accepted their offer impressed Liz no end, but Niall rolled his eyes.

'The government offices will always be quick when a transaction involves money for themselves. But just you wait until you need a permit for something. You'll go grey long before you receive it. They're real devils when it comes to doing a solid day's work for someone who isn't paying.'

Liz shrugged. Niall Flaherty had all the optimism of Schopenhauer.

'I guess I'll soon find out,' she said.

'If anything can go wrong, it will.'

It wasn't until she received a call from Michael that her fond imaginings began to take on a touch of reality. The shrill tone of the telephone interrupted her enjoyment of a musical starring Ginger Rogers and

Fred Astaire, and she picked up the receiver ready to repel anyone's need for a chat.

'Yes?'

'Liz, it's me, Michael.'

'Oh, hello, what a nice surprise. I expect you want news of our progress with the house.'

'That too. But how are you?'

'Oh, you know. Same old thing. Work, work, and more work. You'll be glad to hear the tax people have agreed to accept the estimates for the average value of the house, so I'm planning to transfer the money next week. It's just a question of finding the time to go to the bank and organising it.'

'About that,' said Michael. 'I've tried my hardest, but I can't persuade Blessing to change her mind about a move to Ireland. She's keen to sell George's house and invest in our safari business, and she won't change her mind.'

'Do you want to sell it?' said Liz.

'Not really. But I don't have any choice, unless I'd like to find divorce papers in the mail.'

'I'm sorry. I know you loved the house too, but maybe it's for the best.'

'Probably. It means that I'll need more help from you, and I know how busy you are. Can you possibly find the time?'

Liz stifled a sigh.

'Of course I can. What are sisters for?'

'I hate asking you, but I can't do it from here. The phone lines are terrible to Ireland and there's no way I can organise transfers from here. Are you sure?'

'Don't worry about a thing. Niall Flaherty has already put it on the market. Apparently, there's some local interest, and he has already mentioned an American client who would love to buy it. I'll have to sign the papers for the sale, but I don't mind popping over for a long weekend and seeing Mummy and Daddy again.'

'It seems like a rather sad end to our dealings with the Kennedys, but I can't see a way out.'

'I'm sure George would understand. He loved Blessing and wouldn't have held it against her. He'd be thrilled to help your business thrive in any way he could.'

'You're right as usual. Sometimes I think you're the only sibling who sees things clearly.'

'Not always. Just other people's problems. Mine are a whole other kettle of fish.'

'Is everything all right at work?'

'It's fine, just a bit of a grind. Don't worry about me.'

'At least you have Sean for support. That must be nice.'

'Most of the time. I've got to go now. I've an important meeting tomorrow and I have to revise some papers.'

'Okay. Don't work too hard. Let me know if there's anything I can do to help.'

'I will.'

Afterwards, Liz watched the end of the movie without any enjoyment. She couldn't help brooding over the house and the thought of letting it go. There was no way she could show people around the property and pretend she wanted them to buy it. Niall Flaherty's triumphant tone when she rang him and asked him about offers for the house made her misery worse. His supercilious smirking came down the telephone line in technicolour and got right up her nose. She tried not to mind when he called her most days with news of interested parties and pending offers for the house.

Instead, she heaped praise on his efforts, anything for her brother Michael.

Despite Niall Flaherty's conviction, the house did not sell, and Michael became desperate and depressed as the chance of a windfall receded. Liz sympathised with him, but secretly she crossed her fingers that the house would remain in the family. She tried to persuade their parents to buy it instead. But Bea Green just laughed when she suggested it.

'We're too old for a project like that, and too poor,' she said.

Weeks turned into months, but just when it seemed that the house was fated to rot, Niall Flaherty rang Liz to say that his American clients had seen the house three times and had made an offer for it. Nowhere near the amount he had been asking, but enough to be interesting. Michael received the news with glee.

'I know it's a bargain price, but I need the money. Take the offer,' he said. 'The money will change our lives.'

Liz tried to broach the subject with Sean, who had stayed out of the whole house saga until then, but she couldn't force him to help her. He didn't want to talk about Ireland, and Liz didn't push the issue. His drinking seemed to get worse as she floundered. A deep disappointment made her tetchy and sad, and he wouldn't offer any consolation. Isolated and miserable, she needed to talk to someone who understood, but the long hours at work had precluded any close friendships. Not for the first time, she wondered what she would do if she lost her job.

Finally, she rang her sister Isabella and downloaded the whole sorry story on her. Isabella, not famous for her patience, listened quietly for once. When Liz paused for breath, Isabella tutted at her.

'So why don't you buy it yourself? I know you're pining for it.'

'I'm doing no such thing.'

'Oh yes you are. I saw the notes you made about the shutters on the sideboard when I came to your place last week. You've been decorating that place in your head for months. Why don't you come clean and admit you want it?'

'But what about my job?'

'Your job? I thought you were sick of it.'

'And my flat. If I leave now, I'll lose the massive legacy discount I have on the rent. I would have to pay double if I wanted to move back.'

'I'll take it on if you like. My lease is up next month and I can put the rent into your account. They need never know you don't live here anymore.'

'But Sean, he—'

'Excuses, excuses. Don't give me that. You need a break from your life and this is a golden opportunity to find out what you really want.'

Liz was rendered speechless by this outburst. *It's true though. For once Isabella has hit the nail on the head.*

'Liz? Are you still there?'

'What? Yes. I'm thinking.'

'Don't think too long. You might be too late.'

Liz found Isabella's logical conclusion to be infuriating. It was easy for her to say. She had a peripatetic lifestyle which funded her small rental and minimised her commitments. Liz had a twenty-four-seven job and a semi-live-in boyfriend who took up all her spare time. He wouldn't dream of coming to Ireland with her. *How can I just dump everything? Wouldn't that be running away?*

She tried to push the house out of her mind, but it snuck into her thoughts and sabotaged her efforts to forget it. The final straw broke the camel's back when her team failed to sell their allocation of yet another assetless dotcom at work. Bernie had one of his apoplectic rages and unfairly blamed Liz for the debacle. The tide had begun to turn on the dotcom boom and Liz did not want to experience the carnage she thought would follow. She resented Bernie's apology almost as much as his original rage-fest.

Sean had been unsympathetic.

'You've been getting money for old rope for years,' he said. 'It's about time you suffered a bit. Stop fussing and make me some supper.'

The next morning, still shaking with fury, Liz shut herself into one of the conference rooms at the office, and dialled Niall Flaherty's number. The use of office telephones for personal calls had been prohibited, since one of the junior brokers had spent hundreds of pounds calling his girlfriend in Venezuela, but this act of rebellion made her feel better.

'Mr Flaherty? Hello, it's Liz Green.'

'Ah, Miss Green, how can I help you?'

'It's about the house. Do you still have an offer from the Americans?'

'Yes, the offer still stands, but you need to get your skates on before they change their minds.'

'I'm afraid you're going to have to disappoint them. We can't sell them the house.'

'But you won't get another one. This is your only chance.'

Liz took a deep breath.

'Because I'm going to buy it myself,' she said.

'Did I hear you correctly?' said the solicitor. 'You want to buy the house from your brother?'

'Yes, I do. Please draw up the paperwork. I'll be there to sign it as soon as you let me know it is ready.'

'But it's falling down. You'll have to rebuild it.'

'I have the time and the money, and I fell in love with the house.'

'You're setting yourself up for failure, but if that's what you want… On your head be it.'

Chapter 9

Bernie's eyes opened wide in shock.

'You're kidding, right?' he said, his voice quavering.

'No, I'm deadly serious,' said Liz.

'But this is crazy talk. How can you leave in the middle of a boom? Are you having a breakdown?'

He waited for her to answer but she just smiled at him.

'Maybe you need a holiday,' he said.

'I've made up my mind,' said Liz. 'I need this.'

'Is it the money?' said Bernie. 'Has someone tapped you up? I can match any offer.'

Sweat ran down his face which he wiped off with an old paper napkin.

'Don't be silly. No-one else will have me. I'm not the new kid on the block anymore. I'm practically a dinosaur.'

'But you're my dinosaur. You can't go. I'd be lost without you. Those guys will run rings around me.'

He dropped his head into his hands and his sideburns burst out through his fingers.

'You're killing me,' he said. 'Say something.'

Liz rolled her eyes.

'Okay,' she said. 'Call it a sabbatical if it makes you feel better. One year, and I promise to come back if it doesn't work.'

Bernie looked up, his eyes glinting.

'Six months.'

'Twelve.'

'You should keep the office cell phone.'

'There's no reception.'

'Emails?'

'I doubt very much I can get internet in that tiny village. How about you call me on the landline.'

Bernie grabbed his cell phone and tapped impatiently at it.

'What's the number?' he said.

'I don't know yet, but I promise to call you as soon as I have one.'

'Yeah, right,' said Bernie, putting it in his pocket.

She bit her lip.

'I need a complete break from my life. No exceptions.'

'What does Sean say?'

Liz avoided his inquiring glance. Bernie crowed.

'You haven't told him, have you?'

He rubbed his hands together.

'I'd like to be a fly on the wall for that convo. He'll never let you go back there.'

Liz raised an eyebrow and gave Bernie a hard stare.

'Do you really think I'll let him stop me? In the end, it's my decision, and I've already made it.'

'Good luck convincing him,' said Bernie. 'I'll keep your job open for now.'

Liz shrugged.

'My mind's made up.'

But inside her guts were churning. Bernie had met Sean a few times and been impressed by his straight talking and appetite for life. No one who had met Sean imagined him as a pushover. This would be hard.

Liz planned the moment with military precision, finding time to buy all his favourite things for a massive fry-up dinner. She had always clung to her mother's belief that the best way to a man's heart was through his stomach, and Sean always took bad news better with a full belly. She hummed as she laid the table and lit some candles, not that Sean would notice. He left the domestics to her, something that had started to grate as well as everything else. *As if I don't work long hours already.*

She put an apron on over her dark blue shift dress to prevent the fat from spitting on it, and gave her lips a coating of burgundy lipstick which flattered her pale skin. There was no point cooking until he got home, whenever that might be. *Who knows if he will get side tracked by some welcoming hostelry?*

Sure enough, Sean lumbered in after eight o'clock, his head down. Liz could almost see the black storm cloud floating over his brow. She braced herself for whatever drama he had stored up to take out on her, retreating behind the kitchen counter to start cooking. He stood leaning on his knuckles and swayed slightly. *Drunk again, but it's now or never.* She didn't get the chance to start her prepared speech. Sean thumped the counter with his fist making her jump and turn from the stove. He glowered at her from under his bushy eyebrows.

'Why am I the last to know everything about you? How could you embarrass me like that?'

Liz coloured and a chill rolled up her back. She affected innocence, turning the bacon in the frying pan with the flick of a wrist. *Oh God, he knows.*

'What on earth do you mean?' she said.

'Do you think I'm completely thick, or what?' he said. 'I met your beloved boss, Bernie, by chance this evening in the pub and he asked me what I thought about the big move. I thought he was talking about Danny Mills going to Manchester United. I was mortified.'

Liz moved the bacon around the pan, avoiding his inquiring glance. His brewery breath cut through even the smell of the fat crisping in the pan.

'What did he say?'

'He says you're moving to Ireland. When did this happen? I can't believe you told him before you told me. I laughed at him, but he swore you told him about the move last week and he assumed I already knew. Is it true?'

Liz sighed. *Bernie and his big mouth. Probably did it on purpose.*

'Yes. I'm sorry, darling. I just couldn't find the right time to tell you.'

Because you're always drunk.

'The right time? Are you kidding me? You're moving to Ireland and you haven't bothered to tell your boyfriend of twenty-five years?'

'I'm not moving there, exactly. Well, not forever. I need a break and the chance to buy Michael's house came along just at the right time for me.'

'You're buying that house? Are you crazy? I thought you told me it was a wreck. You can't do it. I won't let you.'

Liz bit her lip.

'I already did,' she said.

'You spent our money without asking me?'

Liz's jaw hardened.

'My money. I spent my money on the house. I told you I needed a proper break from everything,' said Liz.

Sean ignored the pointed remark.

'Could you not go on holiday like a normal person?'

'I am normal, just worn out. I need a change.'

Sean scratched his forehead. He looked straight into her eyes.

'And me?' he said. 'Where do I come in your new plan?'

Liz flinched as he put out his hand towards her. He spotted it. His eyes opened wide.

'Jaysus. You thought I was going to hit you? Have you lost your mind?'

A fat tear slithered down Liz's cheek as she fought for the right words to make things better.

'I need a break from you too,' she said. A sob caught in her throat. 'You're drinking too much and, and…'

'And what?' said Sean, steel in his voice.

'I'm afraid you'll turn into your father. I can't stand it anymore. I'm leaving you.'

There, I said it.

Sean sat down hard on a kitchen stool; his head dropped into his hands. The sound of bacon frying filled the silence. Finally, Sean lifted his head again, the bags under his eyes in shadow.

'But I love you,' he said. 'You're my girl. Don't you love me anymore?'

Liz swallowed.

'I don't know. I'm afraid of you sometimes when you drink too much, and you won't stop, so I'm taking a break before something irreparable happens to our relationship.'

Sean barked out a laugh.

'Irreparable? You don't think buying a house in Ireland and leaving me is the end of us?'

'I don't know. I need time away. Please try and understand.'

Sean stood up.

'Will you come back?'

Liz shrugged.

'That's up to you,' she said.

Sean took a step towards her with his hand and voice raised.

'Oh, so it's my fault, is it? How do I know you don't have some fancy man lined up to replace me?'

Liz noticed the hand and gasped.

'Don't,' she said. 'Please.'

Sean followed her glance and took down his hand, shaken.

'I would never...'

'I'm sorry. It's too late. Isabella will take over the flat next week and I'm leaving for twelve months, or whenever I'm ready to come back.'

Sean spun around and stumbled to the front door, flinging it open so it crashed against the wall. He fumbled in his pocket for the keys to the flat and tossed them on the counter.

'You'll come crawling back,' he said. 'You'll see. You're no match for those culchies, with your airs and graces and money. They'll fleece you for every penny.'

'I'll take my chances,' said Liz.

And he was gone, slamming the door so hard that paint flakes fell from the ceiling.

Liz turned off the hob and sat in her favourite armchair, gripping the armrests like a drowning man with a lifebelt.

'Am I doing the right thing?' she wondered out loud.

But no one answered.

Chapter 10

One of the shutters blew shut with a loud bang as Liz let herself into Kilanon Glebe for the first time as its owner. She had forgotten how many of the windows were broken, and the keen north wind cut through the house, rippling the peeling wallpaper. She wrapped her scarf around her head for warmth and climbed the stairs to the upper floor. One of the bedrooms looked habitable, but she couldn't imagine sleeping through the creaking and banging of the wooden shutters. Anyway, the toilet in the bathroom had cracked and water had seeped into the floor boards which looked dark and rotten. *Imagine falling through into the laundry.*

After months of daydreaming about buzzing bees and ripe fruit, Liz struggled to align this broken shell of a house with her fond imaginings. She had never renovated a dwelling of any kind before. Her flat in London had been spotless with a brand-new bathroom and kitchen when she rented it. The only thing missing were some light bulbs for the spotlights which blew continuously all through her occupation. *Where do I start with the renovations? I must be out of my mind. One thing's for sure, I can't stay here yet. I wonder if I can make the cottage habitable?*

Liz returned to Thomastown and entered Brennan's, the café where she had come with Michael and Blessing on their first trip to Kilanon. Mrs Brennan recognised her and came bustling over.

'So it's yourself, is it? I heard someone had bought Kilanon, but I never imagined it would be you. Is your husband with you?'

'My husband. No, I—'

Mrs Brennan frowned.

'You're not divorced, are you?'

'Oh, no. I'm single.'

'Oh well, there's still time. A woman with money is a great catch for any man around here, no matter how old.'

Liz tried to smile.

'I need to stay somewhere while I get the roof and windows fixed. Can you recommend a B&B around here?'

'Well, there's Ballybreen guesthouse out on the Inistioge road, or the Woodstock pub in Inistioge. They do food too.'

'The pub sounds nice. How do I get there?'

'Just follow the road to Inistioge and you'll see the pub in the centre of the village.'

'Thank you, Mrs Brennan.'

'Call me Kathleen. And you are?'

'I'm Liz. Liz Green.'

'Weren't there some Greens who used to live at Jacinta O'Reilly's farm a decade or so ago?'

'That's us. It's more like three decades though.'

Kathleen knitted her eyebrows together.

'I heard about the shooting of those two poor lads. I remember how shocked we were.'

Liz swallowed.

'It was a horrible coincidence. They didn't stand a chance.'

'But one of them survived, didn't he?'

'Yes, my brother Michael, who you met. But Liam O'Connor died.'

'It must have been terrible for you and your family.'

'It was, but it's in the past now, and I don't want to open old wounds.'

'Of course. Forgive me butting in, I didn't mean to pry. Did you all return to England afterwards?'

'No, we stayed. Ireland had become our home, and everyone helped us and the O'Connors to deal with the tragedy.'

'What happened to your brother?'

'He moved to Kenya and married Blessing, that lady who came with us last time.'

Kathleen sniffed.

'And your parents?'

'They live in Kilkenny now, but I went to London for work and my sister Isabella followed.'

'Half of Ireland went to England for work in those days,' said Kathleen. 'Well, I'm sorry for your troubles. You're welcome home. Let me know if there's anything I can do for you.'

'Thank you, Mrs, um, Kathleen. I suspect I'll be needing tea and comfort in the days to come, so keep the door open.'

'Grand. Of course, I'll keep the kettle on the hob.'

Liz sat in the car for a while with her thoughts racing. It had been naïve to imagine that such a tragic episode would have been forgotten by anyone who had lived in the county at the time. *I hope it doesn't colour my time here. Perhaps I need to accept that people will be curious at first. After all, a local boy died in horrible circumstances, and nothing will change the past.*

She started the engine and pulled out from the kerb. She negotiated the narrow lanes to Inistioge with little bother. Memories of her childhood came flooding back as she entered the small square at the centre of the village and parked in front of the pub. Instead of entering, she strolled down to the River Nore and gazed at the classical ten-arch bridge which spanned the river, its dark limestone arches solid since 1763. The river had crept up its banks due to the winter rains and rushed by in a chocolate stream carrying sticks and oddments of rubbish with it. *How do the fish survive?*

'It's a real beauty, isn't it?' said a voice at her shoulder.

Shaken from her reverie, Liz turned to find Prince Charming at her elbow, or so it seemed to her. A tall, handsome, well-built man of about her age stood looking down at her with a slightly predatory air.

'Yes, I've always loved it,' said Liz, blushing.

'Always? But you have an English accent.'

'It's a long story.'

'One I'd love to hear sometime,' said the man, reaching out his hand. 'I'm Dermot Gallagher.'

Liz took his hand and returned his stare, daring him to look away first.

'I'm Liz Green.'

A shadow passed through his features. Or was it her imagination?

'So, you're the new owner of Kilanon Glebe? That place is a death trap. I can't imagine why you bought it. You must be a glutton for punishment.'

'I fell in love with it,' said Liz. 'And it's not that bad. Just needs a little TLC.'

'Rather me than you,' said Dermot. 'I work with Niall Flaherty, who I think you know.'

'You're a lawyer too?'

'Yes, we're cousins. We run the practice together, although you wouldn't guess it from the way he behaves.'

'You are a bit like chalk and cheese,' said Liz. *Except for the cocky part. That must be genetic.*

Dermot rolled his eyes and glanced at his watch.

'Oh, that's me late again. I'll be seeing you around, I'm sure. Goodbye now.'

'Goodbye Mr Gallagher.'

'Dermot, call me Dermot. Everybody does.'

Liz watched him stride away. Irritation mixed with curiosity swamped her senses. His attraction could not be denied, but he seemed arrogant too, and a bit rude with it. She shook her head to cleanse it of impure imaginings about Dermot Gallagher. After a few minutes, the cold seeped through her coat and into her bones, so she walked back to the Woodstock.

The square was dominated by two churches which faced each other across the road which led to Thomastown, one a large, handsome Gothic style church dedicated to Saint Columcille which loomed large in the small square. The smaller, Protestant church, Saint Mary's, with its square tower had been built incorporating parts of a 13th century medieval Augustinian priory, whose ruins abutted the sturdy church. Behind it, a graveyard filled with ancient gravestones tempted Liz into its mossy surroundings, but she postponed it for another day and instead entered the warm, noisy surrounds of the Woodstock.

Behind the bar, a teenage girl with thick mascara on her eyelashes flirted with one of the locals, who leered at her low-cut blouse. Liz stood patiently at the counter, waiting to be noticed, until another local yelled from his stool.

'Mairead, you've got a customer.'

She gave him a sulky glance and came over to Liz with a toss of her dyed-blonde curls.

'What are you having?' she said.

'Nothing for the moment,' said Liz. 'I need a room for a few weeks, if you have one free.'

A short, plump man, wearing a tight waistcoat and sporting a grey beard, appeared from a doorway behind the bar.

'Leave this to me, Mairead,' he said. 'You're wanting a room?'

'Yes, please,' said Liz. 'I'll need it for at least three weeks, but it maybe longer.'

'Three weeks? Are you a locum or a substitute teacher or what?'

'I bought a house,' said Liz. 'But it's not fit for habitation yet.'

The man's eyes opened wide.

'You're the lady who's bought the Glebe?'

'Yes, that's me.'

'Hey, lads,' he said. 'We have the new owner of Kilanon Glebe gracing our pub with her presence. What's your name?'

'Liz. Liz Green.'

'Like the Queen. We are honoured, your Majesty.'

The locals all laughed at this witticism and Liz blushed scarlet.

'Did you bring your husband with you?' he said.

Liz took a deep breath.

'I don't have one,' she said. 'Do you have a suitable room for me or not?'

'I was only codding,' said the man. 'My name's Billy McNamara. They call me Billy Mac. I have a lovely room for you with its own bathroom if you'd like to take a look?'

Liz relaxed.

'Yes, please.'

The man led her up the stairs and into a cosy room with a double bed and a battle-scarred, oak chest of drawers. A small desk with an anglepoise lamp backed onto the window, which overlooked a scruffy back yard. Empty beer barrels had been piled beside a metal gate, and a cat stalked its prey in the sparse patches of grass along the rotting wooden fence.

'There's not much of a view,' said Billy Mac. 'But this room sits over the storeroom. There is a larger room on the other side of the staircase, but that's over the lounge. This one will be a lot quieter if that's what you prefer,' he said.

'It's perfect,' said Liz. 'How much is it?'

'Well, seeing as you are staying for a good while, I'll give you a discount. It's twenty pounds a night. How does that sound?'

'Great,' said Liz.

'I can add full board for thirty, if that's any good to you?'

'Can we start with full board and see how I get on? I'm not sure how long I'll need it?'

'Grand. Just let me know if your plans change.'

'I'll get my bags from the car then.'

'I'll send Mairead to help you. Are you hungry?'

'Thank you. I'm starving actually. I haven't eaten all day.'

'I've got a nice bowl of Irish stew in the kitchen, if you fancy?'

'That sounds delicious. Can I have a pot of tea as well?'

'Of course. Get yourself settled in and I'll set you a table in the corner. Welcome to the Woodstock.'

Chapter 11

A black cloud of dismay enveloped Sean as he dealt with the reality of Liz's departure. Until the day she left, he had hung on to the conviction she would change her mind and stay in London. He still harboured the hope she would not settle in Ireland and would soon come home with her tail between her legs. He didn't recognise the Liz he knew in this new version. She had been so stuck in her ways for years, they both had. Her decision had been totally out of character and left him confused and lonely.

If the shock of losing Liz made him maudlin at first, his sorrow soon turned into a bitter anger. He could not understand how she would desert him after all those years. It was not as if they had fallen out of love. He still found her attractive and his heart leapt whenever he saw her, just as it had always done. *But did she feel the same anymore? It seemed not.*

The cold chill of doubt froze his heart with grief, but he refused to accept even a tiny proportion of the blame for their break up, complaining at length to anyone who would listen. None of his friends had the gumption to tell him that they too had learnt to avoid him because of his excessive drinking and violent outbursts. The better qualities of the old Sean had long since been diluted with a deluge of alcohol. Self-pity threatened to swamp him, and he took to spending longer and longer in town after work, drinking himself into a stupor and then pouring himself into a taxi for the long ride home.

As the weeks went by, his slim hope of Liz returning to him evaporated and he began to despair. There were plenty of women who were willing to soothe his heartache, but his cack-handed attempts at seducing them put the most ardent off. In the end, his heart just wasn't in it, and he preferred his old friend, alcohol, to numb the pain.

His excessive drinking began to affect his performance at work as he struggled to drag himself in on time and to block out his pounding headaches with painkillers. He found himself dozing off in meetings and then drinking so much coffee to stay awake that he couldn't sleep at night either. He imagined that he had hidden his lack of application well until his boss crooked a finger at him in the office beckoning him into his office. In all his years at work, Sean had only been in the boss's office once, and that was to snog a girl at the Christmas party. He tried to focus on a dull painting of some trees behind the boss's desk.

'This won't do at all,' said his boss, finally.

Sean blinked.

'I'm sorry?' he said.

'You're no longer productive. I don't think you've finished a report this month. I've had complaints.'

'Complaints?'

Sean's eyebrows knitted together as a pulse of pain from his headache hit him between the eyes.

'This is an official warning. Either you buck up, or you ship out. Got me?'

'Er, yes. No, not really.'

'Honestly. I couldn't be clearer. Get out and do some work. Now.'

Sean shuffled out again. His lips felt dry and cracked, and he was dying for a drink. He had exhausted the patience of his friends and their exasperation had penetrated even his thick skin, but he knew someone who could help. Isabella, Liz's sister, had moved into Liz's flat and had stayed in London to complete a documentary for the BBC. She understood him better than anyone, except Liz. And she wouldn't give him grief. Isabella knew better than anyone how he felt about Liz, and how much he missed her.

He had no problem persuading Isabella to join him for a drink after work. They had not met up for more than six months due to the demands of her job. She very rarely spent more than a couple of weeks in the country before bombing off on some exotic assignment. Since she did not have a partner, she had few demands on her spare time. He arranged to meet her in the Duke of Clarence, in one of the booths at the back, and somehow managed to pretend to work for the rest of the day. The resentment he felt at being called out made his hangover worse, and every minute lasted an hour.

Finally, having won half a brownie point for staying after six o'clock, he set out for the pub. A keen east wind blew down Piccadilly, making him wish he had worn his winter coat. He pulled the collar of his jacket up around his ears, but it didn't help much. He staggered into the bar and ordered a double whisky which he threw back in a couple of swallows before making his way to the booths. He took out his copy of the Evening Standard and tried to read it in the dim lighting.

Several minutes later, a cold face with pink cheeks pushed itself into his and blonde curls tickled his nose. He held his breath so Isabella would not notice the whisky on it. She pulled back and inspected him at close quarters.

'You look shite,' she said. 'Are you training to be a zombie?'

'Thanks a lot. I'm just working too hard. You know how it is.'

'Hm. I don't think I do. What are you drinking?'

'I'll have a pint of Guinness please.'

'Do you want another whisky with it?' she said, her eyebrow quivering slightly, but not raising.

He couldn't look her in the eye.

'No, thanks, I'm grand.'

She threw herself off the bench and sashayed up to the bar, her duvet coat failing to hide her still spectacular figure. Sean glared at a man who appeared transfixed by this blonde vision, and he blanched and looked away. The barman ignored the other customers and served her with a massive grin. She flirted with him and bit her bottom lip, a gesture that made him forget to ask for payment until she had turned away. She paid with a cheeky smile leaving the poor man weak at the knees. *Both the Green girls had the same effect on men, and neither seemed aware of it.*

Sean patted the bench beside him and lifted his pint in salute.

'Cheers,' he said.

'Bottoms up.'

Sean knew he should ask Isabella how she had been, and where, and what her latest project was, but he had no interest. His self-pity had swamped his cheerful character and gregarious nature and turned him into a one-track bore. Isabella was not famous for her tolerance, but she had always had a soft spot for her 'bother-in-law'. She did her best not to interrupt the tirade of angst and recrimination that flowed from Sean's mouth. When he finally took a deep breath, she held up a hand.

'Whoa. Stop now. Enough.'

Sean's bravado evaporated and he glanced around the bar as if searching for an escape route. Finding none, he spun his beer mat on the table and pretended to be unperturbed. Isabella fixed him with her famous glare, and then her expression softened.

'Have you finished?' she said. 'Because it's my turn to say something.'

Sean nodded without meeting her eyes.

'Have you ever wondered what happened to me in Sierra Leone?' she said.

'We've never talked about it,' said Sean. 'I guess we've been too busy.'

'I met a man over there, an ex-military guy with PTSD called Pete Hawkins. We fell in love. He saved my life.'

'So why didn't you stay with him?'

'The rebels killed him.'

She held her hand up to stop him saying anything.

'But that's not the reason I couldn't be with him.'

'Was he violent?'

Isabella shook her head and swallowed.

'No. He was a drunk. I couldn't stand the drinking. I didn't want to live with the results of it. He—'

Sean jumped up, almost knocking over the table, and spilling Isabella's glass of white wine over her lap.

'Do you think I'm an eejit?' he said, quivering with anger.

'Sean? What's got into you? Sit down,' said Isabella, regretting her clumsy attempt at a simile.

'You and your sister. Your whole family think they're better than us. I'm not staying here to be insulted.'

'Please sit down. We can talk about something else.'

'Feck off. I'm going to drink somewhere in peace. I'm sick of you and your goody-two-shoes sister judging me.'

Isabella mopped the drink off her lap, to distract her from his attempts to stumble out from the booth. His shame radiated from his body, almost scalding her in its intensity. He walked out and didn't look back at her once. She sighed and stood up too, hoping to get to the local takeaway before they closed. The barman tried to catch her eye as she walked out, but her desire for fish and chips trumped anything he could offer.

Chapter 12

After a comfortable night in her cosy room at the Woodstock Arms, Liz faced the new day with trepidation. *Where do I start?* It seemed logical to fix the roof first to stop the leaks and allow the house to dry out, but having a working toilet was a priority, and to replace the bowl she first needed to put in new floorboards. There didn't seem to be much point replacing the floorboards before rewiring the property, but if the rooms were damp perhaps the system would short continually. *What I need is a firm of builders to take the project off my hands. But how can I choose one?*

Liz returned to Thomastown and parked outside Brennan's café. Kathleen Brennan cooked her a delicious breakfast of bacon and eggs with toast and tea which made Liz feel a lot better.

'Set up for the day,' said Kathleen.

'Except that I seem to be glued to the chair by my breakfast,' said Liz, groaning. 'By any chance, do you know of a reliable firm of builders who could help me with the house?'

Kathleen smiled.

'Well, I don't like to boast, but the Doyle brothers are the best around.'

'Do you know them well?'

'They're also my brothers. There's Noel, Patrick and David, from oldest to youngest. I'm their elder sister. I can ask them if they're busy if you like?'

'Thank you. I don't have a clear plan for the renovation yet, but I definitely need builders. I've got to go and see Mr Flaherty about the deeds to the house today, but I'll drop in later and see if you have any news for me.'

'I've got some shopping to do in Kilkenny, and I won't be in until this evening. Why don't you take my number and give me a call?'

'Okay. Do you want a lift? I'm going there myself.'

'God love you. No, thanks, I've still to organise things around here. We'll speak this evening.'

Liz headed for Kilkenny, still wondering what to do with the house. Despite seeming like a difficult decision to take at the time, buying it had been the easy part. She wished Sean had come with her. He would be up to his neck in builders and electricians by now. *Maybe he would change his mind? Maeve O'Connor might know how to persuade him.* Despite her failure to get him to visit her, she knew him better than anyone. *Perhaps Mrs O'Reilly could help with the builder conundrum too? Jacinta always had a nose for this sort of thing.*

She parked her car outside the Design Centre and walked to Niall Flaherty's office. She rang the bell and waited. The door swung open and to her surprise, Dermot Gallagher stood in the hall.

'If it isn't Miss Green. You're looking ravishing this morning, I must say.'

Liz blushed from head to foot.

'Thanks,' she said.

'Don't thank me. The gods must have been in a good mood when they made the mould,' he said. 'Come in. Niall's waiting for you.'

Still burning from embarrassment, Liz entered Niall Flaherty's office. He didn't appear to notice her at first, his head lowered over a document as he scanned the pages. When he looked up, his face broke into a smile.

'The intrepid Miss Green. How are you settling in?'

Liz relaxed at the warmth of his greeting. He seemed much less stern now that she had made an irrevocable decision about the house. *Perhaps he doubted my resolve.*

'I'm staying at the Woodstock Arms. Billy Mac is taking good care of me.'

'That's great to hear. Billy Mac and I are old friends. He's great gas altogether.'

'He cooks a mean Irish stew,' said Liz.

'I must get down there one of these days. I haven't seen him in ages. Now, where are your papers?'

Niall leafed through a pile of files in his in-tray and pulled one out.

'Ah, yes, Kilanon Glebe. All signed and sealed.'

He took out a deed and handed it to her.

'And now delivered.'

'Thank you,' said Liz, beaming.

She turned the pages of the document and read her name as the owner of Kilanon Glebe. Somehow it didn't seem real.

'I wonder if you might keep it for me,' said Liz. 'I'm not sure about leaving it in my room at the pub.'

'We'd be delighted to guard it in safe custody for you until you need it. Is there anything else we can help you with?'

At that moment, there was a loud knock on the door and Dermot Gallagher entered. Liz noticed a shadow of annoyance pass across Niall's face. Dermot had come in without waiting for permission, and now he pretended to be surprised to see her.

'Miss Green, I didn't expect you to be here today.'

'I was just asking Liz if she needed help with anything,' said Niall.

Dermot raised an eyebrow. Liz smiled at the use of her first name. An air of competition had arisen between the cousins which made the hairs on her arms stand on end.

'Actually,' she said, enjoying the moment, 'I'm looking for some builders to manage the renovation of my house. I've heard the Doyle brothers are excellent.'

Niall rolled his eyes.

'The Doyle Brothers? Who told you that? They're not to be trusted at all.'

'I wouldn't say that,' said Dermot. 'They did a great job on my mother's house last year.'

'What about the Kellys?' said Niall.

'You're joking right?' said Dermot, his brow furrowing.

'Why would I joke? I found them to be excellent.'

Dermot snorted.

'Excellent at spending your money, I'm sure.'

Liz stood up.

'Well, I've got to go now. Thanks for the help. I'm sure I'll find someone suitable.'

Niall shook her hand which almost disappeared into his spade-like one. She felt the callouses on his palms rub against her soft skin. *How un-lawyer-like.* Dermot held the door open for her.

'I'll be seeing you again, I'm sure,' he said, winking.

Not if I can help it.

She popped in for coffee with her parents and spent a pleasant half hour relating her progress to them without mentioning Dermot Gallagher or his cousin. *No doubt they were just trying it on with the new woman in town.*

'Are you planning on visiting Maeve O'Connor? I told her about your move. She'd love to see you. I'm sure Mrs O'Reilly would also,' said Bea.

'I'm planning on popping in tomorrow or the next day. It would be nice to get work started on the house first.'

'Do you have someone in mind?' said her father. 'I'm not really familiar with the builders in this neck of the woods. Ben Hurley retired a couple of years ago and he's the only one I knew.'

'I've had a couple of suggestions. Kathleen, the lady who owns the coffee shop in Thomastown, told me her brothers are builders.'

'Be careful. I've heard there are some real cowboys around.'

Liz smiled.

'I've always fancied being a sheriff. I promise to be cautious.'

'Let us know if you need help,' said Bea.

Billy Mac sat on the fence when asked about builders. He scratched his head and pursed his lips.

'To tell you the truth,' he said. 'It wouldn't be right for me to choose your builder for you. I'll be accused of bias no matter what I say, and people wouldn't like it. Why don't I serve you up a nice helping of bacon and cabbage and you can mull on your decision while you eat it?'

'I can't force you to tell me,' Liz said. 'But I'd love a second opinion.'

Billy shook his head and bustled off to the kitchen, leaving her frustrated. She took a notebook out of her handbag and drew a column down the centre of one of the pages. At the top, she wrote Kelly in one column and Doyle in the other. She chewed her pen absentmindedly as she mulled the pros and cons. Mairead, the bar girl, appeared at her side.

'I heard you were looking for a builder,' she said, twirling her hair around a finger.

Liz looked up at the girl with her spotty face pancaked in foundation, and her dyed blonde hair. *Should I be taking business advice from a teenager?*

'That's right,' she said. 'Have you got any suggestions?'

'I'd use the Kellys if I were you,' said Mairead. 'They're really good.'

'And how do you know that?' said Liz. 'Did they do any work on your parents' house?'

Mairead blushed.

'I just know,' she said. 'You don't have to believe me.'

Before Liz could reassure her, Billy Mac emerged from the kitchen and shooed Mairead back to the bar.

'Honestly. That girl is a pain. What did she say to you?'

'She told me to use the Kellys,' said Liz.

Billy Mac laughed.

'Oh, she would.'

'Why's that?' said Liz.

'She's going out with Brian Kelly.'

'Isn't she a bit young?'

'Beggars can't be choosers around here. There's a lack of women to go around. I imagine you've noticed?'

He winked, and Liz flushed, annoyed to be outed.

'Not really,' she said.

'Oh, go on now,' said Billy Mac. 'A fine young woman like you? I'm sure you've attracted a lot of attention in these parts, or my name's not Billy Mac.'

'By the way,' said Liz. 'I met an old school friend of yours today.'

'Did you now?' Who was it?'

'Niall Flaherty.'

Billy Mac's face lit up.

'Now, he's a great craic altogether, when you get him in the right mood. He's a bit unscrupulous these days, for my taste. Has he expressed an interest? He'd be a fine catch, even for someone as educated as yourself.'

'He's my solicitor,' said Liz. 'And he's too professional for that.'

Billy Mac raised an eyebrow.

'Methinks the lady doth protest too much. You appear to be defending him.'

'Just avoiding gossip,' said Liz. 'Anyway, my food is getting cold.'

Billy Mac narrowed his eyes.

'Well, you'd better eat then. You're going to need all your energy.'

He walked off before Liz could come up with a suitable retort. *How annoying. That's the last thing I need after getting rid of Sean, not that it's permanent. I just wanted a break.*

Chapter 13

The road to Dunbell had not altered since the Greens had taken up residence in Dunbell Farm over thirty years earlier. If anything, the high banks with their luxuriant mix of hazel and oak hedges seemed to loom over the road turning it into a tunnel. Damp, ploughed fields glimpsed through their gateways still glistened in the drizzle, and were blanketed in greedy rooks pulling fat worms out of the thick black soil.

A trace of honeysuckle perfume crept in through the gap in the driver's window and made Liz nostalgic for her childhood. She had not been the happiest of the Green siblings; Isabella took that crown; but she had found a way to manoeuvre through the alien culture in which she found herself. The Greens' kind landlady, Jacinta O'Reilly, known as Mrs O, and the rowdy O'Connor family next door had been the backbone of their new world. Catholic Ireland in the nineteen sixties had been a minefield of unspoken rules and suffocating guilt which marked the whole family and changed their lives forever. Of all the children, only Nuala O'Connor stayed behind in Ireland after they grew up.

Liz pressed the accelerator a little deeper and took the sharp corners with verve. *Slow down, Liz. You're driving like a local.* Like many other pleasures in life, she almost never allowed herself the thrill of hurtling down the narrow lanes, despite longing to drive fast and throw the car around the corners. She was normally far too law-abiding to break the speed limit. Somehow, buying the house in Ireland had released her metaphorical handbrake. She felt free and reckless and young again as the bright green verges blurred into green rivers.

Suddenly, a fat rabbit hopped into the middle of the road and stopped to look around. Liz slammed her feet on the brakes, but the car slid across the surface of the slick tarmac and two wheels dropped into the ditch bordering the tarmac. The rabbit, unperturbed, hopped back into the hedge. Liz jolted forward, but her seatbelt did its job, restraining her in her seat. She undid it, checking herself for bruises. *Damn, damn, damn. Now what?*

Liz got out of the car and surveyed it for damage. It seemed none the worse for wear, but how could she get it out of the ditch? *That'll teach me for driving like James Hunt.* She looked around for help and heard a car in the distance which seemed to be coming her way. Sure enough, a Range Rover appeared and loomed large in the lane as it approached. It drove past her without stopping, but came to a halt in a wider part of the road just ahead of her car. She felt like Marianne Dashwood in Sense and Sensibility. To her chagrin, it was Dermot Gallagher, and not John Willoughby, who jumped out and put his hands on his hips.

'Miss Green, you seem to be in a predicament. Can I offer you a tow out of the ditch, or will your principles not allow you to accept help from a gentleman?'

Her knight errant had to be him of all people. Not Mr Darcy, but George Wickham. Hardly a gentleman. Liz gritted her teeth, but forced out a smile.

'I'd be glad of a tow,' she said. 'A rabbit sabotaged me.'

'From the looks of the skid, you were trying to assassinate it,' said Dermot, winking. 'Let me get the cable set up and we'll have you out of there in two shakes of a lamb's tail.'

Liz tried not to smile. *Caught in the act.* She watched as Dermot pulled the cable from the winch at the back of the Land Rover and attached it to the bumper. He stood up and gesticulated at her.

'Get into your car and steer out as soon as you feel the pull. Don't forget to release the handbrake.'

The Range Rover made short work of towing her car from the ditch and soon Dermot had wound the cable back onto the winch. He straightened up and Liz noticed the mud on his expensive suit. She bit her lip, trying to stifle a giggle.

'Your suit,' she said.

He looked down at his legs and grinned.

'Oh, don't worry about that. I'm sure Siobhan in reception will enjoy sponging me down.'

'I've no doubt.'

Dermot smirked.

'I'm late for an appointment,' he said. 'Try not to crash again. I'm using my van to move some crates later and it hasn't got a winch.'

Liz laughed.

'I won't. Thank you. I don't know what I'd have done without your help.'

'Look, I know we got off on the wrong foot,' said Dermot. 'I can be an arse at times. Will you have that drink with me sometime? I'd really like to get to know you better.'

It would be churlish to refuse.

'Okay, but I'm buying,' said Liz. 'It's the least I can do.'

'We'll see about that.'

And he was gone. Liz got back into her car and set off again, her heart racing. *Was it the near accident, or Dermot Gallagher's rather obvious charms?* She found herself humming along to the radio as she neared the O'Connor's farmhouse, but the sight of the battered building with its white stone wall sucked the joy out of her. Memories of Liam, and the awful day when they lost him, made her drive on instead of stopping. The tug of the past was too strong. She continued down the road until she could pull into the driveway to Gogans' farm. She parked the car to one side and set off up the path to the woods.

To her amazement, they had tarmacked the path, and a small signpost pointed up the hill to Gogans' Wood. *Since when had they called it that?* The cold air stung her face as she strode up towards the trees. *What am I doing here? I should turn back.* But she couldn't. It was as if an invisible force pulled her towards the old IRA training ground. The dark trees closed around her, dripping cold rain on her back. Her breath caught in her throat as she passed the derelict hut used for instruction in bomb making and ambushes.

As she approached the shooting range, her footsteps faltered. *What raw terror must have seized the boys as they were walked up here by the gunmen? Did they make a run for it, or did they go meekly, hoping to talk themselves out of trouble?* She had never managed to get Michael to relate the exact circumstances of that dreadful day. He kept his memories sealed away from everyone except the O'Connors. When Michael had recovered from his wounds, he had struggled over to their farmhouse and told Maeve, Sean and Nuala how their son and brother had died, bravely and without reason.

Liz shivered as she rounded the corner to the area which the volunteers had used for target practice. It had changed little in thirty years, but now Liz noticed a bunch of fresh flowers on the ground and the woman who sat perched on a log beside them. Maeve O'Connor turned at the sound of Liz's footsteps, her face lined with grief. It lit up when she recognised Liz, and she rose to greet her.

'Liz, darling girl, you came.'

'Hello, Maeve.'

'It's so good to see you. I'm sorry I wasn't at the house. I supposed you guessed where I'd be, this being the anniversary and all.'

Liz stood paralysed to the spot. *The anniversary of Liam's death. How could I have forgotten?*

'Come here and give me a hug then. Or are you too reserved and English now?'

Liz embraced Maeve and they stood for a moment listening to the wind whistling through the trees.

'He loved it here, you know,' said Maeve.

'We all did,' said Liz. 'Especially Blue.'

'She was a great dog. I remember when your father bought her from the travellers. We thought she'd die the same night, but Michael wouldn't let her. Liam and Sean loved that animal like she was theirs.'

Maeve wiped her hair from her face.

'And how is my son?' she said, examining Liz's face for clues. 'That bad, eh? Well, let's go back to the farm and have a cup of tea with Mrs O. She's desperate to see you. You'll find her much changed though. Did Sean tell you she had a stroke recently?'

'No, I'm afraid he didn't. Is she all right?'

'You know Mrs O. Even the Lads were terrified of her. She hasn't let a tiny thing like a stroke get her down.'

'And Nuala? How's she doing?'

Maeve's smile wavered.

'Oh, you know my Nuala. As wild as the hedgerows and twice as rambling. I'll tell you all about it at the farm.'

With that, she linked arms with Liz and they started back down the path to the car. Mrs O'Reilly emitted a joyous shriek as the two women entered the kitchen, but she did not get up from her chair. Liz bent over and hugged her, finding only bones under the tweed suit which now hung loose on her frame. Maeve made a pot of tea and warmed some scones in the Aga. The three women sat at the kitchen table with its worn surface scarred by time, like the lines on their faces. Tales of times past filled the air and soon the kitchen resonated with voices long dead as Blue, Liam and Mickey came back to life. With the change in Maeve's mood, her face became lively and animated. Liz was struck by how young and pretty she looked, despite her age. Brian's death had lifted a massive burden off Maeve's shoulders and she had blossomed. *What a pity she spent all her time shut up in the farmhouse tending to the farm. Maybe she should sell it. But where would she go?*

When the subject of Sean came up, Liz found she could not tell Maeve the truth of their parting. She pretended he would be joining her after the end of year accounting season, and Maeve would soon see more than enough of her son. When Maeve left to deal with an issue in the farmyard, Jacinta O'Reilly leaned forward and tapped Liz's hand.

'She's gone now. Tell me the truth about Sean,' she said.

Liz blanched and bit her lip.

'Oh, you know Sean,' she said.

'I do. Is he drinking?'

Liz's eyes opened wide.

'But, how—'

'That boy had the toughest start in life of anyone I've ever met. He absorbed most of Brian's violent rages to save his mother from them. I saw him provoke Brian on purpose to deflect his fury. Michael's back after the CBS priest whipped him had nothing on the daily bruising inflicted on Sean by that scoundrel. May he burn in hell.'

'But he never said anything. I thought his bruises were from his games outside.'

'You didn't see him without his shirt on. His ribs were often purple. He'd sneak in here for some arnica sometimes. That poor little tyke had a rotten life until he found you. Have you left him?'

Liz gulped.

'We're taking a break. Well, I am. He's drinking too much and raised his hand to me a few times. Although he didn't hit me, the thought had crossed his mind. I saw it in his eyes. I didn't want to reach the point of no return, so I ran away.'

Mrs O'Reilly nodded.

'A horrible dilemma. Not one that has an easy solution. Will he stop drinking now?'

'I don't know. I told him we were finished if he couldn't.'

'Jaysus. He'll be in a right state. Let's hope he can find his way out of this alone.'

'I tried, honestly. I've tried for years. He won't listen.'

'Oh Lord, I'm not blaming you, child. Every alcoholic must choose for themselves in the end. Look at his father, Brian O Connor. He chose death rather than give up.'

Shame enveloped Liz as she imagined the misery of Sean's childhood; beaten to a pulp by his father, losing his adored brother, falling behind in school, and getting teased for being stupid. No wonder he had turned to drink. *How had it been so easy for her to blame him when the causes were laid bare for anyone to see? But how could she make him face the past and find a new future without drink.* The thought of asking him to go to therapy had often fleeted through her mind, but she shrank from suggesting it. *Perhaps he would listen now, if he thought she would return to him?*

In the car on the way home, Liz realised that Sean had never really talked to her about the day Liam died and its aftermath. Like Michael, he had clammed up and shoved the memories deep into his brain where they festered and tortured him. As soon as the funeral took place, Sean had become obsessed with leaving Ireland for ever, taking Liz with him. She had been counting the days to leaving herself, so it wasn't hard to understand. But when they were old enough to leave, she ran towards a new life, Sean escaped from his past.

Michael seemed to have dealt with his trauma, perhaps he had talked to Blessing about it and found a way to make peace with the memory, but Sean was still haunted by it and now he had nowhere to hide. He had never dealt with his feelings about Liam's death, and had buried himself in work. Now he was drowning himself in drink. *Give him a chance. Perhaps being on his own will finally bring it home to him; the drinking has got to stop.*

Chapter 14

After his fight with Isabella, Sean found himself even more isolated. He expected her to apologise to him for her insinuation about his drinking, which had cut him to the core. But the telephone stayed silent. Isabella had been his extra sister for most of his life, and her indifference to his suffering hurt him almost as much as her insult. *As if I can't control my drinking. I'm an adult, for God's sake.* He nursed his resentment against the whole Green family. *Why hadn't Michael died instead of Liam?* After all, it was his fault the IRA shot them both. He would still have a brother if Michael hadn't gone walking in Gogan's Wood that day.

Michael himself had told the O'Connors about the confusion over his army haircut and the ensuing tragedy. Sean had listened as Michael had forced out the words, his body still wracked from the pain of the bullets which had narrowly missed his heart. Sean had never sympathised with Michael's side of the story. The fact that Liam had deserted the IRA in the first place, and suffered the fate of deserters from that organisation, had passed over the top of Sean's head. Michael had been in the wrong place at the wrong time, but Sean blamed him anyway. Liam's death had left him alone to deal with his drunken, violent father and to protect his mother and sister. He could not forgive.

He kept his hate inside where it fought with his love for Liz, a toxic brew that needed to be stilled with alcohol.

One evening, he found himself back in The Duke of Clarence, when he noticed Bernie, Liz's old boss, at the bar. While Bernie did not figure high on his list of favourite drinking buddies, it occurred to Sean that he might have news of Liz. He straightened his tie and buttoned his jacket over his wrinkled shirt, and put on a friendly grin.

'Well, if it isn't my old pal, Bernie,' said Sean. 'Can I buy you a drink?'

Bernie looked around in confusion, but seeing no danger in the half-cut Irishman, he smiled.

'Hello, Sean. I'll have a pint of bitter, please.'

'Coming right up. Would you like to join me? I've got a corner table over there. Sit down and I'll bring it to you.'

While Bernie made his way to the table, Sean ordered two pints of bitter, and a shot of whisky which he drained at the bar, before negotiating his way to the table. He put down the pints which slopped onto the table top leaving a pool on its sticky surface. Bernie made an attempt to soak up the beer with an old napkin, but it became soggy before it made much inroad into the spill. Sean did not notice his efforts. He slumped heavily into the chair opposite Bernie, emitting a long sigh.

'So here we are, two orphans, drowning our sorrows together,' he said.

Bernie shook his head.

'I can't believe she's gone,' he said. 'I thought she wanted a raise when she told me she was leaving.'

Sean snorted into his beer.

'At least she told you. She hid the truth from me. I had to hear it from you first.'

'Not that it did me any good. It's costing me a fortune relying on the whippersnappers in her team. They just don't have the experience to root out the best projects from the dross we get offered at the brokers. It's almost impossible to find a new investment. Although…'

Bernie quaffed a couple of inches of his bitter, leaving a moustache of foam on his mouth. He looked around for a napkin and stared in disgust at the soggy one on the table. Instead, he drew his hand across his mouth. Sean's eyes lit up.

'Although what? Have you got something interesting? I could do with some luck.'

'As you should know, a sure thing doesn't exist in this crazy market, but a company we interviewed recently may have cracked the dotcom formula. We're hoping to make a killing on this one.'

Sean gazed at him across the table; his tie dangled into the pool of beer. Bernie did not notice the gleam creep into Sean's eye, and nursed his drink, day-dreaming of millions. Sean grabbed his arm, splashing more beer onto the already glistening table.

'Is there room for one more?' he said.

'Another investor? Sure. Have you got someone in mind? There'd be a decent commission in it for you.'

'I meant me.'

'You? Oh.'

'Of course, me. Who else would I mean?'

'I'd love to give you a piece of the pie, but the minimum investment is two fifty.'

Sean blanched.

'Two hundred and fifty?'

Bernie nodded.

'Look, don't worry about it,' he said. 'I'll find you a cheaper investment soon, if that's what you want.'

Sean lurched further forward and waggled his finger in Bernie's face.

'And who says I can't afford it?'

Bernie avoided his stare.

'Well, Liz, um, told me about your situation. I, er, just presumed.'

'You presumed wrong. I've got the cash in my account.'

'I'm not trying to put you off, but it's always a risk. Are you sure you can afford it? You could lose it all if things go pear-shaped.'

'You let me worry about the money. When does the offer close?'

'In a couple of weeks, so there's still time, if you're sure.'

'It's a safe bet, right?'

'It's not airtight. I can't guarantee anything in this market. You shouldn't risk anything you can't afford to lose.'

Even in his drunken state, this warning alerted Sean's conscience. After all, Liz had worked hard for this money. What if he lost it? He nodded.

'Okay. I'll think about it and let you know.'

Bernie left soon after buying another round of drinks. He chucked his down his throat and stood up.

'Are you off already?' said Sean. 'I thought we could pick up a Shawarma at closing time.'

'It's more than my life's worth,' said Bernie. 'The missus will be at the door with a rolling pin if I don't get home soon.'

After Bernie left, Sean drank two more pints alone at the bar and then tottered out to find a taxi. Thoughts of Bernie's deal did circuits of his brain all the way home.

Chapter 15

Since she could drive past Kilanon on the way home by taking a short detour, Liz decided to drop in and have another look at the house in the hopes she could gain some inspiration. As she approached it, she noticed a small, scruffy, open-backed lorry parked in front. Two men were smoking and pointing up at the roof. *Could Kathleen have already told her brothers about the work? How strange they had come before arranging it with her.*

She pulled up beside the lorry and jumped out of the car.

'That was quick,' she said. 'I didn't expect express service.'

The men did not answer, but stood looking at her with sheepish expressions and taking long drags on their cigarettes.

'I'm Liz Green,' she said. 'The owner of Kilanon. Did you come to make estimates for me?'

The younger man recovered first and elbowed the older man.

'Oh, it's yourself, is it? Er, yes, we wanted to see the house to get an idea of the work to be done.'

'I'm impressed. I thought it would take ages for someone to find the time to do the renovations. Which one of you is Noel?'

The men looked at each other.

'Neither. I'm Ned Kelly, and this is my brother Brian.'

It was Liz's turn to be surprised.

'But how…'

'We heard you were looking for someone, so we took the chance to have a look for ourselves. Didn't we Brian?' said Ned.

Brian grunted and stared at his feet.

'News travels fast,' said Liz. 'But now that you're here, why don't we have a look around?'

She bounded up the steps followed by the Kellys who didn't need a second invitation.

After a tour, they stood outside looking up at the roof.

'You'll need to replace the whole thing,' said Ned.

'Oh, yes,' said Brian. 'The place is falling down with the damp.'

Liz sighed.

'That bad? I thought most of the leaks were over the kitchen and bathroom.'

'There's no point doing a bodge job on it. Half of the rafters are rotten. I recommend we put up scaffolding and take the slates off. Then we can replace the rafters and re-slate the whole thing with the same slates,' said Ned.

'That sounds like a big job,' said Liz. 'How much would it cost?'

'Well, that depends on the state of the slates. If we can reuse most of them, the cost will come down, but I'd say around thirty thousand pounds.'

Liz gulped.

'That's a little more than I was expecting,' she managed.

'Well, like I said, it depends on the slates,' said Ned.

'I'll have to think about it.'

'You'd need to hurry. We've got another job coming up and it will take us months. We can squeeze you in if we start straight away. You won't find cheaper.'

Ned looked at Brian for affirmation and received a nod. *A man of few words.* Liz considered the offer. Their presence seemed to signal the sort of dynamism she craved. Surely one firm of building brothers was much like another. She could supervise their efforts and call it off if she didn't like the way they worked. After all, she had plenty of leeway with her budget. Kathleen would not be happy, but maybe her brothers could do the inside of the house after the roof went on.

'Okay. You have a deal,' she said.

Ned took a long drag on his cigarette and shoved his hand in his pocket, producing a dirty business card. It read 'Kelly Brothers, your friendly local builders' and had a telephone number scrawled on it. Liz took it and put it in her pocket.

'I'll need fifty percent up front,' said Ned. 'To get the scaffolders in and buy the rafters.'

'Will you take a cheque?'

'Of course.'

'I'll bring you one in a day or two, if that's all right?'

'Fair enough. We'll get started right away.'

'Great.'

Ned spat into his hand and held it out. Liz flinched, but she took his grimy hand in hers and shook it.

'Grand. You won't be sorry,' said Ned.

'I hope not,' said Liz. 'Thanks. I'll be in touch.'

She crossed over to her car and waited until they got into the lorry and drove away. Niall Flaherty had not seemed keen on the Kellys, but Dermot Gallagher seemed equally doubtful about the Doyles. *Or was the the other way around? How do I know which to trust anyway? Would either set of brothers turn out to be any good? It isn't as if I could ask Kathleen for her opinion.* And then Liz remembered the way Kathleen looked at Blessing. It put her off a bit. *Maybe Billy Mac would know.*

Kathleen Brennan sniffed when Liz told her of her decision to employ the Kellys.

'It's none of my business who you chose, but I think you're going to regret this. I'll tell my brothers to hold off until the roof's on.'

'Thanks Kathleen. I'm sorry about the roof, but they were already at the house and I decided to go with them.'

'At the house? I don't understand.'

'When I went there this morning. Maybe my lawyers told them I was looking for a builder. Or did they hear it from you?'

'Are you codding me? I wouldn't tell those eejits anything. Anyway, there's no point crying over spilt milk. Let me know when the roof's nearly done and my brothers can talk quotes with you over the inside. Will you be needing central heating?'

'It's basically a shell. It'll need rewiring too.'

'Right. Well, good luck and fingers crossed. Maybe they'll be shamed into doing a good job, what with your brother and all.'

Whatever that meant.

'Thanks, Kathleen. I'm sorry you're disappointed but I am so desperate to get started and they were keen.'

'I'm sure they were. I'm here if you need coffee and a chat.'

Liz did not get a chance to dwell on the events of the day as she found Dermot Gallagher waiting for her in the lounge at the Woodstock Arms when she got back from her visit. His presumption annoyed her, but she had agreed to a drink with him. *Might as well get it over with.* She wound her way through the tables, acknowledging the greetings of the locals, and joined him at the corner table. As she positioned herself across from Dermot, Liz could feel the scrutiny of the whole bar scalding her. All conversation had ceased as people took in this new development. Billy Mac appeared and flicked a tea towel at one of the locals, giving him a pink ear.

'What are you lot gawking at?' he said. 'Have you never seen a courting couple before?'

Liz blushed.

'Oh no, we're not, I mean, we're just having a drink.'

'That's what they all say,' said Billy Mac, and he tapped the side of his veiny nose with his forefinger. 'What can I get yous?'

'A gin and tonic for me, please,' said Liz.

'And a pint of Smithwicks,' said Dermot. 'And some salt and vinegar Taytos.'

Liz didn't like that flavour, but she didn't say so. Instead, she waited for Billy Mac to leave before commenting on Dermot's cheek.

'You don't waste any time, do you?' she said.

'I didn't want you to change your mind,' he said. 'Anyway, I like the Woodstock.' He leaned closer to her. 'So, Miss Green, where were you going at such a lick this morning when you ran off the road?' he said, with a wink, his strong cologne making her wrinkle her nose.

'We used to live at Dunbell, when we were children. I paid a visit to Mrs O'Reilly and Maeve O'Connor, our former neighbours.'

'Jacinta O'Reilly? I heard she had a stroke. I thought she had died. How's she doing?'

'Oh, pretty good, considering.'

'She always was a tough old bird. I heard she let off a shotgun at the Lads once.'

'She did.'

Dermot raised an eyebrow.

'And how do you know that?'

'She was with my father…'

Liz tailed off as she noticed Dermot's eyes get rounder.

'Oh my God,' he said. 'You're the sister of that English boy, the one that got himself shot when the Lads murdered Liam O'Connor?'

His voice had risen in volume and they once again became the focus of all the attention in the pub. Billy Mac set down their drinks with a thump, slopping some of Dermot's pint on the table.

'Keep your voice down, Dermot,' he said. 'You don't know who's listening.'

Liz glanced around at the inquisitive faces. She saw sympathy and curiosity, but no animosity.

'It's okay, Billy. It all happened a long time ago.'

'Were you there?' said Dermot. 'When it happened?'

'No, I was at home with my parents. Mickey, Mrs O'Reilly's farm lad, found them and called the ambulance. We were lucky to save Michael.'

'Jaysus, I'm sorry. I had no idea. How old were you?'

'About fifteen. I left Ireland after the Leaving Cert with Liam's brother Sean and went to work in London.'

'Brian's boy? What's he like? I never met him.'

'He looks identical to his mother but he's more like his father in character.'

'The beauty and the beast.'

Liz laughed.

'You could say that.'

'Do you still see him?'

Liz froze and stirred her drink with a finger.

'Sort of; he's my boyfriend. Or was until recently. We broke up.'

'Did you now? So, how come you bought a house in Ireland? I bet the interest rates are sky high.'

Liz ate a crisp.

'I paid cash,' she said.

'Not only beautiful, but rich too? You must be surrounded by suitors. No wonder you drive so fast.'

Liz smirked.

'I do all right,' she said. 'How about you? Is there a Mrs Gallagher?'

Dermot frowned and took a long slow draught of his beer.

'No,' he said, and sniffed. 'The local girls are too Catholic for me. They're all frigid.'

He dismissed the thought with a shake of his head. Liz changed the subject.

'How long have you worked with Niall?' she said. 'He seems like a good man.'

'Appearances can be deceptive,' said Dermot. 'He's a brilliant lawyer, I suppose.'

He frowned. *Jealous? Maybe.* Liz tried again.

'He certainly did a good job on my house,' she said. 'I've got all the paperwork in record time.'

'I'm not the only one who fancies you then,' said Dermot. 'You need to watch out for our Niall. He's a sly bastard.'

'What makes you say that?'

'I've got my reasons. Anyway, we were talking about you. How's the building going?'

'I took your advice and hired the Kelly brothers.'

Dermot raised his eyebrows.

'You did? I thought you were going to use the Doyles. How's that going for you?' he said.

'Great. They're planning on removing the slates so they can replace a couple of rotting laths next week.'

'Did you pay them yet?' he said.

'I gave them a cheque for half up front, not that it's any of your business.'

He roared with laughter.

'The woman has spirit,' he said. 'Money, brains and guts. Quite a catch.'

'I'm not anyone's prey,' said Liz. 'I'm quite happy being single. I needed a break.'

'Not even for a man with brains and guts? To me, it seems we have a lot in common.'

Liz raised her eyes from her glass and looked him square in the eye.

'Then it's a pity I don't fancy you, isn't it?'

'But you will,' said Dermot. 'I'm irresistible.'

'And who told you that?' said Liz.

'My mammy.'

They both laughed. Liz had no intention of forming a couple with Dermot Gallagher, but he had charm and humour and she had missed the company of an amusing man since Sean had gone under in a sea of drink. She raised her glass and he clinked it with his.

'Here's to your mammy,' she said. 'Deluded, but happy. I bet she's got rose coloured glasses.'

Dermot grinned.

'Speaking of betting, do you like horse racing?' he said.

'I haven't been for years,' said Liz. 'Sean and I used to go to Ascot when my company had a corporate tent.'

'I can't offer you that level of sophistication, but Niall and I are going to Gowran on Saturday to the members' tent. Do you want to come with us? It'll be a laugh.'

Liz rolled her eyes.

'Both of you? Lucky me. Okay, I'll risk it.'

'We'll pick you up here at midday.'

Chapter 16

By the time Saturday came around, Liz found her level of anticipation had built to a crescendo. The thought of hanging out with the handsome cousins made her feel flirtatious. She had never really been out with anyone except Sean. It felt strange to be going on a date with one man, never mind two. *Was it even a date?*

She rummaged through her wardrobe and picked out a light summer dress which highlighted her violet eyes. She settled on a pair of black pumps for her feet in case she had to do lots of walking on the race course. A purple cotton bolero and a large-brimmed straw hat completed the outfit. She posed in front of the bathroom mirror, but it cut off her bottom half, so she couldn't decide how she looked. Grabbing her black clutch bag with the shoulder strap, she descended the stairs into the bar where Billy hoovered the carpet in a vain attempt to clean it. He raised his head to look at her and dropped the nozzle, putting his hands on his hips.

'Don't you look only gorgeous!' he said, and whistled. 'Those boys won't know what hit them. I can't believe you're going with both of them. I'd accuse you of being a witch if I didn't know better.'

'That's for me to know,' said Liz. 'And you to find out.'

'I'd pay good money to be a fly on the wall and watch what happens after those two have downed a couple of pints,' he said.

'I promise to tell you all the gossip, if you make me one of your steak and ale pies.'

Not long afterwards, Dermot put his head around the door of the bar. He had dressed in a tweed suit, and wore a natty brown trilby on his head at a decidedly rakish angle.

'Are you ready to go,' he said. 'We're—'

His mouth fell open as Liz wafted towards him and twirled so that her dress flew out around her in a circle of flowers and perfume.

'Stop the lights,' he said. 'We're after asking Miss World to the races.'

He lifted his elbow so Liz could insert her arm, and he escorted her out to the Range Rover where Niall gunned the engine in impatience. Liz turned to Billy and gave him a big wink. Dermot opened the back door of the car, and a voice came from inside the vehicle.

'I hope you're letting Miss Green sit up front. She's our guest.'

'Of course. I was just checking the leg room.'

Liz smiled at Dermot, and heaved herself up into the front seat of the Range Rover, trying not to flash too much leg. Niall observed her like a cat watching a sparrow.

'Hello Niall,' said Liz. 'Please stop calling me Miss Green. We're almost in the 21st century.'

'It's good to see you too,' said Niall.

Liz put on her seat belt and looked straight ahead. The tension in the car resembled the atmosphere before one of her fights with Sean. She hoped the racecourse wouldn't be too far away, and she breathed a sigh of relief when it turned out to be only ten miles outside

Kilkenny. She had been to the race course once as a child with Mrs O'Reilly, but the roads had been much narrower then, and took longer to navigate. She had a vague memory of loud cheering, and forests of legs encased in tweed surrounding her, so that she imagined herself lost in a strange woollen wood.

They entered the racecourse through turnstiles, and were given tags for the VIP enclosure.

'Right so,' said Dermot. 'Take my arm and I'll get you over to the drinks tent.'

'You should take mine too,' said Niall. 'You can't be too careful.'

Liz linked arms with the pair and felt as if she were floating across the ground so tightly did they support her between them. For some reason she felt like Mary Poppins. *What a weird sensation! I'm not sure I know how to react to this. Maybe I'll just smile a lot and see what happens.*

Soon they were seated in a corner table of the tent which smelled of new mown grass and heated mildew. Dermot ordered pints of Guinness for himself and Niall, and a glass of white wine for Liz. The wine was warm and tasted corked, but Liz raised her glass and toasted the brothers without making a face. Niall got himself a betting card and settled in to scrutinise the runners and riders. He annotated the card and emitted small grunts as he worked his way through the races.

'That'll pay for the petrol,' he said, heading for the bookies' row where the touts were marking up prices on their boards and taking wads of cash from eager punters.

'Do you bet?' said Dermot.

'I have been known to take a gamble,' said Liz. 'But not on horses.'

'You might be good at this then.'

'I doubt it very much, but I might have a flutter.'

Dermot handed her his card.

'Okay, take your pick.'

Liz ran her eyes up and down the lists and sipped her horrible wine. She had no idea how to choose a horse, and she didn't want to be judged by either of the cousins. She spotted a horse called Sean's Choice, and smirked. Now that would be right up his alley. He'd bet the farm on it and make her cheer with him. The hole he had left in her life could not easily be filled, and whether either of the cousins would fit the bill seemed doubtful. The hole in her chest could not be filled with wine. Niall came back to the table, patting his breast pocket.

'There's a few bankers in there,' he said.

'Liz has been running her eye over the betting card too,' said Dermot.

'Seriously?' said Niall. 'Have you done this before?'

'No, but I'd like to give it a go,' said Liz.

'It would be best to spread out your money between the six races on the card. That way you have more chance of a win,' said Dermot.

Niall snorted.

'Fat chance of that,' he said.

Liz raised an eyebrow at him.

'I've already chosen, as it happens. I'd like to put fifty pounds on Sean's Choice to win.'

'Sean's Choice? But he's a hack. He hasn't a chance against these thoroughbreds,' said Niall.

'Are you sure?' said Dermot. 'That's a lot of money to put on one horse. Shall I make it each way instead?'

'No, fifty pounds to win. It's all or nothing.'

She handed Dermot a fifty pound note with a flourish and he trotted out to the bookies. *Now that was dumb. As if you've got fifty pounds to blow on a stupid bet.*

'No wonder you bought the house,' said Niall. 'You've got guts, I'll say that for you. Would you like some more wine?'

'No thanks. I'm not a big drinker.'

'Just a big gambler, then? I haven't got you figured out yet.'

'And you think you will?'

'You can count on it. Shall we watch the first race?'

Dermot joined them as they left the tent.

'Here's your betting slip,' he said. 'Don't lose it.'

'Maybe you should tear it up now, and save time,' said Niall, receiving a punch in the arm for his joke.

The three of them mounted the steps to the grandstand behind the tent, where they had a magnificent view of the finishing straight. A frisson of excitement shot up Liz's back as the horses came under starter's orders.

'Which nag's yours?' said Dermot.

'Inishfree. And he's five to two on,' said Niall.

'What colour is he?' said Liz, more to annoy Niall than anything.

'I don't know but his jockey is wearing maroon with a white cap.'

The tannoy burst into life.

'They're under starter's orders, and they're off.'

The horses thundered past the stand for the first time, sending shivers through Liz's bones. Niall's horse passed them in seventh or eighth place and they rounded the bend and almost disappeared on the back straight. A yell broke out from the crowd as the herd came around the left-hand bend for the last time and raced up the straight. Liz found herself jumping up and down and shouting 'come on Inishfree' at the top of her voice. Dermot and Niall joined in, but all their encouragement did not make a whit of difference. Inishfree trailed in fifth. Niall took one of the dockets out of his top pocket and shredded it.

'Hard lines,' said Dermot. 'Let's have another pint.'

'He would've won if the race had been longer,' said Liz.

'I'm just getting warmed up,' said Niall. 'You watch.'

And they did, with similar results. Liz tried not to gloat, while Dermot revelled in Niall's bad choices. After three races, Dermot announced he would buy them all a burger.

'No cheese on mine,' said Niall.

'Don't get one for me,' said Liz. 'I'm off to forage. I won't be long.'

She left the tent and wandered to the back of the stands where various stall holders had set out their wares. The sun had burned off the earlier clouds and an azure sky hung over the race course. Women wearing short floral dresses with high heels picked their way carefully across the uneven ground. Many of the men had removed their jackets and slung them over their shoulders. Liz bought a cheese and tomato bap, and looked around for somewhere to get juice. At the end of the row of stalls, she noticed a table covered in punnets of fresh raspberries and strawberries, supervised by a short plump woman with bright red cheeks. *She even looks like a berry, but where have I seen her before?*

'Hello, these look delicious. Is it possible to have a mixture of both?'

'No trouble at all. Do you want cream with them?'

'Is the Pope a Catholic?'

The woman smiled.

'You're not from around here, although you have a trace of accent,' she said.

'It's a long story,' said Liz. 'Where are these grown?'

'Near Thomastown, on the back road to Inistioge.'

'Seriously? I drive up and down that road all the time. I've never noticed a sign.'

'We don't have one. Everyone knows where to find us.'

'I love berries. I'll definitely pop in for a visit. What's your name?'

'I'm Lucy Doyle.'

'Any relation to Kathleen?'

'She's my sister. And you are?'

'Liz Green. I'm staying at the Woodstock Arms.'

The woman's eyes narrowed.

'I've heard things about you,' she said.

Liz sighed.

'It's no secret,' she said. 'I'm the talk of the town right now. I owe your sister an apology for a start.'

Lucy patted Liz's hand.

'Don't worry. She'll get over it. Come and see me for a cup of tea and I'll give you a good price on a bulk buy of strawberries. You can make some jam. Kathleen's partial to strawberry jam.'

'I will. Thank you. Can I have an extra serving of strawberries. I've a feeling I'll have to share.'

'Here you go. Put everything in this bag to carry back. Have you made any bets?'

'Only one. Sean's Choice in the last race.'

'A Hail Mary?' said Lucy.

Liz frowned.

'Sort of.'

'No, I'll say one for you. You're going to need it.'

Liz found the men tucking into large fatty burgers with fries. She ate her bap and tucked into her strawberries with noisy appreciation.

'Those look delicious. Can I have one?' said Dermot.

'You can have a whole punnet to share with Niall,' said Liz. 'I'm not sharing mine.'

'These are only gorgeous,' said Niall.

'How are we doing in the betting?' said Liz.

'Terrible,' said Dermot. 'I should have spent my money on fruit instead.'

'We're not finished yet,' said Niall.

The fifth race did not produce any results either, and gloom descended upon the cousins.

'Shall we go home?' said Niall.

'What about the last race?' said Liz.

'Are you sure you want to watch your money going down the drain?' said Dermot.

'Liz is right,' said Niall. 'Let's go up into the stand for the last rites.'

As the horses roared past on their first lap, Liz noticed that her horse was a grey.

'There he goes,' said Dermot. 'At least he's not last.'

'No yet,' said Niall.

As they watched from the stand, Sean's Choice worked his way to the front group of the runners and stayed there.

'Jaysus,' said Dermot. 'Look at him go.'

Liz caught Niall's eye and they both started to yell.

'Come on Sean's Choice.'

Dermot joined in and they all jumped and shouted together, a mad trio among the almost silent crowd. The thundering hooves approached and the grey crept into the lead.

'Oh my God,' said Niall. 'He's going to win.'

And he did, to a groan of disappointment from the crowd. Liz felt a rush of adrenaline swamp her before Dermot and Niall grabbed her and hugged her tight. They whooped and jumped all over the stand, almost falling down the steps. Finally, they calmed down.

'What were the odds?' said Niall.

Liz handed him the betting slip.

'Holy crap, woman. That horse was twenty to one. You just won a thousand pounds.'

Liz's jaw dropped.

'A thousand pounds? Really? I can't believe it.'

'Fortune favours the brave. I'll go and collect it,' said Dermot.

Sitting in the car on her way home, Liz could feel the wad of notes straining her clutch bag to bursting. She resisted the temptation to gloat, but only just. When they arrived at the Woodstock, both men jumped out of the car and walked her to the door. An awkward moment ensued when Liz attempted to go inside. Dermot grabbed her arm and pulled her close for a kiss. Niall stood waiting until Dermot released her, and to her surprise also leaned in and kissed her on the lips. Her lips buzzed with excitement and her heart thundered. *Do I fancy one or both of them? Or just the situation?* She looked from one to the other, unsure what to do next. Luckily, Billy Mac opened the door and pulled her inside.

'You're in trouble now,' he said.

Chapter 17

Sean walked into the boardroom blissfully unaware of the significance of the meeting to which he had been summoned. He had considered skipping it and pretending he hadn't seen the email, but at least, if it went on for hours, he could day dream instead of working. His tongue felt thick in his mouth and his head throbbed with yet another headache. *Do I have time to get myself a glass of water?* He hovered at the door, and squinted around the room, looking for someone he recognised.

'Sit down, Mr O'Connor,' said the sharp-faced woman on the far side of the table.

'And you are?'

'Sheila Walker, head of human resources. Did you bring a representative with you?'

'A what?'

Sean looked around and noticed his boss sitting in the corner. He did not acknowledge Sean, but looked at his watch instead. A shiver ran up Sean's spine and he cursed his hungover state as the gravity of the situation hit him.

'A representative. You are allowed to bring someone with you to this meeting.'

Sean's eyes opened wide. The cogs turned in his head and clicked into place with a thud.

'Am I being fired?' he said.

The woman sighed.

'Haven't you read the documents attached to the formal invitation to this meeting?'

'I didn't know I had to.'

'Mr O'Connor. Your employment is being terminated. Do you understand?'

'Terminated? But I've worked here for years. You can't do that.'

'You've had two verbal warnings and one written one in the last six months. but you've continued to neglect your work and come in late every day. We can't support you any more. The board has decided to let you go.'

Sean groaned and tried to take it in. He'd never been fired before. This couldn't be happening. His emotions whizzed around a roulette wheel and settled on anger. Not the best option.

'Let me go, is it? I'm leaving. I don't need this.'

He shoved his chair backwards.

'You should sign the severance letter,' said the woman. 'It has the details of your rights to appeal, and your package.'

She pushed some papers across the table. Sean didn't even glance at the contents. He took a biro out of his top pocket and signed them with a flourish.

'There y'go. And good riddance,' he muttered.

'But don't you want to discuss this?' said his boss. 'Do you need help of some sort? Therapy or something? We owe you that much after your service to the company.'

'Therapy? It's you that's nuts. You don't owe me anything. I've been thinking of leaving anyway. Can I go now?'

'Will you work out your notice?'

'Feck off.'

'There's no need to be rude.'

'There's no need to fire me either, but that doesn't seem to have stopped you.'

Sean shuffled back to his desk carrying a furled-up copy of the documents and started shoving his belongings into a plastic bag with them. Despite his years in the same office, he had not personalised his desk to any extent. His sports gear stank when he pulled it out of the bottom drawer. *How long has it been since I went to the gym?* He found a picture of Liz in the top drawer, and a packet of polo mints, but nothing else he wanted to take. He embarrassed the other people in the office by shaking their hands and dropping the plastic bag a couple of times. Nobody could meet his eye, but he forced himself to go through with the charade. He took the cactus, that even he had failed to kill, off his desk and gave it to the receptionist before getting into the lift and descending to the street.

Sean threw his key card at the security desk, and waited fuming while they made notes in the ledger before opening the gate for him.

By the time he let himself into his flat, he had worked himself into a state of righteous indignation. *Who do they think they are, firing me after all the years I've worked for them? It's completely out of the blue. Should I sue them? It's Liz's fault. How can she justify dumping me like this? I've stood by her through thick and thin, and yet she has treated me like I'm worthless. I'll show her. I'm going to call Bernie and get my slice of the pie. This investment is my chance to prove that I'm just as good as her. By the time she notices the missing money, I'll have doubled it. She'll see she's not the only one who can make big bucks. That'll make her reconsider. I can't wait to see her face.*

Bernie picked up his telephone at the third time of asking. He let out an exasperated sigh when he realised who was calling him.

'I'm kind of busy right now. Can't this wait?'

If Sean had any lingering doubts about the investment, Bernie's attitude decided him. He squared his shoulders. *Now or never.*

'It's about the investment. Can you still get me in on it?'

He could hear Bernie breathing hard as if he had run up a flight of stairs. Finally, he said, 'Is this Liz's money you're investing? This isn't one of her vetted deals, you know. It's high risk only, for seasoned investors. These young guys don't have her analytical flair. It could go pear-shaped.'

Sean snorted.

'You don't think I'd ask her first? I don't want to donate my guts for garters. I'm not a complete eejit.'

'We do have a tranche left, as it happens. You'll have to be quick though.'

'Sure, and aren't the two accounts linked already since Liz got paid into this one?'

'That's true. Have you read the presentations I sent you?'

'From cover to cover. Don't get your knickers in a twist. I know what I'm doing.'

Sean had tried to read it, but the jargon had defeated him. He wasn't about to tell Bernie that.

'Okay, you're in.'

'Great. I'll go to the bank and transfer the money immediately.'

'Two-hundred-and-fifty-thousand. The float's next Tuesday. We're hoping for a massive spike around lunchtime.'

'Money in the bank.'

'Listen to me. I'm only going to tell you once. Sell the shares as soon as they peak around the one-pound-eighty-pence mark. Don't be tempted to hang on longer. They may well plummet back down as the day traders take their profits. I'm pretty sure they won't recover for months, if at all. The market's been very unpredictable lately. The Dotcom boom maybe over.'

'Tuesday morning. Okay, fantastic. I won't forget. Thanks Bernie. I owe you a pint.'

'I'm serious about this. Sell at one-eighty or you could lose big. Ring our broker. Here's his number. I'll tell him to expect your call.'

'I heard you the first time.'

'I've got to go now. I'll send you the paperwork when the money lands in our account.'

Chapter 18

After her choice of the Kellys to put a new roof on Kilanon, Liz had some bridge building to do with Kathleen Brennan. The woman had been welcoming and kind, and Liz felt as if she might make an implacable enemy if crossed. It occurred to Liz that Lucy Doyle was right and she could use some homemade jam as a peace offering. She got into her car at the first opportunity and set out for Lucy Doyle's berry farm. A warm breeze with the fragrant scent of strawberries blew through the open windows of her car as she drew into the farm yard. She breathed in deeply, luxuriating in the pungent sweetness.

Lucy Doyle looked up from the long chrome display cabinet in the farm shop where she was pricing and stacking the punnets.

'It's yourself,' she said. 'Perfect timing. I was just about to stop for a break. Do you want a look around?'

'That would be great.'

'Follow me then and I'll show you the greenhouses.'

The greenhouses turned out to be polythene tunnels which smelled of hot plastic and pesticides. Row upon row of strawberry plants with fruit at all stages of development sat on trestle tables at waist height. Raspberry plants grew against the walls, supported by lengths of bamboo. Local fruit pickers worked their way down the tunnels with intense concentration.

'How long does it take them to pick the ripe ones?' said Liz

'It's a bit like painting the Forth Bridge. Once you get to the end, you have to start at the beginning again.'

'How many kilos do you produce a year?'

'Tonnes, not kilos,' said Lucy. 'You'd be surprised. There are several fields of these tunnels.'

She led Liz into the packing area where the smell of fruit reached almost unbearable levels on the warm afternoon. *It's like being stuck in a lift where someone has spilled a bottle of children's perfume.* Liz wrinkled her nose in protest.

'You'll get used to it.'

'You've got quite a berry empire here. What's in the barrels?'

'Those are the berries no-one will buy. They are not quite perfect for some reason or another.'

'What do you do with them?'

'We have a buyer in England who takes them off our hands for a song.'

'And how do they use them?'

'They make jam. Why do you ask?'

'Oh, just interested. Can you sell me ten kilos of those, and the same amount of raspberries?'

'The raspberries are all promised elsewhere, I'm afraid. You need to order a week in advance.'

'Okay. Just the strawberries for now then. I'll have to find someone with a big pan.'

'Have you got a recipe?'

'No, but I know someone who has. Thanks a million. I'll be back. Oh, can I have one of your cards as well please?'

'Sure. I'll see you soon then?'

'I hope so.'

Despite the drizzle which had started to fall, Liz had to open the car windows to let some fresh air in. The strawberries were at peak ripeness and the aroma nearly overwhelmed her. A couple of wasps found their way into the car and she jumped in fright as one landed on her arm, almost swerving off the road. *I nearly ended up in the ditch again. Imagine if Dermot had found me there. Or Niall. They'd think I was a lush. But which one would I prefer to rescue me?*

Billy Mac came outside to help Liz bring the strawberries into the kitchen. He popped a couple into his mouth.

'These are only gorgeous,' he said, juice running down his chin. 'I'd like some of your jam if you have a spare pot.'

'You can take as much as you like. I'd be homeless without you. And I couldn't make the jam without your huge saucepans.'

'I use them when there's a big demand or a Feis on. Do you have jars for the jam? I've got boxes of old ones downstairs. I saved them for the nuclear winter, but the chances of that seem to have faded.'

'That would be great. We need to boil them up to sterilise them for use.'

'I'll bring them up so.'

'There's no hurry. I have to get instructions on how to make jam first. I'll be back in an hour or two.'

'Is there anything I can do to help?'

'You could fill one of the pans with water and leave the jam jars in it to boil and sterilise.'

'Grand. They'll be ready when you get back.'

Liz bought a packet of Jacob's Fig Roll biscuits and headed straight for Dunbell farm. She knocked gently on the back door and when there was no answer, let herself in. She found Mrs O'Reilly dozing in her armchair in the sitting room and returned to the kitchen to put on the kettle and lay some cups on a tray with the biscuits. The kettle took an age to boil. Liz smiled to herself, remembering her mother's fights with the Aga in the farmhouse next door. Liz never heard Bea Green swear before in her whole life until she had to cook with an Aga.

Mrs O'Reilly wheeled herself into the kitchen.

'What a nice surprise,' she said. 'And you brought my favourite biscuits.'

'It's a bribe,' said Liz. 'I need your help.'

'And what can I do in this state?'

Liz looked away from Mrs O'Reilly's legs, black and blue in their ancient slippers. She found it hard to associate the broken old body with the vibrant woman who smoothed their path on their arrival in Ireland, and who famously let off her shotgun at the tyres on an IRA vehicle. She had become a legend in her own lifetime with that stunt.

'I'm sorry about your stroke.' she said. But it's your brain I'm after.'

Mrs O'Reilly patted her hand.

'Thank goodness some parts of me are still in working order, eh? Apart from my sharp tongue.'

Liz gave her a quick hug and poured out their tea. Mrs O'Reilly munched her way through three biscuits in quick succession.

'Those were so delicious. I can't resist a Fig Roll. I've only gone and spoiled my appetite for dinner,' she said. 'How's the renovation going? I heard you took on those scoundrels, the Kellys. Whatever possessed you to do that? You should have used the Doyle boys. Too late now though.'

Liz rolled her eyes.

'I knew I should have asked you. I'll get the Doyles to do the rest, I promise.'

'So, what can I do for you then?'

'I need a recipe for jam,' said Liz. 'I bought ten kilos of strawberries and I thought I'd make a few pots.'

'Will I get one? I can't bear that shop-bought jam. It's like nuclear waste.'

'Of course.'

'I'll give you my best recipe if you do me a favour.'

Mrs O'Reilly's favours. Famous for their weighty nature.

'And what's that?'

'I need you to take Nuala O'Connor in.'

'Can I have your second-best recipe instead?'

'But she needs your help. She doesn't have any sisters of her own.'

'She can have Isabella.'

'Has losing Sean made you cruel? That boy has a lot to answer for.'

'No, of course not. It's not his fault. I'm just a bit jaundiced recently, and she's got a reputation for being a bit flighty. The house isn't ready for guests yet, anyway.'

'You'll cope. Nuala isn't like you. She's lost. Please Lizzy.'

'I'm living over the Woodstock pub right now. I promise that as soon as I can move into Kilanon, she's welcome to come and stay with me.'

Mrs O'Reilly nodded and pulled a spiral bound notebook towards her. She wrote with care, the pen grasped in knuckles swollen by arthritis. The writing crept across the page like a spider had fallen into a bottle of ink, but she didn't falter. *What a memory.*

Finally, she ripped the page out of the notebook and handed it to Liz.

'Here you are. Don't be tempted to double the weight of berries,' she said. 'You can cook two batches, side by side if you are in a hurry. And don't forget to add the lemon or the jam won't thicken. You can put the wedges in too as long as you remember to take them out.'

'Do I need to buy pectin?'

'There's pectin in the lemons, but if you simmer mushed green apples for an hour, you should get an apple jelly full of pectin. If you add two tablespoons for every pound of fruit, it will set the jam without lemons.'

'How will I know if it's ready?'

'Put a saucer in the fridge. When you want to test the jam, drop some on the chilled saucer. If the sides crinkle when you run a knife through it, then the jam is ready.'

'All the stuff I never knew.'

'And do you think I am able to analyse a company?'

'Knowing you, Mrs O; I wouldn't put it past you.'

'Don't forget to bring me a pot, or two.'

Liz laughed.

'Are you taxing me now? Okay, you'll get your pound of flesh.'

'I can't wait.'

Chapter 19

A blast of sunlight penetrated the curtains of Sean's lounge and hit him square in the eyes. He screwed them up and rolled off the couch, landing on the empty cans scattered on the floor. He winced as his knee got trapped in a collapsed can, and stumbled to his feet. The smell of his armpits did not help quell the rising feeling of nausea which crawled up his throat. Kicking the cans aside, he dashed for the bathroom and arrived just in time to vomit into the toilet. He sank to his knees, moaning in misery as his stomach heaved and bucked and rejected its contents.

After dragging himself to his feet, he walked straight into the shower where he stayed under the hot torrent until the tank had emptied. He tried to shave, but the lack of hot water made it too uncomfortable. He stood swaying in front of the mirror trying to focus. His mind swam in circles as he chased a vague notion that he had something important to do. *Why did I drink so much?* And then he remembered.

'Jesus, Mary and Joseph! The float. What time is it?' he shouted.

He half ran back into the bedroom, dropping his towel and feeling the chill of the bedroom raise goosepimple on his skin. *Where's my watch?* He located his pile of vomit-spattered clothes and lifted them up in his fingertips one by one without finding it. Then he remembered taking it off in the bar. *Why? And where had it ended up?* He ran downstairs into the kitchen and looked at the electric clock, screwing up his eyes. *Midday? Christ, I must call the broker. Another conundrum. Where's my wallet?*

His wallet, and his watch, were both in the pockets of his sports jacket. He pulled the piece of paper, that Bernie had scribbled on, out of the condom compartment and attempted to decipher the numbers. *Was that a seven or a four? And that squiggle must be a nine, or is it a zero?* He had Liz's office number somewhere. It must have most of the digits in common. He still had about an hour. *No panic. This is going to be one of the greatest days in my life.*

Half an hour later, having dug out Liz's office number and worked out the broker's extension, he dialled, waiting impatiently for it to connect. Beep, beep, beep. Engaged. He tried again, but the line continued to be busy, frustrating all his attempts to communicate with the broker. He tried Bernie's number, but the call cut off each time. *Maybe he turned his cell phone off for a meeting. There must be another way to get through. The laptop. I'll send an email to Bernie.*

He had a light sheen of sweat on his face as he tried to connect his laptop to the internet. He had never before opened the company laptop at home and had only the sketchiest idea of how it worked. Even as he opened the lid, he realised he should return it, but thanked the stars he hadn't yet. The telephone line only reached the door of the lounge so he had to prop himself against the wall while he tried to connect to the company browser. *Why didn't I pay attention in the training sessions for this thing? I can't make it do anything. Should I call Liz or Isabella for help? Definitely not. Think of the awkward questions that would entail.*

As the minutes ticked away, his heart started racing with panic. Finally, he realised that the only way out of this dilemma would be to go to Bernie's office and do the transaction in person. He grabbed his keys and wallet, and ran to the train station where he missed a train when the guard asked for his ticket and he hadn't yet bought one. Swearing and chuntering, he queued up and bought a return ticket to the City. The next train appeared in ten minutes and got him to his destination in fifteen, but panic had now wrapped its tendrils around his heart and he sprinted to the office building as if a tiger was chasing him.

He walked up to the desk, perspiring, and shaking from effort, the shaved portions of his face red and chapped. The security guard looked him up and down and refused him entry. Sean almost burst into tears, but the guard would not listen to reason.

'You must be accompanied by a member of staff or have a meeting with someone logged here in my book. The IRA bombed Docklands not that long ago. Your accent and general demeanour hardly increase my confidence in your story.'

'But I have to see the broker. It's my whole life on the line.'

'I'm sorry sir, but their telephones are all engaged. I must obtain their say so to let you upstairs.'

'You don't understand. I'll lose all my money.'

'I'm sorry, sir. Mr Sternberg, Bernie, will be back from his meeting shortly. If he says it's okay, you can go up with him.'

So began the longest, and shortest, ten minutes of Sean's life. He watched the second hand of the large, chrome-plated clock hanging over the reception. It seemed to fly around the face, but Bernie did not arrive. A quiet desperation settled over Sean as it dawned on him that he might be too late. He tried to justify his risk to himself as the seconds ticked by, but the feeling of guilt grew and obstructed his throat so that he almost choked on it. A glint of sunlight flashed across the lobby as the doors opened and Bernie walked in, patting his pockets for his key pass. He spotted Sean lurching towards him and his face fell.

'Jesus, man, what are you doing here? Did you sell…'

His voice tailed off as Sean shook his head.

'Follow me. Quickly. We may be in time to save something.'

Bernie nodded at the security guard who handed Sean a pass and made him sign in to the ledger. They passed through the gates and took the express lift up to the brokers' floor. As the doors opened, Sean felt his heart drop in his chest. All of the telephone receivers were lying on the desks off the hook. *No wonder I couldn't get through thought Sean.* An eery silence met them as the brokers still in the room stared at their screens in disbelief.

'The shares are suspended, Bernie,' said one.

Bernie swallowed.

'How much?' he said.

'Ten pence,' said another.

'But I paid a pound a share,' muttered Sean, mostly to himself.

'Why didn't you call them?' said Bernie. 'I told you this might happen. The shares were one-pound-seventy-eight when I left for the meeting.'

'I slept in,' said Sean.

'You slept in? Were you drinking last night? You told me you'd stay at home.'

'I did, but I had a few cans of beer watching a movie.'

'We're screwed.'

'It's my money.'

'It's Liz's money. She'll never forgive me.'

'But at least we'll get ten percent, right? That's better than nothing?'

'They'll go down the drain after this. There's no rescuing this dog,' said the original broker.

Sean shut his eyes tight and opened them again, hoping it would turn out to be a bad dream, but the pale faces of the brokers had all fixed on his. A chill rose up his spine and he almost fainted with the horror of what he had done. How could he ever tell Liz? Bernie tried to put a hand on his shoulder, but he shrugged it off, shaking his head. He couldn't face Bernie's judgement or the brokers' distain. He spun around and marched back to the lift, pressing the down button again and again, jabbing it with his finger.

When the lift finally arrived, he got in without taking his leave of Bernie. He waited for the doors to shut before turning around to face the exit. The lift sped down to the lobby. Bile rose in Sean's throat, but he had nothing to vomit. He took the underground to Victoria station where he installed himself in the darkest corner of his favourite bar. He ordered a pint of Guinness and a whisky chaser and began to drink again. He had no intention of stopping until he passed out.

Chapter 20

The Kellys had removed all of the slates from the roof of Kilanon and the house resembled an eight-year-old with a gap in their front teeth. An operator had driven a rented crane up the driveway and parked it alongside the main house. He manoeuvred the massive new rafters up onto the roof joists under the direction of Ned Kelly, who chained smoked with stress. Liz leaned against her car and watched proceedings with bated breath. The old crane wheezed and creaked under the weight of the rafters and she tried not to imagine the damage if one of them crashed through the loft into the bedrooms below.

Her mobile telephone rang making her jump. She recently invested in one so she could make calls away from the noisy pub phone at the Woodstock, but so far she had only given the number to a couple of people. She grabbed it from the front seat of the car and raised it to her ear.

'Hi, Liz. It's Niall Flaherty. Are you busy?'

'Niall! I'm busy avoiding a heart attack right now. They are raising the rafters onto the roof and I can't bear to watch.'

'Why don't you jump in the car and come for a coffee with me? There's a new place beside the cathedral I want to try.'

The crane groaned under the weight of another rafter and convinced Liz in an instant.

'I'll be there in twenty minutes,' she said.

Butler's Café sat on the corner of Parliament Street and Vicar Street, opposite St Canice's Place, a short lane which led up to St Canice's Cathedral. Niall jumped to his feet as she entered the café and kissed her cheek, lingering one second too long. She looked at him from under her lashes, her violet eyes flashing with amusement.

'Where's the fire?' she said.

'The what? Oh, I just thought it would be nice to see you.'

'Have you ordered?'

'Not yet. I, er, have you ever been to the Cathedral?'

'I must have, but I don't remember it well. Aren't there some medieval tombs or something?'

'Or something? What about the tower?'

'I've never been up there.'

Niall grabbed her hand.

'We can have coffee later,' he said. 'If we go up the tower, we'll need cake too.'

They walked up St Canice's Place to Church Lane and in through the metal gates to the Cathedral. In front of them the round tower with its Pisa-like lean loomed over the church.

'Let's go inside first,' said Niall.

They entered through the main door and gazed up the aisle towards an enormous, magnificent, stained-glass window.

'Wow, that's stunning,' said Liz. 'How has it survived?'

'Oh, it didn't. Cromwell's soldiers destroyed the original 13th century window. This copy was made in the 19th century.'

They walked over the worn black, red, green, and white marble tiles in the Cathedral floor, representing the four provinces of Ireland and set out in diamond patterns over the interior of the church. To the sides of the nave were alcoves which contained sarcophagi of medieval knights rendered in black Kilkenny marble, still holding their swords, and wearing chainmail. Liz stroked the dogs which lay under the chain-mailed feet and wondered if they were buried with their masters. She admired the sarcophagi of noble women with their amazing two horned headdresses.

'Who are the people represented on the sides of the tombs?' she said.

'Those are the tomb weepers. St Peter, St Paul, St Thomas and so on. I don't remember. Have you seen enough?'

'For today, yes, but I'll definitely be back. I'd forgotten how wonderful it is inside.'

'Are you ready for a climb?'

'Sure. Let's go.'

The interior of the thirty-metre-tall round tower had a series of internal ladders comprising seven floors and one hundred and twenty-one steps in total. Liz made Niall go first as she did not want him staring at her bottom all the way up to the top. The summit had a viewing platform with a chain-link fence and a circular bar at about stomach height. The view of the surrounding town and countryside took away Liz's breath, and she stood mute in appreciation. Niall lurched into her, pale and sweating.

'Are you okay?' she asked.

'Oh, yes. I have a tremendous fear of heights. I don't know what possessed me to come up here.'

He put his arms around her waist and his chin on her shoulder. She felt the warmth of his body pressing against her back. He pretended to be looking at the view, but his breathing had gone shallow and she could feel his heart thundering in his chest.

She unfolded his arms and pushed them away.

'Time to go I think,' she said. 'Before we forget why we're here.'

And why are we here?

He didn't move. Instead, he held her again as she turned around to face him, and moved in so close their noses touched. He shut his eyes and leaned in to kiss her. She responded with confusion, but kissed him back anyway as it seemed polite, and then drew away.

'That's enough of that,' she said. 'I've got to go back now. The Kellys will destroy the place if I don't keep an eye on them. I don't know why you thought they were the best. Their equipment is prehistoric, and they are always late, or don't turn up at all.'

'This is Ireland,' said Niall. 'Expect the unexpected.'

But whether he meant the kiss or the Kellys, Liz couldn't tell. She bought herself a takeaway coffee and a brownie at the café, as she still had the craving, and drove back to Kilanon. Niall had left the Cathedral without waiting for her, or coffee, but he turned and waved as if nothing had happened between them. Maybe it hadn't. Liz couldn't figure either of the cousins out. *Were they simply so competitive they couldn't let one of them go out with a woman without trying to seduce her themselves? Or did they both fancy her?*

Of course, the main question was not who fancied her the most, but whether she fancied either of them at all. Lust played a part. She had never been through a barren patch like most women she knew. Sean had always provided for her sexual needs and she had never tired of his passion for her. Now she had nagging feelings of want and desire which she could not satisfy, and the cousins were making them worse.

The truth, which she could not admit to herself, was that she missed Sean, and the cousins were only a side show compared to him. She enjoyed being courted and the thrill of the chase, but she longed for the sound of Sean's dirty giggle in her ear and the feel of his fingers slipping under her shirt and tracing the outline of her bra. *Would she ever get back with him? Did she even want to?* She looked up the drive at Kilanon, and saw the Kellys having yet another cigarette break. One of these days they would burn the place down with a misplaced butt. She sighed and drove up to the house.

Chapter 21

Sean woke to find Isabella Green sitting on the window sill in his room like a be-jeaned guardian angel, her eyebrows knitted together in fury. A faint smell of disinfectant hung in the air, and the walls of the room were painted a sickly green which advertised their location. *How on earth have I ended up in hospital? And what was Isabella doing here?* He groaned as the light penetrated his brain, and illuminated all the dark corners he wanted to keep hidden. *Oh God, let it not be true.*

'What's going on?' he said. 'How—'

Isabella sighed.

'You're a right eejit,' she said. 'You almost died. Liz told me you were drinking a lot, but I never imagined this.'

'Did I have an accident?'

'You could call it that. Bernie found you passed out in the street outside the Duke of Clarence and called an ambulance.'

'So how did you know—'

'He rang Liz's flat and I answered the telephone. The nurses told me you collapsed from alcohol poisoning so I came over to make sure you were all right.'

'You did? But what about—?'

Isabella cut him off with a tut.

'Honestly,' she said. 'You're never going to get it, are you? You're stuck with the Greens, with all of us. We're your extra family.'

'You're not mad at me?'

'Water under the bridge, you big eejit.'

Isabella jumped down from the window sill and sat on the edge of his bed. She poked the drip in his arm, making him squeak with indignation.

'What on earth drove you to drink so much?' she said. 'You could have died.'

Sean squirmed under the glare of her lion's eyes as the memories of the awful day seeped from his brain.

'I lost her money, Izzy. All of it.'

'Whose money? I don't understand.'

'Liz's. Oh God, she'll never forgive me. I should have listened to Bernie, but I forgot and—'

'What's Bernie got to do with this?'

'He told me to sell them straight away.'

'To sell what?'

'The shares. I bought some shares in a dotcom company Bernie raised funds for. I wanted to impress Liz by doubling her money. She thinks I'm a loser. That's why she left me; you know.'

'So why didn't you sell them?'

'I got drunk to celebrate the float of the company, and I overslept. The shares doubled in the first hour and then collapsed. They got suspended at ten pence. Even if they get restored to the market, they've lost ninety percent of their original value.'

Sean put his head in his hands and moaned.

'I'm so completely screwed. What am I going to do now? She'll never take me back.'

Isabella pushed Sean to one side of the bed, almost knocking him onto the floor and stuck her legs out straight above the covers. She pulled a pillow from under him and stuck it behind her back.

'You're such an amadan. I can't believe you let her go in the first place.'

'She left me. I didn't let her go.'

'Semantics. It was one hundred percent your fault. Do you want her back?'

'Of course I do. She's the blood in my veins.'

Isabella snorted.

'Ha! It sounds like alcohol is the blood in your veins most of the time. You've got to stop drinking. She'll never take you back like this.'

'But I don't know where to start. I've been drinking all my life.'

'Can't you stop?'

'I have done in the past, but the booze always lured me back. My whole social life is structured around drink. It always has been.'

'She won't take you back if you don't stop drinking, so that's the only choice you have. And that's if she forgives you for losing her money.'

'Oh God. The money. How's she going to renovate her house without any cash? You haven't told her, have you?'

'I didn't know what you'd done until just now. But she'll find out the next time she tries to draw a cheque on the account. It won't be a secret for long.'

Sean covered his face with his hands.

'Jaysus, I'm a fecking loser. She'll never forgive me, and I wouldn't blame her.'

Isabella patted his hand.

'Is there any chance of repaying the money before she finds out?'

'Not a snowflake in hell.'

'She'll need help then, because her renovation project just became a DIY. You've got to offer to help her. You're pretty handy, aren't you?'

'I used to be. But she won't forgive this. I've lost her for good now.'

'And how do you know that? If you hadn't been so stubborn you would still be together. Liz loves you, I'm sure of it, but she won't take you back, unless you are sober. Why should she?'

Sean sighed.

'No reason at all,' he said. 'I've screwed up so badly. How do I begin?'

'My friend Fred joined his local AA meeting and went from there.'

'Is he still sober?'

Isabella avoided his pleading glance.

'Actually, he's dead. Got shot by the Taliban on a reporting mission. But he had stopped drinking altogether.'

'I'm not sure which is worse, Liz or the Taliban. She'll be incandescent with rage when she finds out.'

Isabella stood up.

'Do you want me to tell her?'

'Would you?'

'On one condition. You go straight out to here to your nearest AA venue. Can you do that?'

'I can.'

'Okay, I'll get my courage up and give her a call.'

'Tell her I'm sorry.'

'You can tell her that yourself; if she ever rings you again.'

She kissed him on the temple and jumped off the bed, turning to look him in the eye. He could feel sweat break out on his forehead under her intense scrutiny. He broke eye contact, and looked out of the window where a flock of starlings had gathered on a nearby rooftop. Isabella opened the door of the room, wavering at the entrance until he returned her glance.

'You've really screwed up this time,' she said. 'Even Liz has her limits.'

After Isabella had left, Sean lay in bed, wrestling with his thoughts. *Bernie is to blame for all this. He said it was a sure thing. He led me up the garden path. There's no way I'm going to sit in a group with all those losers. I'm not an alcoholic. I can stop drinking by myself.*

Once the doctor had signed him off, he signed his release form under the stern eye of a staff nurse who had the air of someone who had seen it all before.

'You're a very lucky boy,' she said, fixing him with a steely stare. 'You almost died and your liver is hanging on by a thread. If I were you, I'd stop drinking before it's too late.'

'I'm in control of this,' said Sean. 'And not the other way around. I just had a few hard days.'

'That's what they all say,' said the nurse. 'You'll be back. Let's hope you survive the next time too.

'I'm perfectly capable of stopping,' said Sean. 'Don't class me with those losers.'

But, despite his certainty, he lasted barely two days before a bottle of Jameson's winked at him from the shelf of the local Tesco supermarket. Stuffing it in his rucksack, he rushed home to pour himself a strong one with a cube of ice. The golden nectar trickled down his throat and sat hot in his stomach.

'Jaysus, that's the right stuff,' he said. 'There's nothing wrong with a drink after a hard day on the job search.'

He sat on his well-worn couch and watched the news and weather forecast. *Shite as usual.* Before he knew it, he had downed five or six shots of whisky. Suddenly, a sharp pain in his liver made him wince and bend double just as the telephone rang. He stumbled over and grabbed the receiver, pulling the whole apparatus off the sideboard and knocking over a Belleek vase given to him by his mother. It shattered the glass coffee table in front of the couch.

He reached out and lifted the receiver to his ear.

'Sean? What the hell's going on there?'

Liz.

'Nothing. I jush dropped the phone.'

'Are you drunk?'

'No.'

A long silence.

'I'll call you some other time.'

'Please, don't hang up. Why did you call?' He steeled himself. 'Did you speak to Isabella?'

'No, why?'

'Oh, no reason.'

'Actually, I spoke to your mother and Mrs O'Reilly. They sent their love to you.'

'Did they? That's nice, I s'pose.'

'Mrs O'Reilly told me you used to provoke your father so he'd hit you instead of your mother. Is that true?'

Sean sniffed.

'I don't want to talk about it.'

'But is it true?'

'Sometimes. Other times he just hit us both anyway.'

'Those bruises you used to have were not from hurling with your friends, were they? Why didn't you tell me the truth?'

'I don't know. I thought you guessed.'

'I'm not psychic. But I could have done something if you'd told me.'

'Like what?'

'I don't know. Called the police or something.'

Sean laughed softly.

'Don't be an amadan. The gardai back then thought men should hit their wives to keep them under control. They probably still do.'

'You've never told me anything about Liam either. After he, I mean, you know.'

'After they murdered him? You never asked.'

'I'm asking now.'

'I'm tired, darling, and I've had too much to drink. Call me again and I promise I'll tell you things.'

'You will?'

'Cross my heart and hope to die.'

'Okay. Bye then.'

'Bye, darling.'

Chapter 22

Billy Mac stood at the bottom of the stairs and roared for Liz.

'There's some English girl asking for you on the phone.'

She jumped about a foot in the air with fright, and wished she had the gumption to tell him to come upstairs and knock, rather than bellowing like a stranded bullock. She smoothed down her hair and opened the door.

'Coming,' she said, and skipped down the steps.

Billy Mac passed her the receiver but did not show any sign of leaving the phone booth.

'Thanks a million,' said Liz, with her hand over the mouthpiece. 'What would I do without you?'

Billy Mac got the hint, and Liz shut the door behind him, squashing herself into the ridiculously small space.

'Hello?' she said.

'It's me,' said Isabella.

'What a surprise! I didn't know you were in the country, well, in London anyway.'

'I'm working on a documentary.'

'That's nice. So, what's your big news?'

'I don't have any. Why do you ask?'

'Oh, Sean asked me if you'd called. I presumed you had a new contract or something.'

Isabella sighed.

'Are you alone? I need you to stay calm.'

'Are you pregnant or something?'

'No, nothing like that. This is about Sean.'

'Sean? Oh God! Is he okay?'

'Sort of. He asked me to tell you something important, and to be frank, I've been avoiding this call.'

The knot tightened in Liz's stomach. *Could he have found someone new already?* She crossed her fingers.

'Spit it out,' she said.

'He invested your savings in a Dotcom float,' said Isabella. 'But the shares crashed and burned, and he didn't manage to sell them on time.'

'Is all my money gone?' said Liz.

'Nearly everything. I'm sorry. I should have told you earlier.'

Liz felt a cold shiver up her spine.

'But how did he know what to invest in? Sean doesn't know anything about shares.'

'Something to do with Bernie. I didn't really understand. He said it was a sure thing, but then it wasn't.'

'Oh God. I can't believe it. How did he miss the crash? I…'

Liz trailed off when Isabella didn't answer. She swallowed hard.

'He slept through it, didn't he? Drunk again, and this time, he's ruined my life as well as his.'

'He wanted to prove he could make money too, to win you back. He was desperate.'

'Desperate? I knew he was struggling, but I never expected him to touch my savings. Bastard.'

'I told him to go to Alcoholics Anonymous. He promised he would and he told me to tell you he'll pay it all back.'

Liz barked out a laugh.

'With what? Bottle caps? I can't believe it.'

'I'm so sorry. I don't know anything about it beside what he told me. Why did he still have access to your bank account?'

'It never occurred to me to change it before I left. I suppose I assumed we'd get back together. How could he do this to me? What on earth am I going to do now?'

'You could sell the house in Ireland and come home. At least you'd get some of your money back that way.'

'But I don't want to. I love the house. It's my home now.'

'I'm so sorry to give you the horrible news, but Sean couldn't face you himself.'

'Thank you for telling me. It must have been very hard for you to make this call.'

'That's okay. What are sisters for?' said Isabella. 'Sean is destroyed you know. He almost drank himself to death the other day. He ended up in hospital.'

'Is he better now?'

'I think so.'

'At least he didn't manage to kill himself. I'm so sick of feeling sorry for Sean. He just ruined my life, and I'm meant to care what happens to him as usual.'

'You have a right to be angry. I'd be livid, but you're so brainy, you'll figure this out.'

'Maybe, but that money represented twenty years of my life I'll never get back, and Sean threw it away in an instant without asking me for permission. You can tell him from me that I never want to hear from him again. Never, ever. I've had enough.'

After an exchange of goodbyes, Liz replaced the receiver, her hand trembling with the fury coursing through her veins. She backed out of the booth. Billy Mac hovered at the entrance to the passageway.

'Is everything all right?' he said. 'You're as pale as a ghost. Will I make you a nice cup of tea?'

Liz tried to push past him, hating the tears which threatened to escape from her eyes.

'Is it Sean O'Connor?' said Billy Mac, putting his hand on her shoulder. 'I don't like to interfere. Only Mairead said that Mrs O Reilly told her mother that you have been courting him all these years.'

'Trust Mrs O. That woman's a human foghorn,' said Liz, forcing a smile. 'No secret is safe with her.'

'I didn't mean to intrude now. You just look so shocked.'

'Oh Billy. I'm going to need that tea. And so are you after I tell you what's happened. I don't know if I will be able to pay your bill any more.'

'The bill? That's the last thing on my mind, you eejit. Sit down and I'll make us a pot of tea.'

Liz sank gratefully into the worn velvet of the corner snug and waited for Billy to come back with the tea. She frowned as she tried to remember all the recent cheques that she had issued which were likely to bounce.

'Turn that frown upside down, pet. Here's the tea,' said Billy Mac. 'Now tell me all about it and we'll sort something out.'

Billy nodded gravely, and sipped his sugary tea, as Liz unburdened herself to him. As she spoke, Liz felt like a massive weight lifted off her shoulders. Somehow telling a stranger seemed infinitely easier than someone who knew her, and would judge her against her own ludicrous standards. Liz tended to be hard on everyone, but no one suffered her intense scrutiny more than herself. Her inner voice had criticised and cajoled her all her life, leaving her exhausted with its demands.

Liz found herself telling Billy about the Green family's arrival in Ireland, the weird customs, the overbearing Catholic Church, her growing isolation. She explained how Liam and Michael got shot, and how Liam's death was the catalyst for Sean's and her departure to look for work in London.

'Sure, didn't half the population go to England in dem days,' said Billy, rubbing his chin. 'You've been together since then? But how come you didn't marry him?'

'I don't know,' said Liz. 'In the beginning, I left Ireland because of the pressure to get married and have children. I wanted a career first. The whole nine yards. Sean would have been happy to get settled down, but I told him to wait. Instead, we both graduated as accountants. Then I got a job at a London brokers office and discovered my skills as an analyst. I moved into the centre of town, but Sean stayed in the flat in Croydon.'

'You don't live together?'

'I wanted to, but he seemed content in Croydon and I worked a seventy-hour week. The years flew by without us noticing. The more successful I became; the more Sean drank. He started turning into his father.'

Billy Mac nodded.

'Oh, I remember Brian O'Connor. A vicious brute. He got barred from here after attacking the previous owner. I'm surprised Maeve managed to survive him.'

'I don't think Sean has ever recovered from losing his brother or having Brian as a father. I have to confess that I never really thought about it. I was so wrapped up in my own career. And we were blissfully happy for years until drink got in the way.'

'And now he's gambled away all your savings? Saints preserve us.'

'Well, not quite all. Luckily, I bought the house over here before then, so I've got that anyway, and there's a few thousand in my other account but—'

Liz clamped her hand to her mouth.

'Oh God, the Kellys. They've paid to put up the scaffolding and they've only repaired half of the roof. The cheque I gave them will bounce. And what about yours? I'm so sorry, Billy. I would never have done this to you on purpose.'

'Don't fret. We'll sort that out another day. First you need to tell the Kellys about their cheque. They're not what I'd call reasonable people, so you need to do that first. Can you pay them anything at all?'

'I'm not sure. I'll go straight there tomorrow and see what I can negotiate.'

Liz returned to her room, fretting, and writing endless lists of her assets, trying to make the numbers add up. Her whole world had collapsed around her and the dream of doing up Kilanon now seemed stupid and impossible. Despite her vow about Sean, Liz could not resist the need to call him and find out the truth. *Has he really lost all my money? Has he finally stopped drinking? I spent my entire adult life with him. Could it be over for good?*

She went back downstairs to the payphone and dropped all her change into it. The ring tone droned on for ages before Sean picked up the receiver.

'Yesh?'

Drunk. I should have guessed. A feeling of inevitability swamped her.

'Sean, it's me, Liz.'

'Darling? I hoped you'd call.'

'And I hoped you'd be sober.'

'I've only had one. I—'

Liz snorted.

'Isabella told me you had promised to stop, but I knew it was too good to be true.'

'Don't be like that. I meant to go to the meeting, like I said I would, but…'

'But what, Sean. What's the excuse this time?'

'I lost my job. It was a terrible shock, and I've been depressed.'

'Depressed? What about me? I'm the one who should be depressed.

'I've been missing you too.'

'Missing me?' Liz's voice took on an edge. 'So much that you lost all my money?'

'She told you then? I'm so sorry. It was a mistake. I—'

'A mistake? You lost my life's savings. How could you? Did you do it on purpose, to spite me, or what? You promised to look after me, and love me; not ruin my life.'

'But Bernie—'

'Don't Bernie me. You're the one who invested my money in that pile of crap. I don't know why I bother to call you, when all I get is some lame excuse from a drunk. We could have tried again, you know. But now I never want to see you again. Ever.'

'I'll pay you back. Every penny. I promise.'

'Yeah, sure. No problem now you don't even have a job. I can't wait until you win the lottery. Goodbye, Sean. Have a nice life.'

Liz put down the receiver and sat on the floor with the dust and the beetles, staring at the wall, whose thick paint had dripped down onto the skirting board. She stayed there for a long time.

Chapter 23

Daylight poked its way into Liz's room to find her red-eyed and wide awake. She could not get her head around Sean's betrayal. The final straw? The one that broke the camel's back? All those years together now seem like a bad joke. And as for Bernie, I'll kill him next time I see him, if the other investors haven't already finished the job for me. How could he have accepted the money from Sean, knowing it was mine? Surely, he knew where it came from? Maybe he wanted to get back at me for leaving? Bernie could be vindictive, but whatever possessed him to take money from Sean in this market?

She went downstairs and made her way through the bar into the kitchen. The smell of rancid beer and cigarettes made her queasy. Liz wrinkled her nose in disgust. *Billy Mac should give that carpet a clean, or better still throw it out and buy something less seventies. Those swirls only increased her nausea.* She made herself a pot of strong tea and a couple of slices of toast. After pouring herself a mug of tea, she slathered butter on the toast and added some strawberry jam she found in the cupboard. The tea made her feel life could be worth living but the jam tasted like chemical sludge, and it had the same colour.

Yuck, that's truly disgusting. Time to open one of mine, I think.

After breakfast, she begged a handful of fifty pence pieces for the call phone from Billy before he had realised what they were for.

'I'll give you a lend of the telephone in my office if you pour me a cup of tea. You can't have those bankers thinking you're not a professional,' he said. 'If the bank manager hears the coins dropping, he might panic or could realise how bad things are.'

'He must have noticed the absence of money in my account.'

'But that doesn't mean they will have made any assumptions about it. Call them and sort things out. Try and stop them bouncing your cheques for now.'

Liz took a deep breath and put in a call to her branch of Barclays in Knightsbridge. A flustered middle manager put her through a rigorous identity check before confirming the account had a balance of five hundred and sixty-eight pounds, before pending cheques were cashed. Liz got a sinking feeling in the pit of her stomach.

'I recently wrote one for fifteen thousand pounds made out to a Mr Edward Kelly. Can you please find out if it got cashed or not?'

'This is most irregular. Can't you wait for your statement?'

'I do apologise. I'm in Ireland and my statement has not arrived yet.'

The manager huffed and the line went silent for a few minutes. Liz crossed her fingers and implored the fates to take pity on her. Alas, they were otherwise engaged.

'Hello, Miss Green. Yes, the cheque has been presented, but rejected due to the lack of funds in your account.'

'Oh, I'm so sorry to hear that. Can I make a transfer from my savings account?'

'I'll send you a form to fill out. Or you can fax it to us to speed things up. You know you have to give one month's notice of any withdrawal?'

Liz sighed. The only fax number she had belonged to the lawyers' office, but beggars can't be choosers.

'Can you fax it to me, please. I'll give you a number.'

She read it from her address book. The manager coughed.

'You realise you have a premium account, madam? I see you have withdrawn most of your money lately. The premium account costs a lot more to run than an everyday one. Would you like me to downgrade your account?'

No, I would not, but what choice do I have?'

'Um, sure, that sounds sensible for the moment as I have all my cash tied up elsewhere.'

'I'll send you a new bank card. Shall I send one to Mr O'Connor as well.'

'There's no need. Send them to me and I'll see he gets it.'

There was a pause. Liz could almost here the cogs grinding at the other end of the line.

'Are you sure you want to keep Mr O'Connor on your account?' said the woman. 'Only…'

She hesitated.

'Only he seems to have withdrawn all my money?' said Liz, and sighed.

'Well, it seems a bit odd. I don't want to interfere in your finances, but are you sure everything is okay?'

Liz sighed.

'Everything is fine, but Mr O'Connor has his own accounts now, so why don't you downgrade my account for the time being and remove him as a signatory?'

'Understood. I'll fax you the form this morning.'

'Thanks,' said Liz. 'I really appreciate your help.'

And she did. *It's a pity I didn't do this before. Too late now.*

She put down the telephone and looked out of the window at the river making its merry way down to New Ross. She had the urge to jump in and swim with the current for miles and miles. *What a disaster. But who would have predicted it? Sean never showed much interest in her money. Apart from the pub, he never spent money on anything.* She shrugged. *Time to plead my case with Ned Kelly.*

Liz drove to Kilanon at a sedate pace as she struggled to formulate a plan in her head. She had zero experience with budgeting after earning a lucrative salary for years. Having grown up in relative poverty, compared to her peers in England, she had experienced a longing for unaffordable luxuries like Levi's jeans and tennis lessons. The Greens had hit rock bottom when their father's business partner had bankrupted them, but her parents had struggled to give them some semblance of the middle-class life they left behind. Instead of boarding school with her friends, she went to a free convent school in Kilkenny with a hockey pitch that also served as cow pasture. She had been old enough when they left England to notice the difference and mourn her old life.

Liz had hated the convent but the nuns had responded to her thirst for knowledge with the full force of their teaching skills. She had taken several accountancy exams in Dublin after her Leaving Certificate, while waiting for Sean, who was younger than her, to catch up. As soon as he finished school, they took the ferry to England and a new life together.

In the end, she hadn't needed any accountancy qualification to get her foot in the door of the brokerage. She took a position as a temporary secretary replacing a woman on maternity leave and never left. Her young boss preferred to spend his lunchtimes boozing in the pub, and she found herself holding the fort on various key moments. Her quick brain and detailed analysis of complex company profiles soon brought her to the attention of Bernie Sternberg, who poached her from the sales desk and installed her in his team of analysts.

Liz had to put up with a barrage of sexist remarks and innuendo about what she did for Bernie in order to get the job, a barrage which only got worse when the men discovered she had started in the company as a temporary secretary, but Liz didn't care. With her accountancy qualification, she could run rings around most of them, and she outlasted all the old crew who knew about her origins. Her earning power increased as she became near indispensable to Bernie. Once she started earning a healthy amount, she bought anything that took her fancy, until she ran out of things she coveted and started spending her money on holidays instead. But now the worm had turned and she had to persuade the Kellys that she was good for the money. But could she kid a kidder?

Liz pulled into the driveway and drove towards the house. The scaffolding still climbed the walls to the roof where half of the roof had been re-slated, but a gaping hole still exposed the new support beams they had installed there. Liz jumped out of the car and approached a pile of ivy they had stripped from the wall and the gutters. A few pieces of broken slate were scattered on the ground, their weathered exteriors a contrast to their virgin interiors. *Where are the rest of the slates? This is a disaster. What if it rains?* Liz looked up at the azure sky. She hadn't experienced a summer like it since 1976, but one sharp rain shower would soak the interior of the house and all the floorboards from top to bottom. She had to find Ned.

She got back into the car and headed for Kilkenny. On her way she stopped and wound down the window to ask passers-by if they had seen the Kellys. It didn't take her long to track them down. They were fixing a roof on someone's barn with a load of weathered slates. She sat in the car for a while admiring their skill, and then went over to the truck and pulled out a slate. Underneath it, she caught sight of some lettering etched into the surface. She moved it around in the sunlight until the writing became clear. Kilanon Glebe 1890.

'Hello there,' said a voice, and Ned Kelly approached her. 'How can I help you, Mrs?'

'I think you know,' said Liz. 'These are the slates from my house.'

'And what if they are?' he said. 'Didn't your cheque bounce higher than the clouds leaving me out of pocket. I'm only taking what you owe me.'

'But what about my roof?' said Liz.

'Hard lines,' said Ned. 'It's not my problem any more.'

'And the scaffolding?'

'Oh, that's not mine. It belongs to Kevin Furlong. He'll be along shortly to take it down.'

'But he can't. I mean I'll stop him.'

'You and whose army?' said Ned, smirking. 'Have you got any cash?'

'Not on me.'

'Well, you'd better think fast. You need a tarpaulin over the hole before the weather breaks.'

'But what about my slates?'

'It's too late now. You'll have to look elsewhere.'

And he turned away from her and lit a cigarette. The smoke blew into her eyes making them water. She didn't want him to think she was crying so she got back into her car and drove away, tingling with the fury that rose within her. *Nothing will stop me doing up my house. Nothing. If I have to do it all myself, I will. The bedrooms at the east end of the house are now under a new roof, I'll fix them up and move in. There's got to be a way of making money out here. I'm not giving up.*

Chapter 24

After Liz had hung up, Sean sat on the couch with the receiver in his hand, surveying the destruction in front of him. The shattered glass from their last conversation still carpeted the rug under the coffee table, mixed with the shards from the vase. The bottle of whisky perched on the wooden surround of the table, taunting him. Shame and grief flooded his senses as he relived the call. *She's just angry. She'll come round. But what if she doesn't?*

He sat there deep into the night, staring at the bottle. Finally, he picked it up and took it into the kitchen.

'We're breaking up,' he said, as he poured it down the plug hole in the sink. 'And this time, it's for good.'

He went back into the sitting room and moved the frame of the broken table from the fleece rug where it stood, breaking the legs off and dismantling it. Then he rolled up the pieces of the table in the rug with all the broken glass and tied it at both ends with a piece of string he found in the kitchen. He took the bundle downstairs and threw it in the skip behind his building. He returned upstairs and had a shower, throwing his filthy clothes into the washing machine with his equally grubby sheets.

He laid clean linen on the bed, and put on a clean t-shirt and boxer shorts which he dug out of his almost empty chest of drawers. Then he made himself a cup of strong coffee, and rejecting the sour milk in the fridge, he piled in a few teaspoons of sugar. He collected the Yellow Pages telephone directory from the table in the hall, and sat back on the sofa, placing his coffee on the carpet with exaggerated care. Then he searched for the section for Alcoholics Anonymous and rang their central number. Soon he had the time and place of a local meeting happening the next evening, before he had a chance to change his mind.

Despite every possible excuse running through his head from the minute he woke up, Sean distracted himself by spring cleaning the house and doing three more loads of laundry which he carried down to the local laundrette to dry. Before he knew it, the time to leave for the meeting had arrived. Somehow, he hauled himself out of his flat and down the stairs to the street. He arrived at the church hall wrapped in a heavy overcoat, the collar turned up to protect him from the biting wind and the possibility of someone recognising him attending the meeting.

He entered with trepidation, as if expecting a trap. The inside of the hall had a glum, mundane air, at odds with the fear tearing at his guts. White plastic chairs were set out in two concentric circles in the frigid church hall, which echoed with his footsteps as he approached them. He sat down in the outer ring of chairs as close to the exit as he could. His craving for a drink screamed inside his head, but he fought his instinct to stand up and head for the nearest bar, using the memory of what he had done to Liz. The awful truth of his cavalier loss of her money kept him in his seat despite his desperation to leave. *How could I have done that to my girl? My only true love.*

Sean kept his head low as the hall filled up. Some people greeted each other with shy nods of their heads, but most just sat quietly looking at their hands in their laps. A short man with a bushy grey beard and massive eyebrows came in and sat almost directly across from him in the inner circle of chairs.

'Hello, my name's Andy Travers, and I'm an alcoholic,' he said, his dark eyes sweeping the room. 'I'll be leading the meeting this evening. I see we have some new members. You're welcome. There is no judgement here.'

Sean flushed and stared down at a piece of chewing gum stuck onto the wooden floor in front of his seat.

'Helen, can you please read the 'How it works' section from the Big Book. And then Sally can run through the twelve steps.'

Relieved not to have to contribute, Sean listened to the women reading. He brindled as she mentioned God. *What's God got to do with this? I could leave now if I stood up.* As if psychic, Andy coughed to interrupt.

'Remember that God stands for any power higher than yourself. You must hand over control of your addiction and deliver yourself to the programme for it to work. Does anyone want to get us started tonight?'

He sat down again and waited. His gaze swept the rows of chairs, pausing an instant on Sean's face, making him looked fixedly at the floor. A man got to his feet; his body almost cadaverous in its thinness. He wiped his long thin nose with a filthy handkerchief.

'Hello, I'm Robert, and I'm an alcoholic.'

'Hello Robert,' chorused the group.

'As you know, I've been coming here for six months now, and I still find it hard to admit the truth. Sure, I've always liked a drink, but I've held down a good job and paid my bills despite the difficulties caused by my drinking.'

He stopped and swallowed a sob. Another man reached up and patted his shoulder.

'But now, I'm alone. My wife took the children and left me. She says she doesn't love me anymore. She can't bear the waiting between the bouts of drinking. I have managed to give up several times, for several months, but I always start again. She can't stand knowing that I'll fail again. The hope has killed her love. Hope is a dreadful thing. So, this time it has to be forever. Drink has finally destroyed my life, but I'm lucky to be able to choose sobriety before it kills me. I feel blessed to have this knowledge, to be able to accept the finality of my choice. With your help, I will never go back. Thank you.'

Sean found that a huge lump had welled up in his throat and he could not look up from his lap where his tightly clasped hands were white and bloodless. *Had Liz felt the same? Had her lost hope killed their love? He couldn't bear to imagine her disappointment and hurt every time he fell off the wagon. How had she stuck it out so long? To think that he had accused her of having a fancy man, when he had been having an affair for twenty years with a demanding mistress who wouldn't let him go.*

Sean squirmed on his seat. *I hate this. Why did I come?* Suddenly, he got the feeling that someone's eyes were boring into him, like hot coals on a nylon carpet. He raised his head and stared across the circle. A man gazed at him, his face white and drawn. A wave of nausea hit Sean as he looked into the eyes of his older brother, Liam. *But how?* He rubbed his eyes and tried to focus, but tears made his vision blurry. The man stood up. *Could anyone else see him?* They didn't appear to notice the man who seemed transfixed. Sean could see his face clearly again. Liam, thirty years older, but a doppelganger of terrifying similarity. *It must be the drinking.*

Sean staggered to his feet in panic, bumping into a couple of people in his haste to exit the hall. The clatter of plastic seats hitting the floor as he blundered through them followed him outside. He leaned against the stone wall of the church and retched until he thought his stomach would turn inside out. When he had calmed down, he took in some long cold breaths and pressed his forehead against the cool stone worn smooth by the touch of thousands of hands.

Sean tried to rationalise what he had just experienced. It had seemed so real. He could remember the last time he had seen Liam with such clarity. Tom Green and Mrs O'Reilly had arrived at Dunbell triumphant after rescuing his brother from the clutches of the IRA. Liam had been installed in Michael's bedroom while they made preparations to ship him over to George Kennedy's house in England. The night before the shooting, Sean had sneaked over to the Green's house with some of Liam's belongings, and crept up the stairs to Michael's bedroom. He found Liam packing an old suitcase and put the things he had brought on the bed. Liam had beamed at him.

'So, shorty, will you miss me then?' he said.

'Of course, but at least I won't be worrying about you dying all the time.'

'I'm immortal. They can't kill me. Come here.'

Liam's voice had caught in his throat. He held out his arms and grabbed his little brother roughly, squeezing him too tight. Sean breathed in his brother's cheap cologne and the damp smell of a sweater dried in the Irish climate. A sneeze threatened as the short hairs on Liam's neck tickled his nose. After a few seconds, Liam rubbed Sean's hair briskly, disturbing his careful parting.

'Whoa. Don't do that. I spent ages getting it to stay flat,' said Sean.

'There are more important things in life than hair. Get going. Da will be home from the pub soon, and Mammy needs you.'

'Do you have to go?'

'Feck off now. I've got stuff to organise.'

Sean remembered jumping up and kissing his brother on the cheek before running down the stairs, embarrassed, afraid his brother would make fun of him or punch him. But Liam never followed him. He never saw him again. After the shooting, the police had taken the body away covered in a sheet and they wouldn't let him touch it. After the autopsy, they sealed Liam into a coffin and delivered it to the funeral parlour where a wake was held. A dreadful occasion he had blotted out from his mind. Brian O'Connor wouldn't let him go to the funeral, saying "he's not even your real brother". Sean had clammed up from then on, keeping his pain deep within, a dark hole he could never fill, not even with booze.

The door of the church hall opened and Sean cowered behind a buttress. Andy emerged holding a bunch of leaflets. He spotted Sean shaking with fear in his hiding place and approached him.

'Are you okay?' he said. 'You went as white as a sheet in there.'

He looked down at the patch of vomit on the pavement.

'You didn't drink before coming to the meeting, did you? No one may attend if they have been drinking.'

'I didn't drink,' said Sean. 'I haven't had a drink for three days.'

He stared at his shoes, unwilling to look up.

'Can I ask you a question?' he said.

'Sure, I'm listening.'

'I heard that drink can cause delirium tremens.'

'The DTs? Yes, it's true, but you have to be pretty far gone to suffer. Why do you ask?'

'I think I saw a ghost, just now, in the hall.'

'A ghost? I suppose you could have been hallucinating, but it's unlikely.'

Andy rubbed his beard.

'Was it someone that you knew?'

'My brother.'

'Oh, I'm sorry.'

'He died a long time ago.'

'Maybe he's haunting you for some reason. I expect you know what it is. When you feel like talking about it, the meeting will listen to you without judgement.'

'I'm not even convinced I belong here yet.'

'Admitting you do is the first step. I've got to go back inside. Will you come with me?'

'No, not this time. I need to go home and process my thoughts.'

'Okay, it's your choice. I brought you a handful of beginner's leaflets. Have a read and ask me if you come up with any questions. Giving up drinking is hard, but not giving up is much worse. Trust me, I know.'

Andy held out his hand and Sean shook it, finding it hard to let go. He felt like a shipwrecked sailor who had found a lifebelt in a stormy sea. Andy's smile was kind as he extracted his hand from Sean's grasp.

'What's your name, son?' he said.

'Liam, Liam O'Connor.' *Why did I say that?*

'Well, Liam, when you're ready, we can help you,' said Andy, and went back into the hall.

Despite his good intentions, the shock of seeing Liam's ghost triggered the drinking reflex in Sean. He bought a bottle of cheap whisky at the off licence on the way home and such was his desperation to take the edge of, he twisted the cap off and took a swig before he reached his flat. He sank onto a bench at the park and sucked on the bottle, feeling the liquid burn its way down to his stomach. His Dutch courage replenished, he hurried to his flat where he bolted all the locks, his heart thundering in his chest. He poured himself another drink, diluting it with several cubes of ice, and lay on his bed swirling the drink in his glass and listening for the clink of the ice cubes as they hit the sides.

He noticed a corner of the floral wallpaper had detached itself from the wall over the blocked-up fireplace and hung down, tempting him to get up and tear off the whole strip. His landlady would be hysterical. She barely tolerated him recently, especially as he had been twice late with the rent. His salary had not risen in years, mostly due to his inability to arrive on time for a job he hated, and now he had lost it too. He had never been honest with Liz about how bad things were. Shame crushed him as he imagined her reaction to his plight. He didn't need her to tell him whose fault it was – he knew.

Chapter 25

After her meeting with Ned Kelly, Liz drove to Kilkenny to collect the form Barclays Bank had faxed to her. Despite her agitation she couldn't help hoping that Dermot would be there. His transparent brand of charm had not fooled her, but she imagined she had detected some chinks in his armour. There was more to him than the brash exterior he projected. At least he might distract her from the dilemma in which she found herself. To her disappointment, she met Niall in the entrance to their offices. She hadn't seen him since their tour of the cathedral and their awkward kiss. He beamed at her. In his hand, he held a fax with the logo of Barclays Bank at the top.

'Miss Green. You'll be wanting your fax, I suppose? Can I tempt you to a cup of tea while you fill out the form?'

So, he's read it then? Does he realise I've run out of money? Thank goodness I paid the final lawyers bill before Sean's disastrous decision. I still have some credit with them, I suppose it wouldn't be correct to ask for the money back? Liz had overpaid the bill to cover expenses which had not materialised, so at least her legal costs were covered for the foreseeable future.

'Oh, hi Niall. Sorry about that. I didn't know anyone else with a fax and the post takes ages from England.'

'Don't worry yourself about it. Come in.'

He put his hand on the small of her back and guided her into his office. She sat in one of the large chairs furthest from his desk and crouched over the low coffee table to fill in the form. She could feel his intense gaze sweeping her for clues as she laboured over it, and the tip of her tongue emerged from her mouth in concentration. She reddened under his scrutiny. *Why couldn't they make these forms simpler?* Finally, she finished and sat back in her chair with a sigh of relief.

'Is it an important matter?' he said.

So, he hadn't read it, or was he pretending? You could never tell with Niall. Dermot was as transparent as a sheet of glass, but Niall had the opaque quality of smoke and mirrors. She couldn't tell what went on behind those cool grey eyes.

'Just transferring some funds into my current account.'

'So, you're fine for money then?'

What sort of question was that? Niall pursed his thin lips.

'Only I heard that Ned Kelly told anyone who'd listen about you bouncing cheques all over town.'

He sat back with his fingers interlaced and watched her react to this gem. The statement hit Liz with the force of a sledgehammer. Her eyes widened and she swallowed.

'I should've known I couldn't keep a secret in Kilkenny,' she said. 'It's all my stupid fault. I forgot to organise a transfer to cover the cost of fixing the roof. It's all sorted out now. Well, it will be, when I fax this order to the bank.'

She tugged at her shirt and rolled up her sleeves trying to seem unconcerned, but the colour rose higher in her cheeks and a smirk crept onto Niall's face.

'I could still sell the house for you if you wanted,' he said. 'Of course, the price would be about half the estimate, what with the roof gone and so on.'

Liz searched for something sarcastic to say, but she held off as she didn't want to burn all her bridges with Niall.

'How nice of you to offer,' she said. 'If I ever sell it, you'll be the first to know.'

She flicked her hair back behind her ears and wet her lips with her tongue. She could almost feel his ears prick up in anticipation.

'Where's Dermot, by the way? I had hoped to have lunch with him.'

Gotcha. Niall's eyes narrowed and turned colder.

'Lunch? With Dermot?'

'Oh yes, I've been seeing him. Didn't he tell you?'

It was Niall's turn to flounder.

'Oh, yes, of course. I forgot.'

Now that's interesting. Dermot hasn't told you, has he? Perhaps he wanted something you don't have for once. But she didn't voice the words out loud.

'Anyway, I'll go and get this sent,' she said. 'Thanks for the use of the fax. I owe you one.'

Niall rubbed his chin.

'Maybe you'd like to buy me a drink sometime, if you're not too booked up with my cousin that is.'

Liz raised an eyebrow.

'And what makes you think I'd agree to that?'

'Well,' he said, grinning now. 'If you're going out with my cousin, you must be desperate, so I figure I stand as much of a chance as he does.'

Liz guffawed. *What a cheek these two had! Mind you, I haven't had this much attention in years. It is kind of exciting.*

'I'm not finding your approach very flattering,' she said. 'But it can't do any harm.'

'I was thinking we might go to the Bridge in Irishtown.'

'Who's going to the Bridge?' said Dermot, who came in on a cloud of cologne.

'Oh, hi,' said Liz. 'Your cousin wants me to go for a drink with him.'

A black cloud passed across Dermot's features.

'And wasn't I after thinking the same thing,' he said.

They glowered at each other, puffing out their chests like cockerels in the farmyard. Liz felt a shiver of anticipation rise up her spine. *Dare I? You're only young once, Liz Green, and not for much longer.*

'Great, she said. 'It's a date.'

The two men looked at her in confusion.

'Both of us?' said Niall.

'That's a bit weird,' said Dermot.

'Come on now. It will be brilliant, just like the races,' said Liz. 'What do you say?'

'Why not?' said Niall.

Dermot rolled his eyes, but he nodded. Liz grinned.

'I could get used to this.'

In the car on the way home, her excitement fizzled out as she remembered her plight. It was all very well carrying on with both of the cousins, to distract them from her dilemma, but she had real world problems to solve. The first of those owned the scaffolding company. As soon as she got back to the Woodstock, she searched the yellow pages for his number.

'Hello, Kevin Furlong here. Who's calling?'

'Oh hi, it's Liz Green. Your scaffolding is up at my house, Kilanon Glebe.'

'Oh, right. Ned Kelly paid me until the end of this week but then I'll be taking it down.'

'Please don't do that. I had a problem with my bank in London, but it's fixed now. I can pay you, just not right now.'

'I'm not a charity, Miss Green. Ned tells me your cheque bounced. I won't work on promises. You need to pay me in cash on Monday morning for the following week or it comes down.'

'You'll have your money. I promise.'

'I'll believe it when I see it.'

Liz replaced the receiver to find Billy Mac standing behind her. She jumped.

'You shouldn't creep up on me like that,' she said. 'You put the heart across me.'

He smiled.

'I haven't heard that phrase in a while,' he said. 'Listen, about the cash you owe me—'

'I'm so embarrassed about it,' said Liz.

'Let me finish. I have a proposal for you. It's probably not up your street, but Mairead is pregnant.'

Liz wrinkled her brow.

'I'm sorry Billy. I've no idea what you mean.'

'She can't do as many shifts in the bar. I wondered…'

Bar work. Jesus. This is a nightmare. Liz forced out a smile.

'Oh, um, sure. If you train me how to use the cash register. I haven't poured a pint for years, but it must be like riding a bicycle.'

Billy beamed at her.

'Look, I know it's not the perfect solution, but I need help and you need money. Why don't we give it a whirl for now? Until you sort yourself out, I mean. You'd be doing me a massive favour.'

'No, it's you who are doing me the favour. I'm so grateful,' she said.

'Magic. Can you start tonight?'

'Tonight it is, then. Oh, but I can't work on Thursday.'

'And why is that?'

'I'm off to the pub with Niall Flaherty and Dermot Gallagher.'

'You're playing with fire.'

'I'm a big girl. I know what I'm doing.'

'I doubt it. Those two are trouble.'

Chapter 26

Liz resigned herself to her fall from grace, having landed with a resounding thump which left little to her imagination. She had covered two of Mairead's shifts at the bar and had been subjected to the locals' humorous take on her predicament.

'How the mighty are fallen, eh?' said one. 'Little did I realise that I'd be served by Lady Muck tonight or I'd have worn my tiara.'

Billy tried to mitigate the worst of their comments, but even he couldn't diminish the combined effect of Ned Kelly's bounced cheque, and the novelty of having Liz working behind the bar. Liz kept her head down and didn't rise to the bait, but internally she seethed with resentment. *If I ever see Sean O'Connor again, I'm going to punch his lights out.* She hadn't made many friends yet, but she had a secret weapon sitting on the shelf in Billy Mac's kitchen. She needed to make up with Kathleen if she wanted to get her roof finished.

The threatening grey clouds overhead as she drove to Thomastown focussed Liz's attention on the imperative of getting the roof fixed before the autumn rains set in and wrecked the floors at Kilanon. It might withstand a few short showers, but even that much water would be hard to dry out again. She parked nearby and sat in her car, steeling herself for her visit to Kathleen Brennan's café. Lucy had assured her that Kathleen couldn't resist a pot of delicious jam, but the gesture seemed unlikely to defrost her after what had happened over Liz's choice of builder. Liz berated herself for picking the Kellys and the loss of her slates. *Was it Dermot or Niall who had recommended them? Too late now.*

She opened the car door and slipped across the square, picking her way through the potholes in the gravel. To her dismay, a hand written sign hung on the door which proclaimed that the café would be closed for the day. Liz pressed her nose up against the glass and spotted Kathleen sitting beside a table at the far end, glaring at the piles of paper in front of her. She knocked on the glass with the ring on her finger and Kathleen's head shot up. She frowned, but she beckoned Liz in, mouthing 'Push'.

Liz pushed the door hard and the doorbell jangled like her nerves as she entered the café. Kathleen did not welcome her in. She stayed sitting at the table waiting for Liz to say something.

'Hi Kathleen. Long time no see.'

'I expect you've been busy bouncing cheques,' said Kathleen, a malicious smile creeping onto her face.

Liz bit her lip.

'Not since I tried to swindle the Kellys. Your brothers had a lucky escape.'

'I hadn't thought of it that way. I suppose they did.'

Liz approached the table and reached into her bag.

'Look, I'm sorry we got off on the wrong foot. I should have listened to you. The lawyers confused me with their bad advice. Anyway, I came to make peace with you.'

She took out the jar of strawberry jam and put it on top of a pile of receipts.

'Your sister told me this is your favourite. I made it with her berries. Oh, no, I'm such an eejit…'

A large blob of jam had fallen onto the receipts from the side of the jar. Kathleen took one look at Liz's face and guffawed.

'You certainly are. Don't worry. Even you couldn't make this situation worse. Doing the accounts every year is a living nightmare. I haven't eaten any breakfast yet. Let's have a cup of tea and some toast.'

Twenty minutes later, Kathleen licked her fingers and smacked her lips.

'Excuse the bad manners,' she said. 'I don't think I've ever had such delicious jam. I've eaten three pieces of toast already.'

'It's pretty good,' said Liz. 'We can thank Mrs O for the recipe. It's a pity we burned the first batch. Mairead had to go to the toilet and forgot to take it off the heat.'

'You'll have to make more and sell it. I'd buy some. My customers would love to have the opportunity to take a pot home with them. Can you make raspberry jam as well?'

'Sell it? I hadn't thought of that.'

'There's plenty of shops around here who would like some up-market jam to sell. Their customers can afford to pay for quality.'

'I suppose I could give it a go. I don't have anything else to do right now, except, well…'

'Well what?'

'I'm a qualified accountant. Not qualified exactly, I can't sign off your accounts, but I could assemble them ready for sign off, if you wanted. I did all the exams in Dublin years ago.'

Kathleen's eyes widened and she rubbed her chin.

'You don't say. I'm not sure I'd trust an accountant who bounces cheques, but I'm pretty desperate.'

'I'll never live that down, will I?'

'No, but who cares? Can you balance the books for me? We could work out a deal.'

'Have you got the latest regulations for filing them?'

'I have the government booklet, but I can't make head or tail of it.'

'Can I have a look?'

Several hours later, Liz stood up from the table and stretched out her back.

'Do you need more tea?' said Kathleen.

'Not right now. I'm making good progress, but my back complained.'

'If it's okay with you, I'd like to see Kilanon. I'm not opening the café today anyway. Do you fancy a quick spin?'

'That would be great. I need a break. Shall we go in my car or yours?'

The sky had cleared and the sun shone on the hedgerows as they drove to Kilanon Glebe. A scatter of hens played chicken at the roadside. As they approached the house, Liz felt depressed to see the gaping hole in its roof. To her horror, the scaffolders had arrived and were dismantling the top storey of the framework. She jumped out of the car and shouted up at them to stop. A man appeared from the back yard and approached the women.

'We have every right to take down the scaffolding,' he said. 'Seeing as we aren't being paid.'

'I'm Liz Green. It's my fault Ned couldn't pay you.'

'The famous Miss Green. Well, I'm sorry, but no payment, no scaffolding.'

'How much do you need to leave it up for a month?' said Liz.

'Five hundred pounds.'

'Do you take cash?'

'Have you got any? I heard otherwise from Ned Kelly.'

Liz opened the car door and reached into her glove compartment. She felt for the fat bundle of notes from Gowran. She had stuffed it there, intending to deposit the money in the bank, but, somehow, she hadn't got around to it yet. She counted out ten fifty-punt notes and handed them to him as Kathleen's eyes nearly popped out of their sockets. Kevin Furlong held one of the banknotes up to the light and screwed up his eyes.

'Have you been printing these yourself,' he said.

'The bookie gave me new notes,' said Liz. 'Do you want them or not?'

'The bookie?' He scratched his head. 'No wonder your cheques are bouncing.'

Liz held out her hand to take it back, but Furlong shook his head and stuffed the money into his pocket.

'No, I'll keep it,' he said. 'I'll leave the scaffolding up for now so.'

'I'll organise some roofers as soon as I can.'

'Oh, I don't care about that. If you keep paying, the scaffolding will stay where it is.'

Liz thanked her lucky stars again for the fortunate bet. Now that the scaffolding had been saved, she intended to persuade Kathleen to get her brothers to fix Kilanon's roof. The bemused scaffolders replaced the missing struts and planks, and drove off again.

'Well, aren't you the dark horse?' said Kathleen. 'Bouncing cheques. Bundles of cash. Are you a drug dealer?'

'It's a long story,' said Liz. 'I don't think I believe it myself. Trust me. I'm as confused as you are.'

Kathleen roared with laughter.

'So, show me this house of yours,' she said.

Liz took Kathleen on a tour of the house where she noticed the floorboards had become damp from the summer drizzle. *How long before they start rotting?* The toilet had sunk further through the floor of the bathroom and looked as if it might break through any day.

'That looks as if it's on its last legs,' said Kathleen.

'I'm desperate to fix it, but…'

'What about your bookie?'

Kathleen's eyes had a wicked twinkle. Liz grinned.

'I won't be trying that again. Actually, I'm planning on prepping some of the rooms myself. I had planned on using my savings to fix up the house, but, well, it looks like I'll be doing a lot of it myself.'

'Do you want to tell me about it?'

'Not really. I might cry, and I'm sick of weeping.'

After a walk around the back yard, they entered the orchard full of trees groaning with ripe fruit.

'Would you look at that,' said Kathleen. 'And they're all going to waste. Do you mind if I collect some for the café? I can make all sorts of cakes and desserts with them.'

'Not at all. I might take some plums home to the pub and see if they make good jam.'

'Now you're talking.'

Kathleen collected an apron full of cooking apples and plums from the orchard before returning to the car.

'If you don't mind,' she said. 'I'll come and collect the rest of these. We have a shed to store them and I can use them well into winter.'

'I don't see why not,' said Liz. 'As long as I can sample the wares.'

Kathleen smiled.

'Maybe we can set up some shelving in one of the sheds at the back here. I could talk to my brothers, if you like.'

'I'd love that, but I simply can't afford it right now. I've hit a bump in the road as far as money is concerned. That bundle of cash is all I've got right now.'

'Oh, no. I don't expect you to pay them. I wondered if you fancy doing their accounts as well. It's a big job. Their business model consists of plastic bags full of miscellaneous receipts and handshakes instead of contracts. I know they pay a lot to get their accounting done. Perhaps we could come to an agreement?'

Liz frowned.

'Like what?'

'Well, I have some old slates that came off a barn in my mother's house. I planned to use them someday, but they're just covered in creepers and returning to the earth. If you will finish sorting out my accounts, I'll give you the slates.'

'Wow. Yes. That sounds fantastic.'

'And if you do my brothers' accounts, I'm pretty sure they can fix that hole in your roof, maybe they'd throw in the bathroom if you pay for the floorboards.'

'That would be fantastic. Can you ask them?'

'I'll need a bribe.'

'More jam?'

'Lots more jam.'

'I need the wiring fixed too.'

'I'm sure we can sell enough jam for that. Why don't you expand your production? I'm sure you can sell all you can produce.'

'I don't think Billy Mac would appreciate me taking over his kitchen. He's already started tutting.'

'And why don't you convert the sheds? They appear to be waterproof. If you can get someone to put in suitable wiring and concrete floors, they'll be perfect.'

'But how would I pay for that?'

'Kilkenny County Council gives grants to small start-up businesses. They gave one to me. It's not onerous, just time consuming.'

'I'll look into it straight away. Thank you.'

Liz drove home from Kathleen's café in a state of rare excitement. *If I can do people's accounts, maybe I can fight my way out of this hole. It will be slower than I hoped, but it gives me the option of moving into Kilanon and saving money and time. I don't mind doing shifts for Billy Mac, but it isn't exactly lucrative work.* She put the plums into a ratty plastic bag which she found in the trunk of the car, and entered the Woodstock, whistling. Billy Mac waited for her behind the counter. He crooked his finger at her and indicated a rumpled figure asleep in one of the snugs.

'Is this yours?' said Billy Mac.

Liz crept over and lifted the curtain of hair even though the identity of the owner was obvious. Nuala looked just like her mother, only rounder. Her knees poked out from under her gingham frock. They were grazed and weeping. Liz shook her head.

'I'm afraid so,' she said.

'I'm not a charity,' said Billy Mac.

'Neither am I,' said Liz.

'You'll have to send her away then.'

'I can't. She's like family. Can I have another bed in my room? Just for a few days?'

'Yours is a truckle bed. All you need to do is pull out the lower mattress. I can give you some bed linen, but how am I supposed to cope with the flood of

171

hormones? One pregnant single woman is bad enough.'

'She's pregnant? Oh, now I understand.'

'I wish I did. You'll bankrupt me.'

'Listen, I've got a plan. Come into the kitchen with me and I'll explain. Have you done your accounts yet?'

'Are you kidding? I leave them until the last minute, and this year, I'm afraid to do them at all.'

'Let's have a cup of tea.'

'Let's have something stronger.'

Chapter 27

Despite all his best intentions, Sean could not deal with the trauma of seeing Liam again without resorting to drink. He bought a couple of six packs in the off license when he got up the next day, and put them in the fridge, drinking them lukewarm when he couldn't wait for them to cool. He told himself it did not matter and that he would go dry again when he finished them, but the days went by, and he visited the off license every time he ran out of drink.

After a while, beer did not take the edge off any more and he started to buy spirits, kidding himself that he would drink them dilute. He bought branded whisky at first, but his funds ran low and he changed to supermarket own-brands instead. Soon he found the effort of carrying heavy bottles of mixers home too great, and he began to drink the spirits neat with ice. His awful hangovers prevented him from searching for work and his savings dwindled. This made him reduce his intake during the week, but his weekends were a blur of drink and headaches. His life spiralled out of control and he didn't care enough to do something about it.

One evening, after a few whiskies, he had drifted off to sleep on the couch, when he heard the buzzing of the Entryphone. *Who the hell turned up at this hour of the night? Maybe one of his drinking buddies had wandered by with a six-pack?* He rolled off the cushions and stood up, reeling from his drunken state. All that whisky on an empty stomach had gone straight to his head. He shook himself awake and stumbled into the hall.

'Hello?' he said, pressing the entry button. 'Battersea dogs' home at your service.'

But no one answered. Sean stood swaying for a minute and then headed for the kitchen to make some toast. He put two slices of thick white bread into the toaster just as someone knocked on his door. He tottered back into the hall. Laboriously, he slid open the bolts and pulled the door towards him, scrunching up his eyes to peer into the stairwell. A man waited outside; his face familiar. Sean jumped backwards in panic and tried to slam the door, but a sturdy leather brogue prevented him. Sean hyperventilated as the man stepped into his flat. Liam's ghost. Sean staggered away, shielding his eyes, and moaning in fear. The man watched him with eyes full of sympathy and not the judgement he had expected.

'How did you find me?' said Sean, looking behind the man into the corridor. 'Am I on Candid Camera or something?'

'The night you came to AA, I followed you home intending to question you, but I wimped out. I tried to forget I'd seen you, but your face appeared in my dreams. So here I am.'

'But who are you?' said Sean. 'Is this some sort of trick? I don't understand.'

'I could ask you the same question,' said the man. 'You look so like her, I had to find out.'

'Like who?'

'When I was sixteen, I travelled to Ireland on a school coach tour. We did all the usual sights and ended up at the Cliffs of Moher on a windy afternoon. Another tour bus pulled alongside ours and it was full of girls. I attended an all-boys school and we were pretty innocent in those days, so we were all a bit shy. Then a girl with wild red hair stepped off the coach and into my heart. She caught me looking at her and smiled. I thought I would faint with excitement. Despite the best efforts of our teachers to keep the two groups apart, we mixed and chatted and found out we were staying in the same cheap hostel. And, somehow, she and I ended up in a shed together later that night. I don't think we were the only ones who had a liaison. We only had one night together, but I've thought about her every day since then. We wrote to each other for a while, but she stopped answering. Not knowing what happened to her broke my heart.'

The man flapped his hands around like a bird with a broken wing, a gesture that Sean recognised. He sat down on the couch and indicated the grubby armchair to his companion. The man ignored him and sat beside him on the couch. He raised his hand as if to touch Sean's face, and dropped it again as Sean's eyes widened in alarm.

'What was her name?' said Sean, although he knew.

'Maeve…' said the man.

Sean swallowed. He tried not to breathe out whisky fumes as the shame of being drunk engulfed him.

'My mother's name is Maeve,' said Sean.

'You look just like her. I…'

The man searched in his pockets in vain for a handkerchief, but found none to stem the flood of tears which had leaked from his eyes. Sean ran to the kitchen and grabbed the roll of kitchen towel. He tore off a few sheets and folded them along the perforations before handing them to the now sobbing man.

'I'm sorry,' said the man. 'I thought I'd never get the chance to meet my son. It's a little overwhelming.'

'Your son? I'm not—'

'Oh, I know it's only biological. I wouldn't blame you if you had no interest in getting to know me.'

'It's not that. I—'

'Please, hear me out. We haven't even been introduced. I'm Matthew Harris. I guess you are the result of me getting your mother pregnant. I would have married her if I'd known. For some reason, she stopped answering my letters. I didn't know why. I guessed she had found someone else.'

He paused. Sean gulped.

'They forced her to get married,' he said. 'She had no choice.'

'She could have married me, if I'd known.'

'I think my grandmother hid your letters. My mother thought you'd abandoned her.'

'And I thought she'd dumped me. Life is unbelievably cruel, isn't it?'

Matt sniffed and dabbed his nose with the kitchen towel.

'Anyway, when I saw you in the church hall, I knew fate had brought us together for a reason. If you agree, I want make up for lost time. We can heal together. I'd like to be your sponsor at AA. What do you say?'

Sean gulped. He wanted to tell Matt the truth about Liam, but the love emanating from the man made his head spin. *What would it feel like to have a father who didn't beat you and judge you unworthy? A father who loved you despite everything. How could he turn that down?* He nodded, mute with desire. Matt beamed and held out his arms.

'May I hug you? I know it's not very macho of me but I've waited all my life for this.'

'So have I,' said Sean.

The two men stood and embraced, awkwardly at first, but soon Sean relaxed and dropped his head to Matt's shoulder smelling a faint odour of Eau Sauvage mixed with damp tweed. Finally, they drew apart. Matt looked Sean square in the eye.

'Is she still alive? Your mother?'

Sean bit his lip.

'I'm so sorry,' he said. 'She died of cancer years ago.'

Matt flinched and a look of intense pain flashed across his features. At that moment, Sean nearly came clean, but he wanted Matt all to himself, and if Matt talked to Maeve, Sean's lie would come out immediately. *I just want a chance at happiness. Is that so wrong?* He waited. Matt shrugged.

'I'll have to get to know her again through you then, if that's all right.'

Sean nodded mutely.

'Have you got any photographs?'

Sean pictured the album in his dresser, with its photographs of the O'Connors and Greens, one of his most treasured possessions. There were not many photographs of Liam, but he would have to remove them first.

'I lent my album to a close family friend, Isabella Green. She wanted to copy some of my photos. I'll get it back and show it to you next time we meet.'

'I'll look forward to it. I have to go now, but I'd like to be sure you'll come back to the meetings. There's no doubt you inherited your genetics from me, and I can help you conquer the need for drink if you'll trust me.'

Matt took a pen from his pocket and scribbled on a bus ticket which he handed to Sean.

'Here's my phone number. Call me any time, day or night, if you feel yourself failing.'

'I'll be there,' said Sean. 'You can count on it.'

After Matt had left, Sean mulled on the enormity of his lie. He blamed the fact he had been surprised and drunk for going along with Matt's passionate need for redemption. He would tell him the truth next time they met. Definitely.

Chapter 28

To Liz's surprise, Nuala O'Connor settled into life at the Woodstock without making a ripple. Liz had taken a dim view of having to share her room with someone who got up to go to the bathroom constantly during the night, but Nuala soon won her over. Her cheerful demeanour defeated Billy Mac, who became quite solicitous of his surprise guest. Despite Liz's gentle prompting, the identity of the father of Nuala's baby remained a mystery, and Nuala seemed disinclined to discuss her pregnancy with anyone. However, the minute she met Mairead, all her barriers came down. They squealed in delight and felt each other's blossoming bumps. The terrible twins, as Billy Mac called them, joined forces, and spent hours together, stirring the vats of bubbling jam and whispering confidences.

Within days, neither Liz nor Billy Mac could remember how things had been before she arrived. Since Nuala had such a positive effect on Mairead, he soon forgot all his objections to her staying, and made her constant cups of tea and snacks. 'For the growing baby'. He forgave Liz on the spot when she offered to balance his accounts for him and to keep them up to date.

'Tis a very strange family we are, to be sure,' said Billy Mac, but the grin never left his face.

The arrival of Nuala O'Connor coincided with a massive upsurge in orders for Liz's jam. Kathleen had been right about its popularity. Liz could hardly keep up with her orders and then other people started to call and make inquiries. To Liz's surprise, orders spiralled upwards to a point where she had both Nuala and Mairead working almost full time in the kitchen. The women got on like sisters from their first meeting and became inseparable within days. Liz bought an extra two-ring gas stove and a bottle of gas, and Billy Mac made them work down one end of the kitchen while he cooked for the bar.

Lucy Doyle soon organised a supply chain for Liz, even getting her husband to deliver barrels of fruit to the Woodstock. Since Liz's operation used the fruit almost instantaneously, she could use the ripest strawberries and raspberries which would not travel well to England. Lucy gave her a great price as these would otherwise have been dug back into the soil. Liz travelled to Carlow to the sugar beet factory to buy sugar in bulk, and used the apples from Kilanon's orchard to make pectin.

'There's a great profit in this jam,' she said to Billy Mac, one day over coffee. 'I'm thinking of printing up some labels instead of just writing on labels with a Sharpie.'

'That's a great idea. What will you call it?'

'Kilanon Country House jam.'

'I think that's a great plan. But you can't use my kitchen any more if you go industrial. I'm already struggling to make pub food in there. The locals won't eat cream teas instead of steak and kidney pie.'

'Oh God no. I wasn't thinking of using your kitchen much longer. I've already taken advantage of your generous nature. Mairead's boyfriend is wiring up one of the sheds in the back yard and soon it will be sealed and ready for action.'

Billy Mac raised an eyebrow.

'How did you swing that?'

'I told the girls I'd have to shut down operations, if I didn't find somewhere fast. Mairead threatened to reveal the name of the baby's father, so he's doing it in his spare time.'

'Doesn't everyone know already?'

'He doesn't realise that.'

'It's a great idea, but how are you going to pay for the equipment? And you'll need a license from the council.'

Liz's hand flew to her mouth to stifle a gasp.

'A what? It never occurred to me. Are you serious?'

'You're running a business making food. I'm sure you need a licence once it goes beyond the phase of giving jam out free for favours.'

'I never thought of that. Where do I go?'

'I got mine from the Kilkenny County Council trading standards office. Well, I didn't get it, exactly. I inherited it from the former owners. I only had to renew it.'

'No time like the present. I'll go there straight away.'

'And my accounts?'

'They're nearly finished. I promise to get them done in the next couple of days. Do you have your permit here? I'd like some tips so I can fill out the forms correctly.'

'I'll make you a copy. Have you thought about the accountancy as well?'

'Thought what?'

'You might need some sort of company for that business too.'

'Blimey, this is getting complicated. Okay, I'll find out.'

On her way to Kilkenny, Liz pondered the wisdom of leaping feet first into both a jam making and an accountancy business at the same time. She mourned her old life and the massive salary that had allowed her to accumulate savings and a pension other people could only dream of. And it took one silly decision from Sean to wipe a large chunk away and completely change her life. She found herself missing Sean. He'd love the jam business and the fact she had finally used her accountancy skills. But she wouldn't call him. *If he's still drinking, he's on his own.*

She parked her car in the municipal car park and made her way to the offices of Flaherty, Gallagher and O'Brien. It occurred to her that she'd never met O'Brien. *Maybe he had an office at the back of the building?* As she approached, Niall and Dermot emerged deep in conversation. She shrugged and turned to go back to the car. Niall noticed her.

'Hey, Liz, were you coming to find us?'

She smiled.

'I was, as it happens, but I see you are busy.'

'Never too busy for your company,' said Dermot. 'I know we were due to go to the pub soon, but we're off for a coffee. Do you want to join us?'

'That would be nice. I wanted to ask for some advice, so you'll have to set the clock running.'

'Try us,' said Niall.

They walked together towards Kilkenny Castle and entered the Design Centre. A heavenly aroma of coffee and cakes met them as they climbed the stairs to the second-floor café.

'I can hear the carrot cake calling,' said Dermot.

'Me too,' said Liz

'You'll get fat,' said Niall.

'We'll be cuddly together,' said Dermot.

They loaded up their tray and made their way to the cash register. Niall took out his wallet, but Liz held up her hand.

'If I'm going to subject you to my musings, I'd better pay,' she said.

'In that case, I'll have cake too,' said Niall.

Liz rolled her eyes and waited for him to choose a slice of coffee and walnut, before paying. They sat in a corner table near one of the round windows looking over the courtyard. The old stables had been adapted as workshops and she felt a frisson of excitement. *Maybe Kilanon could pay for itself.* She lifted a forkful of cake to her mouth and let the icing melt on her tongue.

'This cake is heaven,' she said, shutting her eyes.

Niall leaned over and brushed a crumb off her chin. She jumped back, startled, her eyes wide.

'Um, you had something sticky there,' said Niall, avoiding her glance.

'What did you want to tell us?' said Dermot.

'Oh, yes, it's about my businesses.'

'Your what? When did this happen?' said Niall.

'I asked myself the same question on the way here,' said Liz. 'I'm making jam for sale, and doing accounts for people.'

'Don't you need a license for jam production?' said Dermot.

'I've kept all the receipts.'

'It's health and safety you need to worry about. The EU regulations are pretty stringent.'

'They are? It's only jam.'

'It's illegal jam,' said Niall.

'Can I try some?' said Dermot.

Liz snorted and Niall rolled his eyes.

'Shut up, Dermot. Where are you going to make this jam, Liz?' said Niall

'I'm already making it, but I want to set up a commercial operation.'

'But where would you put it?' said Niall.

'There are farm buildings around the back yard at Kilanon Glebe. One of them runs the length of the yard. It would be ideal for a small production line.'

Niall shot a glance at Dermot, and smirked, but Dermot was gazing at Liz.

'Aren't the buildings falling down?' said Dermot.

'They're in pretty good shape. I'm having them wired and sealed. When they're finished, they'll be ideal.'

'The Council will want to inspect the premises before giving you a licence,' said Niall.

'I'll need to buy equipment first, but it's taking the last of my savings to get the buildings fixed up,' said Liz.

'Aren't the government giving out grants for local start-ups?' said Dermot

Niall coughed.

'Let's not put the cart before the horse,' he said. 'I recommend you talk to the permitting department of Kilkenny Council. They'll sort you out with an application. And why don't you get a loan to tide you over? The house should be good collateral.'

'Ask for Flinty Maguire. He's a friend of ours. He'll see you right,' said Dermot.

'Gosh, thanks, I should've guessed you'd have contacts all over town. I'll go to the bank this afternoon.'

'Which bank do you use?' said Niall.

'The Allied Irish branch in Irishtown.'

'I know it well. Let me know if you need a reference. Who's your manager?'

'I think his name is Quinn. I'd better apply for that permit as soon as possible.'

'I know Mark Quinn. He's a bit of a stickler for the rules, but if you need help there, just give me a call. The Council office is also in Irishtown. Maybe you should go this afternoon. You don't want to risk getting shut down,' said Dermot.

'Once you fill out the applications, we can run the process for you if you like,' said Niall. 'You've still got credit with us.'

'It won't be quick,' said Dermot.

Liz sighed, and shelved the idea of telling them about the accountancy company. *That could wait.*

'If you'll excuse me, I forgot to make a call. See you later,' said Niall.

'Do you want me to come?' said Dermot.

'No, you're all right. Finish your coffees and have a browse. There are lots of great things to buy here.'

He hurried out, looking over his shoulder. Liz shrugged.

'Your cousin really is a hard man to fathom,' she said.

'I wouldn't dig too deep if I were you,' said Dermot, his brow furrowed. 'How about a trip to the cinema this week?'

'Actually, I could do with your help. I remember you said something about a van?'

'Yes, I've got an old Ford Transit I bought for my parents' fruit and veg business.'

'Well, Mrs O'Reilly has offered to lend me some furniture for Kilanon, and I need to move it over.'

'No problem. I can do it on Friday, if you'll go to the cinema with me afterwards?'

'It's a deal.'

Chapter 29

Sean spun the red chip using his thumb and forefinger and watched it pirouette until it clattered down onto the table, landing on the white chip he had already placed there. He found it hard to believe he had managed one whole month of sobriety already. Matt had taken on the role as Sean's sponsor with the agreement of Andy, despite Andy's initial resistance to the idea. As part of the deal, Andy made Sean go to the beginner's meeting held once a fortnight in the hall first.

Sean had attended the meeting two days after Matt had come to his flat. He found himself accompanied by about a dozen other new recruits who all looked wan and nervous. They were presented with white chips as a symbol of the start of their journey to sobriety. The meeting had calmed some of his fears about being ridiculed or exposed after Andy had assured the people who attended that anonymity would always be respected. He told them about his addiction and how AA had saved his life. Then he opened the meeting for questions.

'Why is the focus on staying away from one drink one day at a time,' said one young woman. 'I'm fine until I have too many. That's my real problem.'

A hum of agreement rippled around the hall.

'The first drink triggers the compulsion to drink more. The key of staying sober is avoiding that first drink.'

'But how?

'Apart from the initial promise to yourself? For me the key at first was never getting too hungry, angry, lonely, or tired. These are all triggers, because they make you feel resentful that you can't have a drink. They make your self-pity grow and your craving for just one gets even stronger.'

'What if I'm teetering on the brink?' said another.

'Call your sponsor. Remove yourself from the temptation. Come to a meeting for support. Work on the twelve steps. There's nothing easy about this. It's a lifetime commitment.'

Sean had not asked any questions. He had read and reread all the literature, desperate to win Matt's approval. In reality, he had swapped one addiction for another. Alcoholics Anonymous became an obsession with him and for the first period of his sobriety, replaced drink, filling that gap in his life. His other obsession, Matt, did everything he could to pass his experience on to the younger man, patiently explaining and listening to Sean on his bad days. They attended the same meetings together, Matt picking Sean up at his flat to make sure he came.

Despite his theoretical following of the precepts, Sean had not shown any inclination to follow the twelve-step program. If Matt had noticed this, he did not force the issue until Sean started to find fault with every tiny thing. He complained at length about the cheap coffee at his contract job, or the crush on the trains to work.

'Are you looking for an excuse?' said Matt.

Sean had reacted as if he had been stung.

'What do you mean?' he said.

'You know exactly what I'm asking. What is the first step in recovery? Do you even know?'

Sean hung his head.

'I don't need the twelve steps,' he said. 'I haven't drunk anything for weeks.'

'Willpower can only take you so far. You need to change your behaviour and let the past go, or you will never get past the first hurdle.'

'And what is that?'

'Acceptance. You must accept that you are an alcoholic, that you have no control over the small things in life. Without acceptance you are always on day one. I want to help you, but you must first help yourself.'

He put his hand on Sean's tense shoulder.

'Let go,' he said. 'I'm here to catch you.'

Sean bit his lip.

'I'm afraid. I don't know how to do this.'

'No one does. That's why you're stuck with me. Why don't you show me the photograph album? I've been pining for a look at your mother for weeks.'

Sean couldn't help smiling. He had never thought of his mother in any other way than the bullied martyr of his childhood. Matt's idea of her as some kind of Valkyrie had been surprising. It made him mourn the woman she was, before she met Brian O'Connor and had the fight and joy beaten out of her. He took the album, now carefully censored, out of the top drawer in the dresser, and handed it to Matt. The best photograph of Liam was now hidden in the compartment of his wallet reserved for condoms.

Matt sank onto the couch and opened the first page with reverence. Small noises of appreciation escaped him as he drank in the images of Maeve as a young woman. His eyes shone, and he looked twenty years younger, as he poured over the photographs in the album. Sean felt a pang of guilt as he watched the transformation. *I'm digging myself deeper and deeper here, but how do I escape?* Then Matt ran his finger over a photograph of Maeve with Sean in her arms, and a shadow passed over his face as he traced the faint bruise mark under her eye. Sean held his breath as he watched the turmoil in Matt's expression. Finally, Matt spoke.

'He hit her?'

'He used us all as punchbags, but mostly her.'

'Did he drink too?'

'Yes.'

Matt went quiet again. The muscles worked in his jaw. He opened the album again and removed a photograph of Maeve as a teenager. He held it out to Sean.

'This is the girl I remember. I'll never forgive myself for abandoning her. And now I'll never get to meet her again. So close, and yet so far.'

He kissed the photograph.

'But you didn't. She…'

But there were no words. Matt had left with the photograph, his shoulders slumped, promising to get a copy and then return it. He had not asked any more questions about the family. Nuala did not get a mention, but then she looked like her father who only featured in one photograph. Sean had often thought about cutting Brian out of that one, like he had cut him out of his life, but in the end, he left it in there. After all, Brian was dead now, what harm could he do anyone?

Sean picked up the chip and spun it again, watching it revolve and fall to the table. *That's what happens if you stop moving. I'm afraid to accept the truth in case it's too painful when I do. How did I get myself in this mess? I want a drink so badly, but I want sobriety more. The pain of acceptance will fade, but first I have to take that step. Am I ready?*

He spun the chip again.

Chapter 30

Noel Doyle patted his pocket and beamed at Liz.

'We'll have that bathroom in working order for you by the end of the week. Would you like me to inspect the septic tank for you while I'm at it?'

'The what?' said Liz.

'The septic tank. These old houses are too far back from the road to be integrated into the local sewage systems. They have their own tanks for bathroom waste which need to be emptied every now and then.'

'Oh,' said Liz, trying not to imagine the contents of such a thing. 'Yes, please.' She rubbed her nose. 'What happens when it's full?'

'I've got a friend who'll pump it out for you. Just don't let it overflow. Do you know where it is?'

'I've got a plan of the house here somewhere. I'll fetch it for you.'

Doyle spread the map out over the bonnet of Liz's car, carefully avoiding the glistening bird droppings newly deposited on its shiny surface.

'I wouldn't park under the tree next time,' he said, looking upwards at the rooks' nests.

Liz rolled her eyes. She took out a tissue and dabbed the mess away, looking around for somewhere to throw it. Doyle shrugged and took it from her with his thick fingers. He leaned over the plan.

'Let's have a look then.'

He scanned the plan from left to right using his podgy finger, which resembled a cheap pork sausage.

'Well, there's the tank,' he said. 'It's right at the back of the orchard. We should find the metal cover easy enough. And…'

'And what,' said Liz, alarmed at his change of expression.

Doyle scratched his head, making flakes of dandruff float down onto the plan. Liz pretended not to notice.

'Did anyone tell you about the backyard?' he said. 'Only, according to this plan, it's not part of your property.'

'I don't understand,' said Liz, but a chill crept up her back.

'You don't own it,' said Doyle, stabbing at the plan with his finger. 'It's not included within the boundaries of the plot.'

'But how can that be?'

'Oh, it's quite common over here. Property registration is still not compulsory in Ireland. The new computerised system contains some information, and some are on paper records. There are others written on deeds in people's safes, and in desk drawers, signed by some fella who emigrated to America a hundred years ago.'

'But how can I find out?'

'Mostly, people don't bother. They just leave the problem to the next generation in their will. It's still a bit of a mess to tell you the truth. A friend of mine bought a new house and discovered that the builder owned the driveway.'

Liz examined his face to see if he was joking, but its placid expression told her nothing.

'Let's go and inspect the contents of the tank. They've probably settled over the years. You should be grand for a while.'

Doyle used a crowbar to level off the lid of the septic tank and gave Liz the thumbs up.

'That should be fine for a couple of years at least, unless you fill the house with people. Just get someone to check it every now and then. I'll write down the name of my friend with the slurry truck for you.'

When Doyle had left to buy the new floorboards for the bathroom, Liz went upstairs to inspect the main bedroom. She had made good progress with stripping the wallpaper from the walls, helped by the grooves left by the electricians who had rewired the house, leaving traces in every room. The heavy Georgian door creaked as she used a piece of sandpaper to remove a stubborn lump of gloss from one of the panels. Her City manicure had long given way to ravaged cuticles and a myriad of mysterious scratches on her hands, but she revelled in her new situation.

She might not have any money, but she had left all her stress in England, and she felt ten years younger. Now that the roof had been completed, she had spent the last of her savings on getting the house rewired and buying some replacement floorboards. With her lawyers' help, it had been a simple process to apply for the grant. Flinty, from the grant office, had telephoned Mark Quinn at AIB and assured him the grant was a certainty. The bank had then lent her money on the strength of her grant application. The loan would be enough to get the out-buildings fit for purpose and buy some jam boilers and bottling equipment. She figured that with electricity and plumbing sorted out, she could move in and decorate the rooms one by one as she received income from the manufacture of the jam and occasional accountancy gigs, paying off her loan as she went.

Despite her optimism, the conversation she had just held with Noel Doyle had perturbed her more than she wanted to admit. He had been so blasé about it, but she didn't feel comfortable knowing that the out-buildings didn't belong to her. There must be a process she could follow to claim them. The sound of a car's horn disturbed her thoughts. She ran downstairs and flung open the front door to find Dermot outside with a battered transit van.

'I brought you the furniture from Mrs O'Reilly's farmhouse,' he said.

Liz couldn't decide whether to be thrilled or horrified. She hadn't warned Mrs O that Dermot would be passing by yet. *What on earth would she have made of him?*

'Are you going to help me or just stand there looking gorgeous?' he said, opening the back doors of the van.

Liz smiled and rolled up her sleeves.

'I thought you'd never ask,' she said.

Liz had always been quite athletic, but they struggled to lift the heavy furniture up the stairs and into the bedrooms. Liz sat on a chair and watched as Dermot re-assembled the bed in her room, admiring the sinews in his forearms and the bulge of his biceps in his t-shirt. When he had finished, they pushed it up against the wall. One of the legs jammed against a loose floorboard, sending Liz flying. Dermot picked her up off the floor and kissed the elbow she was rubbing with grave attention. He bent down to examine the board and lifted it out of the floor.

'Jaysus. Would you only look at that?'

'What? Don't tell me I have rats. Have you found a nest?'

'No, it's a box. I'll take it out.'

'A box? How exciting. Maybe it will contain hidden treasure and solve all my problems.'

'It's a bit light for doubloons. '

Dermot prised the metal box out of the hole and popped open the lid. Inside was a plastic bag.

'So, it's not old then. What a disappointment,' said Liz.

Dermot put his hand into the bag and pulled out a bundle of letters and papers. He handed the first letter to Liz who sat on the bed to read it. Her eyes flickered from side to side, and then she smiled.

'Oh, how romantic. They are love letters from George Kennedy to Lee. I wonder why she put them here. You can read one if you want. They're both gone now. I don't expect they'd mind. I'll have to send them to their son Ben. He'll be amazed.'

She continued to read. Dermot flipped through the stack of letters, unwilling to intrude on the love story. He unfolded a document and his eyebrows flew up. He shut it again, glancing at Liz and then he shoved it into his pocket. He carefully went through the rest of the correspondence to make sure there were no more bombshells in the stack.

'They were such a lovely couple,' said Liz, looking up with tears in her eyes. 'I wish I'd met Lee. My father says she was a real Irish firebrand.'

Dermot sat beside her.

'Her parents stole this house from Niall's grandparents, you know.'

Liz dropped the letter.

'They stole it? How?'

Well, not exactly. But Niall's grandfather gambled away the family money and Joe Kennedy, Lee's father, bought the house when Niall's grandfather was made bankrupt.'

'That's hardly stealing, is it?' said Liz, pursing her lips.

She replaced the letter in the plastic bag with the others and put it back into the box. Dermot lifted her chin with his finger tips and gazed into her violet eyes.

'I didn't mean to upset you.'

'You haven't.'

'Let me kiss you better.'

'We're supposed to be unloading the rest of the furniture.'

'It can wait.'

Chapter 31

Sean glanced around the café and spotted Isabella sitting in a booth with shiny red plastic benches. As usual she had attracted the attention of all the men in the place with her tousled blonde curls and lion's eyes. She looked up from her full English, and grinned at him, ketchup on her upper lip. He shook his head as he approached.

'You eat like a horse,' he said. 'How do you stay so slim all the time? I'm bursting out of my jeans.'

'That's a beer belly.'

'Steady on.'

Isabella patted her stomach.

'I'll be working on one myself if I keep eating these. Actually, you're looking pretty good. Have you stopped drinking?'

'I followed your advice and went to my local AA meeting.'

'It seems to be working then? That's great. What's the big drama anyway? You never call me for a chat these days, so it must be important. Have you made up with my sister yet?'

'She won't have me. I think she's found someone else.'

'Liz? Don't be silly. She's an old maid. Who'd fancy her?'

Sean glared at her.

'Well, me, for a start.'

'I'm sorry,' said Isabella. 'It must be hard for you after all those years together.'

'At least it made me stop drinking.'

'I thought that was the AA.'

'It is, only…'

'Only what?'

'I met a man there who says he's Liam's father.'

Isabella's eyes nearly popped out of their sockets.

'Liam's father? But how do you know?'

'We've had some long chats.'

Isabella punched his arm hard.

'Wait, you've met Liam's father, and you haven't told anyone?'

Sean sighed and picked his nails.

'It's complicated.

Isabella snorted.

'Complicated? Are you nuts? You've got to tell Maeve. She has a right to know. I presume you've told him about Liam.'

'That's just it. I haven't told him anything. Oh God. Izzy. I've made a hames of everything as usual. No wonder your sister left me.'

'He still doesn't know about his son?'

Sean swallowed.

'He thinks I'm his son. And worse still, I told him Maeve had died because I didn't want him to find out that I'd lied to him.'

Isabella sat back and observed him over the rim of her mug of tea.

'But why would you do that?' she said.

'I panicked. I thought he wouldn't be interested in me if I wasn't Liam, and I needed a father other than

Brian O'Connor. A father who loves me and doesn't treat me like a punch bag.'

Sean's head sunk into his hands and Isabella's fury dissipated. She patted his arm.

'What am I going to do?' he said. 'I've fecked this up too, haven't I?'

'It's not terminal,' said Isabella. 'You can tell him the truth.'

'But he'll hate me. He won't let me explain. He's not a patient man.'

'You must tell him before he finds out. There's no option.'

He knew she was right. Invariably, the Green sisters got to the kernel of every matter. But he didn't get the chance to confess the truth before it came out by mistake. Matt came to his house to watch a DVD at the weekend and they ordered a pizza to eat in. Sean insisted on paying to celebrate his continuing sobriety. After much debate about the merits of pineapple on pizza, they settled on a large one, half pepperoni, and half Hawaiian, and ordered it on the telephone.

'Shall I order a bottle of Coke?' said Matt.

'I'd prefer Sprite if that's okay with you.'

'They're all the same to me.'

Once the pizza had been ordered, Sean put out a couple of glasses and some kitchen towel on the coffee table in front of the television.

'You're spoiling me,' said Matt.

'Feck off.'

The pizza took about half an hour to arrive, and when it did, the doorbell sounded just as Sean had gone to the bathroom.

'Matt, can you pay the pizza guy, please? My wallet's on the table,' he said

Matt picked up the wallet and opened it to take out some cash. As he ferreted through the partitions, a small booth photograph caught his eye. He pulled it out and his eyes widened. The delivery man leaned on the doorbell making Matt jump. He opened the door and grabbed the pizza, thrusting the money into the man's hand. Then he threw the pizza onto the table, knocking a cup onto the floor where it shattered.

'Whoa, look out for my crockery,' said Sean, appearing from the toilet. 'I don't have much left…'

He tailed off as he saw Matt's white face and realised what he had in his hand.

'Where on earth did you get this photo of me as a kid?' said Matt, holding it out. 'I've never even seen it before. Why is it in your wallet?'

Sean's blood ran cold. He swallowed hard.

'It's not you,' he said. 'You'd better sit down.'

Matt sank to the couch, the picture still in his hand.

'What's going on?'

'I never intended for this to happen. You have to believe me.'

'For what to happen? Make sense.'

Sean took a deep breath.

'You're not my father,' he said.

'I know that. I'm just the biological beginning of your story. Your—'

'You don't understand. My name is Sean O'Connor, and my mother is Maeve, but my biological father was Brian O'Connor, also a drunk.'

'But I don't understand. How old are you?'

'Younger than I look. I'm an alcoholic, remember, like my father, Brian.' Sean bit his lip. 'Do you remember when I first noticed you in the meeting?'

'Yes, you ran away that night. We weren't sure what had happened to you.'

'Why do you think I recognised you?'

'I never thought of that. I guess I was so stunned when I realised who you were, I didn't wonder about it.'

'That's just it. When I saw you, I thought you were Liam.'

'Liam?'

'The boy in the photo. My older brother. He looked just like you. Identical in fact.'

Matt raised his head.

'Your older brother? Oh my God.'

Sean ran his fingers through his hair and blew his cheeks out.

'I wanted to tell you the truth so many times, but we have such a strong connection. I convinced myself I was your son too.'

'But where is Liam?'

Sean blanched.

'I'm so sorry,' he said. 'Liam died decades ago. The IRA shot him.'

The colour drained from Matt's face.

'Oh my God,' he said. 'The bastards killed my son?'

'It was a mistake,' said Sean. 'My brother found himself in the wrong place at the wrong time.'

Matt looked Sean in the eye.

'And your mother?' he said.

Sean tried to smile.

'She's very much alive, and still living in Ireland.'

Matt stood up.

'I can't stay here,' he said.

'Please don't go. You may not be my father, but our bond is real.'

'But you lied to me. You let me think my son was alive. I'm not sure how I can forgive you for that.'

'But Matt—'

'Don't talk to me now. I've got to go.'

'Please…'

But Matt had reached the front door and, in an instant, he had left. Sean stood horrified in the sitting room and then he noticed Liam's photograph on the floor. He picked it up and rubbed the face gently with his thumb.

'You may be the one who's dead,' he said. 'But at least you never killed anything. I destroy everything I touch.'

Chapter 32

Exhausted by the combination of jam making and late-night accounting, Liz stopped by at Doyle's farm to pay Lucy for her last delivery of fruit. The rear-view mirror reflected her tired face back at her, as she dabbed some concealer on the bags under her eyes. Once inside the dairy shop, she leaned against the counter, yawning while Lucy printed out the receipt. Lucy raised her eyebrows.

'You look exhausted,' she said. 'Are you burning the candle at both ends?'

'A little. I'm spending most of the day painting and sanding at Kilanon, and then the evenings bottling jam at the Woodstock. We are flooded with orders, and Billy Mac's kitchen is not big enough for large batches of jam. I could do with a mechanical stirrer of some sort too. The girls will soon be too large to get close to the saucepans. They're both close to giving birth. I don't know who will win.'

Lucy nodded and then she held up her finger.

'Hang on a second.'

She opened a drawer and started to rummage through a pile of old receipts and notes written on post-its.

'No, it's not here,' she muttered, and opened the drawer below it. She took out a stack of business cards, many stained with berry juice and flicked through them. Finally, she held one up in the air, in triumph.

'Here it is. I knew I still had it somewhere.'

She handed it to Liz.

'Copy down the number,' she said. 'The Conran family used to make jam until they switched to cider. It's a long story, but not one I've time to tell you today. Anyway, I'm pretty sure they had a couple of jam boilers on their farm. You might be able to buy them.'

Liz wrote down the name and number into her address book.

'This is great, thanks. I'll call them straight away.'

'Tell them Lucy sent you.'

The telephone line crackled as Liz waited for an answer to her question.

'Let me get that straight,' said the voice. 'You want to buy our jam boilers?'

'Well, at least one of them, if that's okay.'

'Okay? Are you codding me? I'd give them away free. They're hanging around here reminding me of what happened. It would be a relief to get them off my hands.'

'When can I come over?'

'Is tomorrow good for you?'

'Tomorrow? Okay, I'll sort out a van. What size are they?'

'Thirty-five litres. You'll need an estate car or a small van to take them away. I've got a forklift here so I can easily load them for you, but you'll need help unloading them at your place. Where are you based?'

'Kilanon Glebe.'

'The old Kennedy place? I thought that had fallen derelict.'

'Not yet. I'm hoping to move in soon.'

'You can tell me all about it tomorrow. Just come to the dairy before midday and I'll get you sorted out. Do you want an old apple press too?'

'An apple press? No, I don't think so.'

'Don't worry about it. I'll have the jam boilers ready for you.'

Liz rang Dermot Gallagher next.

'My van? Tomorrow morning? Sure, no problem at all. I can't drive it myself, but my cousin will help you. He owes me a favour. Are we still on for the pub?'

The next morning, Liz found herself in the front seat of the Ford Transit, held in with a fixed seatbelt, surrounded by choking Players cigarette smoke. She gritted her teeth. *Keep telling yourself how cheap he is.* Luckily, they didn't have to drive too far. They drew into a farmyard near Clonmel, and Phil Conran emerged from the cowshed, his boots covered in manure. Liz jumped out and shook his hand. He looked her up and down.

'So, you're the woman with the bouncing cheques,' he said.

'I brought cash,' said Liz, trying to smile.

'Grand,' he said. 'Let's get them into the van then.'

He made the driver reverse up to the doors of one of the barns and opened them. Inside, Liz spotted two large, stainless steel drums side by side.

'They look perfect,' she said. 'Exactly what I need.'

Phil Conran jumped onto his forklift and lifted on of the drums off the floor. He drove up to the van and stopped, rubbing his chin.

'That accent's not from here,' he said. 'How did you find me?'

'I'm from London. Lucy Doyle told me about you. I had explained to her that I was struggling to fulfil the orders after I set up the business with the help of my lawyers. They also helped me buy the house and pay the death duties.'

Phil Conran lowered the lift bed to the ground.

'Which firm are you using?'

'Flaherty, Gallagher and O'Brien. Niall—'

'Niall Flaherty? That snake? You're working with him?'

'Not with him. He's my lawyer.'

'A likely story.'

He started the forklift and took the jam boiler back inside the barn. Liz stood beside the van with her mouth open, speechless with astonishment. Phil Conran slammed the barn door shut again, dislodging plaster from around the hinges.

''Feck off,' he shouted, purple with fury. 'You've got some cheek turning up here with your posh accent, acting all nicey-nicey with me.'

Liz stared at him in shock.

'I'm sorry,' she said. 'I don't—'

Conran strode over and shoved his fist in her face.

'You've got thirty seconds to leave, or I'll set the dogs on you.'

She gulped and backed into the door being held open by the now panicky driver.

'Get in,' he said. 'There's a couple of Dobermanns behind the garden gate. They're massive feckers.'

He drove off as Phil Conran turned the air blue with a string of bad language.

'What the hell was that about?' said Liz.

'No clue,' said the driver. 'He started acting funny when you mentioned Niall and Dermot. Before then, I thought he might give you the boilers for free.'

'It's a big blow,' said Liz. 'We'll have to order a new one and keep making the jam by hand for now. I don't know how I'll keep up with the orders.'

Despite the valiant efforts of Dermot's cousin to start a conversation, Liz remained silent on the way back to the Woodstock. Phil Conran's violent reaction at her mention of her lawyers had shocked her to the core. *Why had he reacted like that?* The cousins had been so helpful to her since she had arrived. She found it hard to believe they had done something to rile the man up so much. There was only one way to find out.

Despite her tiredness, she got into her own vehicle and drove to Kilkenny. She parked outside the offices of Flaherty, Gallagher and O'Brien and marched in. The receptionist, Siobhan, looked up from her work and smiled.

'Is it Dermot you're after?' she said.

On receiving an answer in the affirmative, she showed Liz into Dermot's office.

Dermot looked up from his desk and beamed at her.

'Well, if it isn't the prettiest girl in Kilkenny,' he said. 'What can I do for you?'

His smile evaporated when he took in Liz's tight jawline and glazed eyes. He drew a chair up to his desk and gesticulated at it.

'Sit down, before you fall down. What on earth is the matter?'

'Maybe you can tell me?' said Liz, pulling at her blouse and avoiding his gaze. 'I had the doubtful pleasure of meeting Phil Conran this morning.'

Dermot's expression did not change. He swallowed.

'Phil Conran? Now that's a blast from the past. How did you come across him?'

'Lucy Doyle told me they might sell me some jam boilers, so I rang them and organised to collect them.'

'So that's why you needed my van? I wish you'd told me.'

'You didn't ask.'

'What sort of problem did you have with Phil Conran?'

'When I mentioned that you and Niall are my lawyers, he threatened me and threw me off his farm. So now I have no boilers, and I'm stuck with these huge orders I can't fill.'

Dermot pulled at his collar.

'That man's a menace,' he said. 'If you'd told me that you were going to see him, I'd have warned you about him.'

'But why does he hate you so much?'

Dermot stood up and turned his back on her, cracking his knuckles as he stared out of the window. Liz waited.

'His business went bankrupt and he blames us for it.'

'Why?'

'Because he can't accept that he is the one at fault. He over-reached and grew too fast, and the bank foreclosed on his loans.'

'But what's that got to do with you?'

'We failed to save his business from the inevitable collapse. We tried, but he was up to his neck in debt. It was hard on him, but not our fault.'

Dermot turned back to face her and his expression softened.

'I'm sorry that happened to you. He can be pretty intimidating. Will you come and have a quick drink with me? The sun's already over the yard arm.'

Liz felt her anxiety dissipating.

'That would be nice,' she said.

'And meanwhile, I'll have Siobhan make some calls, and see if we can replace those boilers.'

Chapter 33

Sean stood outside the church hall, his hands deep in his pockets, watching people file inside to the meeting. Anonymous beings with hidden lives. Some of them gave him sheepish waves or a thumbs up. *How ordinary they looked; people's mothers and fathers, sons and daughters, all slaves to alcohol, lives ruined by their addiction. Did they look at him and see the same thing? How had it come to this?* He longed for the night to be over. *Would Matt understand how his deep need to be loved had led to his disastrous lie?*

Andy Travers appeared in the distance, striding towards him along the pavement lined with plane trees, kicking a fizzy drink can along the road with all the enjoyment of a small boy. He gave it a final belt and mouthed 'Goal' as it flew through the gate and landed at Sean's feet. Sean picked it up and dropped it in the rubbish bin.

'Man U?' he said.

'Liverpool,' said Andy.

'I'm going to speak today,' said Sean.

Andy grabbed his arm and looked into his eyes.

'That's fantastic news,' he said. 'Everyone finds their voice eventually.'

'No, it's not. Someone here is going to get hurt by what I say. Please can you make sure he doesn't leave until I finish speaking.'

Andy scratched his head and pursed his lips.

'You mean Matt? I noticed you two had stopped hanging out together. I can try, but I can't stop him leaving if he wants to.'

'I know that, but he trusts you.'

'I'll see what I can do. But I can't promise anything.'

'Thanks.'

Andy disappeared into the dark interior of the church, pressing the flesh, and murmuring greetings. Sean waited until the last minute before he entered the hall, watching the clouds congregate over the hall like speech bubbles of doom. Forcing his feet to move, he shuffled inside. He noticed Andy had managed to sit beside Matt, and headed for a seat almost directly opposite them. He wiped his sweaty palms on the thighs of his trousers, his mouth dry.

The preliminaries seemed to take forever, and he mumbled along with the others without understanding the words or caring what they meant. The smell of cheap coffee drifted across the hall, but he craved something stronger to help him through this. He caught Matt glancing at him, but did not acknowledge the gesture.

Finally, Andy opened the meeting to contributors, and Sean leapt to his feet, almost knocking his chair to the ground in his haste to be the first. Once standing, he hesitated as nausea swamped him, but the need to make things right again overcame his reluctance. He cleared his throat and swallowed a couple of times, forcing down the panic which rose up his gullet.

'My name is Sean, and I'm an alcoholic,' he said.

Andy's eyes opened a little wider and Matt's jaw dropped. Murmurs of welcome swelled around the hall, and he could feel many pairs of expectant eyes on him. Most people spoke eventually, but he had avoided opening his soul until this moment. People were bound to be curious about his story. *What would he even say?* Matt stared at him, waiting. Too late to back down now. He folded and unfolded his arms, and finally he spoke.

'My father, Brian O'Connor was a drunk. He beat my mother most days when he came home from the pub. I tried to stop him, but he used to throw me aside, or beat me too. I had an older brother, Liam, but he never helped me protect my mother. He had a different father whom he had never met, and he hated Brian. He left home as soon as he could, and joined the IRA. I loved him a lot, even though I felt abandoned. Then one day, he came home, and for a short while we were happy. My father didn't touch my mother for fear of a reprisal from Liam. But Liam's past caught up with him, and the IRA shot him dead for running away. They called him a traitor. He was seventeen.'

Sean choked back a sob. The woman sitting beside him squeezed his hand and he managed to soldier on.

'I swore I'd never be like Brian. I left Ireland as soon as I could and came here, hoping to forget it all and start a new life. And for a while, I succeeded, but I never felt free of the misery. The only thing that could push the pain away was drink. My girlfriend tried for years to help me, but I couldn't be helped. I pushed her away and replaced her with booze. And then I nearly hit her one night. I had turned into my father. She finally dumped me, and I don't blame her.'

He wiped his nose on his sleeve.

'But then I came here. And a miracle happened. Not the one you're expecting. Liam's father is in this room,' he said, to a gasp from the listeners. 'He looks just like him. I guessed who he was almost immediately, although I first thought he might be a ghost. I look just like my mother, and he thought I was his son, and he wanted to sponsor me and take care of me.'

Sean bit his lip and swayed on his feet. He saw Andy nodding at him.

'I should've told him then that I wasn't Liam. I wanted to, but he wanted me to be Liam, so much, so much, that I wanted to be Liam too. I needed someone to care about me. I've lost my life-long girlfriend because of my drinking. My job too, and my whole life is going down the toilet. This man saved me with his love. I should've told him the truth from the start, but I had been drinking when I first met him and my judgement was flawed. I know it's not an excuse, but the chance to have a loving father blinded me to the consequences of the lie. And as time went on, it got more difficult to tell the truth. I found a reason to carry on, to give up drinking. I felt like I had come home.'

Sean lifted his head and looked Matt in the eye.

'I'm so sorry, Matt. I never meant to hurt you. I was so desperate for a different life, a new start, that I forgot the effect it would have on you. You have every right to hate me. I deserve it. Drink has now robbed me of both my fathers, because Brian O'Connor died of liver failure when I was twenty-three. If I don't give up, it will be me next.'

Sean shrugged and sat down again. He felt empty, but somehow cleansed. The main door of the hall opened and closed, and the hall reverberated with the slamming of the door on the frame. Matt's seat sat empty. Andy took the meeting to its close, nominating other speakers and handing out tea and coffee. Sean stayed sitting in his chair until almost everyone else had left. Some people touched his shoulder in solidarity as they went by. Finally, he stood up and made for the door. Andy, who had been tidying up the coffee cups, gave him a thumbs up.

'That was brave,' he said. 'It's never too late to apologise. Give him time. He'll come round.'

'But what if he doesn't?'

'You can't control his actions, only your reaction to them. If he decides not to forgive you, he will have to live with it as well. I don't think he's that sort of man. He loves you because you are your mother's son, he can't help it. Your main job is to stay sober and not let this be the excuse you use to go back to booze. Can you do that?'

'I hope so. One day at a time, or one hour. Somehow.'

'I'll be here if you need me. Keep coming to meetings.'

'I need to be worthy of his love. I have no choice.'

'You should do it for yourself. And you did a brave thing tonight. You spoke from the heart. Liam would be proud of you.'

Chapter 34

Weeks went by in a blur as Liz struggled to get the house fit for habitation, and filled orders for jam from what seemed like the whole county. Nuala and Mairead did their best, but Billy Mac lost his patience with the whole operation, and ordered them out of his kitchen. Liz transferred the equipment to the backyard buildings at Kilanon and awaited the arrival of two new jam boilers she had ordered from England. The end of the summer fruits season approached and she had a breathing space while the plums ripened. She busied herself sourcing Seville oranges from a supplier in Dublin with the intention of adding marmalade to her repertoire during the winter months.

As the house started to come together, Liz became anxious about the permits from the council. Every time she saw Dermot, which had become a frequent occurrence, she asked him about progress, but he always managed to avoid a direct answer. She had so far avoided sleeping with him, using Sean as an excuse. Instead of putting him off, as she had hoped, it made him more attentive. Sometimes, she considered giving in to him, but something stopped her.

Since Dermot could not be persuaded to tell her about the permits, she called Niall at his office, a move she soon regretted. He asked her to come in and bring the plans of the house with her. She pretended not to have a copy, but Noel Doyle had given her one, and she had never been any good at lying.

'Do you have a copy or not?' said Niall.

'I do, but there's a problem. Or at least it might be a problem. I don't know.'

'You'd better bring it to me then. I'll soon tell you.'

After putting it off as long as she dared, Liz drove to Kilkenny with the map in a plastic folder on the seat beside her. She almost crashed the car retrieving it from the floor when it slid off going around a sharp bend. Her nerves jangled as she entered Niall's office and he did not smile or compliment her as he usually did. He looked at her over the top of his half-moon spectacles.

'So, Ms Green. What haven't you been telling us?'

Liz flushed.

'It's here on the map. I assumed you knew about it as you organised the surveys for me. Did nothing about it emerge from your due diligence?'

It was Niall's turn to look uncomfortable.

'Nothing about what?'

'The out-buildings. They're not part of the property. Or at least they are, but not on the plan I have.'

Niall almost grabbed the plan out of her hand.

'And where did you get this?'

'From the builder. I don't know where he got it.'

He examined the photocopied markings and seals before opening the plan and spreading it on the table at the side of his office. He leaned over it, muttering, and tracing the property boundaries with his index finger. As Liz watched him, her dread increased. She had never expected such a thing to be possible at the gateway to the third millennium. Niall straightened and pushed his glasses up his nose.

216

'This is awkward,' he said. 'But not terminal. Not yet anyway.'

'I don't understand. Noel Doyle said it happens all the time and not to worry.'

'Is he a lawyer?'

'No, he's a builder.'

Niall sighed.

'He's wrong. But what do you expect from a builder?'

He sat behind his desk and indicated that Liz should sit down too. She folded the map again and put it back in her folder, holding it on her lap.

'May I keep the plan?' he said.

'It's my only copy. I'd rather you didn't.'

'I'll give it back. I need to make my own copy to keep with your registration.'

Liz frowned, but she dropped the plan on his desk out of his reach. Niall interlaced his fingers and pursed his lips.

'This might explain why the government are taking so long to make a decision on your grant. Their decision-making process can be opaque, but there will usually be a reason if they don't decide with a few weeks. You'll need to apply for ownership of the out-buildings at the registry office. It shouldn't take them long to run a check for you. If no-one else has applied for them, you will get a prior claim registered and they'll be yours in fifteen years.'

'Fifteen years? But what about my grant. The bank has been agitating for me to pay the loan back. It was only supposed to be short term.'

'They would never have lent you the money if they had known you didn't own the outbuildings. You should have told them.'

'But I—'

But she had known about them when she asked for the loan. It just never occurred to her that there would be a problem.

'The Archive for the Registry of Property is in Waterford. I suggest you go down there and make a search application.'

Liz calculated that she could get to the Registry Office before it closed, and picked up the plan again.

'I'll go straight there, but I need this,' she said. 'I'll make you a copy.'

Niall grimaced, but he nodded.

'Bring it to me as soon as possible.'

Liz left his office immediately. On her way to Waterford, she tried to quell the panic in her stomach. She had scored a definite own goal, but why hadn't the lawyers spotted the problem with the outbuildings? She had paid for a survey, quite a large amount of money, to get the best company for the job. They came highly recommended by Niall. But they had somehow missed this rather obvious problem. *Why hadn't they warned her?* Annoyance filtered into her driving, and she honked the horn impatiently when a driver in front of her dithered at a turning. The driver waved cheerily at her, misinterpreting her fit of pique as a friendly salute, and she felt ashamed.

The Registry Office was located on the road to the Ursuline Convent. Liz remembered playing ferocious hockey matches against their students in her teenage years, followed by match teas of sausages, baked beans and chips. *I definitely had a faster metabolism then.* She pulled into the car park and walked into the new building to the inquiry desk. The young man at the desk of the Registry Office looked as if he had spent his entire life underground. Indeed, with his spatula-like hands and plastered-down black hair, he resembled a mole more than an archivist. He wrinkled his nose as her when she asked for the search.

'A search? For the owner? Oh dear, well, I suppose we can do that. Which county?'

He pulled out a form which still had carbon paper between the leaves and proceeded to fill it out in tiny, precise lettering as Liz answered his questions.

'You're supposed to fill this out yourself,' he said. 'But people's writing is so atrocious. It's easier if I do it.'

'How much do I need to pay?' said Liz.

'Oh, nothing. It's a public service. But you could give me a kiss,' he said.

Liz jumped back in alarm and he laughed, a strange hissing sound.

'Ha ha. Got you there. Only codding. Hiss, hiss, hiss.'

Liz pretended to smile.

'How long will it take?' she said. 'Only it is rather urgent.'

'For someone as beautiful as you, I can offer the express service.'

'And how long is that?'

'As long as it takes. Here, take a card and I'll give you a call when I get a result. Don't worry. Your expression of interest is now registered. All being well, the property will be yours in 2015.'

He winked at her, and Liz sighed. *So much for the dream home in Ireland.*

Chapter 35

The ferry lurched and bounced over the waves on the Irish Sea, throwing Sean against Matt as they hung onto the railing of the upper deck. Sean's skin had turned a sickly green colour and he fought the inclination to vomit again.

'Do you mind going by sea?' said Matt. 'I'm determined to recreate my first trip to Ireland.'

'It's a bit late to ask me that now,' said Sean, retching.

Matt smirked and patted him on the back.

'I can see her now,' he said. 'Our bus pulled up to the car park at the Cliffs of Moher at the same time as another full of school girls our age. We were spotty, gangly and awkward, and the girls ignored our pathetic attempts at attracting their attention.'

'Arsing about and shouting?' said Sean, who had heard this story rather often by then.

'That sounds about right. Anyway, I noticed one of the girls standing apart from the others, staring out to sea with a look of wonder. Her long red hair flew behind her like a pennant and her skirt wrapped around her shapely legs.'

'That's my mother you're talking about,' said Sean.

'She told me she had been named after Queen Maeve, the notorious warrior queen of Connaught. I thought she was the most beautiful girl I had ever seen. Did you know that Maeve means she who intoxicates?'

Sean shook his head. He did not recognise his mother from Matt's imaginings in the shadow of a woman who had crept around their house in his childhood. The woman who had protected them from Brian O'Connor and spent twenty years black and blue with bruises. The woman he had left to her fate as soon as he could scrape up a few grades at Leaving Certificate and escape to England with Liz. He had never wondered how Maeve, and Nuala, his sister, had coped without either brother, trapped in that farmhouse with a violent drunk. His shame at deserting them had not reduced after Brian died, and he had not visited the land where he learned to feel worthless. Not even for his father's funeral, although Liz had gone. Liz, the fearless, fighting his dragons for him, and now off on a new quest, leaving him behind.

'I didn't,' he said. 'Until you told me about twenty times.'

Matt laughed.

'I can't wait to see her. Will she still remember me? I'm so nervous. I feel like I'm sixteen again.'

Sean rolled his eyes and tried to concentrate on the horizon, searching for the ribbon of land which would signify this part of the ordeal had come to an end.

Matt hired a car in Dun Laoghaire, 'in case she wants to go to the Cliffs of Moher', and Sean acted as navigator as they drove south past summer hedgerows, and fields of rapeseed and sugar beet. The smells and sounds of the countryside dredged up an intense nostalgia which threatened to overwhelm Sean as he drank it all in. In his mind's eye, he could see Blue again, bounding through the fields and looking backwards to make sure Sean and Michael were following her. Panicked rabbits shot into hedgerows ahead of her, but she rarely focussed long enough to catch one. Blue, gone with those innocent days, buried under the oak tree in Mrs O'Reilly's front field.

All too quickly, they approached Dunbell. Matt's carefree air evaporated, and he chewed his cheek as they pulled up beside the white painted stone wall outside Maeve O'Connor's farmhouse. Matt showed no signs of exiting the vehicle. He bit his lip and ran his hands through his hair.

'We should have warned her,' he said. 'What if she won't talk to me?'

'Now is not the time to have doubts about this trip,' said Sean. 'I gave up my job to come with you.'

'You did what? But that's a crazy thing to do.'

'It was only a contract. They'll have me back if I ask them.'

Matt wiped his hands on his trouser legs and pulled at his shirt. Then he grabbed the door handle, but he didn't open the door. He turned to Sean, patting his hair down again.

'How do I look? What if she doesn't recognise me?'

'I recognised you, and I've never seen you before.'

Matt grinned, but took his hand off the door handle.

'Am I mad? Is this a fool's errand?'

'You're not backing out now,' said Sean. 'Not after you made me cross the sea in that rust bucket. Get out of the car.'

Matt opened the door and got out, stretching his legs. Sean gave him a shove and he tottered into the yard. He looked around at the aging barns and the tractor up on bricks. He flexed his back and stretched upwards, groaning.

'You stay out here and relax,' said Sean. 'I'll prepare the ground.'

'But I want to come in now.'

'She'll kill me. If she does agree to see you, she'll be wanting to look nice. Be patient for a few more minutes. I'll call you, when we're ready.'

'Okay. But don't take too long.'

Sean rolled his eyes and headed for the back door, his own excitement rising as he anticipated his mother's reaction. The door hung open and he knocked softly.

'Is anyone about?' he said. 'Can a parched man get a cup of tea around here?'

He stepped into the kitchen where his mother was sitting at the table with her mouth open. A half-eaten biscuit hovered in her hand. Mrs O'Reilly sat opposite her in a battered wheelchair. The two women spotted him and squealed with delight. Maeve stood up and took him in her arms, wordless with happiness. He felt her wiry strength against his back as she held him for an age. He opened his eyes to find Mrs O'Reilly beaming at him from her wheelchair.

'You came home at last?' she said. 'Let him go, dear. You're going to suffocate the poor lad.'

'And he'd deserve it, staying away for so long.'

Maeve released her grip and sank into her chair. Sean leaned over and gave Mrs O'Reilly a cautious squeeze.

'Honestly, do you call that a hug? I won't break you know,' she said.

'What a lovely surprise,' said Maeve. 'I can hardly believe it. We were just talking about you and…'

She tailed off. High points of colour appeared in her cheeks.

'What is it, Mammy?' said Sean.

Maeve stood up slowly and her hand rose to her mouth. She pointed at the doorway where Matt stood staring at her. A gasp escaped from her throat.

'And who's this?' said Mrs O'Reilly. 'Whoa! What are you doing?'

Sean had taken the handles of her chair and swung her around. They headed for the door, leaving Matt standing there staring at Maeve who seemed transfixed.

'I'll tell you outside,' said Sean. 'Trust me. You need to give them a minute.'

'But who is he? He looks just like Liam.' She gripped at the wheels of the chair, trying to turn back into the house. 'Oh, my goodness. How could you take me away at such a moment?'

'How could you stay?' said Sean. 'Give them a minute. They've waited a lifetime for this.'

'Will you tell me everything?' said Mrs O'Reilly. 'And not leave out one tiny detail?'

'I promise. And will you tell me what you know about Liz? I need to know everything.'

Back inside the farmhouse, the couple stood staring at each other, struck dumb by their reunion. Maeve had her hand on her heart as if to stop it bursting from her chest. Finally, Matt stuttered.

'You're still so beautiful. I hoped, well, I dreamed, of this moment, but I never imagined...'

'But how? Where? I don't understand.'

Matt closed the gap between them and put his hand on her face. She leaned into his palm and shut her eyes. He kissed the corner of her eye feeling the wrinkles under his lips. She opened them again and he fell into their deep pools of sorrow, feeling the gap of years melt away in her warm gaze. He leaned his forehead against hers and he sighed.

'It's a long story,' he said. 'Have you got time for it?'

'We have all the time in the world.'

Chapter 36

Liz reached over and wiped a drop of gravy from Dermot's chin. He grasped her wrist and pulled her towards him. She wiggled free, snorting indignantly, and she noticed Billy Mac staring at them from behind the bar. He had not been in favour of her dating either cousin, but then he had assumed the role of surrogate father to all three women and took himself quite seriously. She winked at him and he busied himself shining a pint glass with a grubby cloth. Dermot patted his distended stomach and sighed.

'I think I ate too much again.'

'You don't have to eat my leftovers every time,' said Liz.

'But Billy's pies are delicious. I can't leave any to be thrown away.'

'You'll need new trousers if you keep this up.'

Dermot drew in his stomach.

'Nonsense. There's plenty of room in these.'

'Billy does cook well. He uses his mother's recipes. He won't share them though. I tried.'

'I could never refuse you anything.'

'So you keep saying. Let's go for a stroll along the river.'

'But it's raining.'

'I thought you couldn't refuse me. Anyway, that's not rain, it's mizzle at most.'

'Mizzle? What's that?'

'Not rain. Come on.'

They stepped outside and wandered along the bank causing the ducks to scatter and plop into the placid waters. Dermot put his arm around Liz and tried to pull her towards him again. She put her hands up to prevent him from reeling her in. He tutted and dropped his hands.

'Why wont you let me kiss you. Is it Niall?'

Liz raised her eyebrows.

'And what's he got to do with anything?'

'He says you like him more than me.'

Her cheeks burned with indignation. *The cheek of him!* Dermot's pout made her bite her lip to keep in a guffaw. He had the grace and maturity of a five-year-old boy. She put her hands on her hips.

'And have either of you thought to ask me what I think?'

Dermot avoided her eyes. He shrugged.

'It's okay. I'm used to it. What Niall wants; Niall gets.'

Liz grabbed his arm and turned him towards her. She stood on tiptoe and planted a firm kiss on his lips. He wrapped his free arm around her waist to hold her close and stuck his tongue in her mouth. Liz squirmed but he held her firmly as he French-kissed her with gusto. Finally, he released her, beaming, and wiped the back of his hand across his mouth. Liz didn't move. Her mind had filled with a mixture of feelings; disgust being foremost. Suddenly, she really missed Sean, and she acknowledged the gaping hole he had left in her heart, her life, if she were being honest. Dermot, flushed with triumph, imagined her smitten and did not pick up any of her negative vibes. He patted her head as if she were a cow or a dog.

'Well, there's a turn-up for the books,' he said. 'You're full of surprises, Liz Green.'

'That's me,' said Liz. 'I've got to go now.'

Dermot's mouth drooped and he stuck out his bottom lip. *What a man-child! And he kisses like a dishwasher.* She restrained the urge to clean her tongue with a tissue.

'Are you my girl now?' said Dermot.

Liz grunted and tapped her watch, striding towards the Woodstock. For a minute she thought he would follow her, but he remained gazing over the weir, and hardly noticed her go. Liz felt guilty at encouraging him. The truth which surfaced as soon as she kissed him, floated, and taunted her. Sean. She still loved him, despite everything. *How annoying!* It wasn't that she didn't fancy Dermot, despite the sloppy kissing; she did, but the same way she fancied Robert Redford and Paul Newman in the movies. An attractive package, but only for window shopping. Fun, but no spark.

***

The early morning drizzle had given way to a weak sunshine which bounced off the wet leaves, almost blinding Sean as he set out along the back road towards Inistioge. His heart felt as if it would burst with hope and love as he anticipated seeing Liz again. He hoped she had missed him as much as he had pined for her. She couldn't have forgotten all the good times they had together. He would persuade her to try again.

A loud honk made him jump off the road into the ditch. A laughing farmer with a bright red face leaned out of the window of a battered Ford Escort and offered him a lift. Sean jumped in beside him and endured an ancient cassette of America country music played at full blast for the trip. The farmer belted out the songs in a voice only his mother would love, but Sean didn't mind. His good humour could not be diminished. When they reached Thomastown, the farmer let him out with a cheery wave and Sean almost immediately got a lift with a nun who was driving to New Ross.

He grappled with his seatbelt as she shot off toward Inistioge. She drove as if the Four Horsemen of the Apocalypse were on their tail. A decal proclaiming that God was her co-pilot did not convince Sean of his likelihood of survival. He smiled at her through gritted teeth as she threw the Ford Fiesta around the corners on the wrong side of the road.

'There you go now,' she said, leaving him on the far side of the bridge from the Woodstock. 'See you in heaven.'

You'll be there a lot sooner than me if you keep driving like that thought Sean, but he nodded and smiled. He started to cross the bridge remembering the times he and Liz had sneaked away to Inistioge to kiss and cuddle, and swim in the river's turgid waters. He wondered how Matt and Maeve were getting on at the Cliffs of Moher. Their newly kindled relationship seemed to be perfect, but you could never tell. He wished he had already reunited with Liz and didn't have such an awkward meeting ahead of him. *Should I have let her know I'd be coming?*

His answer came with brutal swiftness as he noticed Liz on the other bank standing beside a tall and very handsome man he didn't recognise. When she reached up and kissed the Adonis who stood beside her, Sean felt as if someone had put his heart in a vice. Her laughter rang out and bounced off the water reverberating in Sean's ears. He dropped onto his backside and hid behind the stone wall which followed the arch of the bridge. He lowered his head into his hands and forced air into his lungs. The pain in his heart almost made him cry out. Mrs O had been right. Liz was the one and had always been his only one. *How can I live without her?*

He jumped to his feet and walked away as fast as he could without running, unwilling to draw attention to himself. *What if she sees me and calls me over?* Cold sweat dampened his t-shirt just as the breeze picked up and the rain fell harder, like a punishment. He felt as if he was suffocating. *I've lost her and it's all my fault.*

Chapter 37

Michael wiped the sweat off his brow with the sleeve of his t-shirt adding a damp stain to the patchwork of paint and bleach marks. The palm-leaf roofs of the new tourist bungalows shimmered in the heat. Several geckoes lurched from side to side on the walls, lifting their comical suckered feet in the air to regulate their temperatures. A large hornet flew by on an unknown errand, making Michael duck out of its path. Blessing appeared at the back door with a jug of ice-cold lemonade. Condensation dripped onto the ground from the jug, producing small puffs of dust.

'Come into the shade and have a break,' she said. 'It's sweltering out there.'

'It's baking,' said Michael, striding over with a big grin on his face. 'But it's nearly done. We can start advertising as soon as the electrics are in.'

'They look fabulous, darling. It's been worth the effort.'

'I wonder how Liz is getting on with the house. I don't know how she kept going after Sean lost all her money.'

'Any woman who conquered the male bastion of City brokers must be made of tough stuff. You don't need to worry about her.'

'But I do. It's a massive burden to take on alone.'

'And how do you know she's alone?'

The shrill tone of the telephone prevented Michael's indignant reply. He sighed and went to answer it.

'Let's hope it's not another booking we have to turn down,' he said.

He picked up the receiver and a huge smile spread over his features.

'Well, speak of the devil,' he said. 'If it isn't the prodigal sister.'

'Prodigious to you,' said Liz. 'No wonder my ears are burning.'

'How's it going?' said Michael. 'I heard all sorts of over-the-top rumours from Isabella. She should write a gossip column when she's finished being a foreign correspondent.

'There's been lots of water under the bridge since we last spoke.'

'Not all turbulent, I hope.'

'A mixed bag. You'll never guess what happened to Maeve O'Connor.'

'Surely you mean Nuala? Nothing ever happens to Maeve.'

'It has now. Sean found Liam's father.'

'How extraordinary. But isn't he dead?'

'No silly. His real father. Matthew Harris. And he's brought him back to Ireland to meet Maeve again.'

'How on earth did he find him?'

'I'm not entirely sure, something to do with Alcoholics Anonymous, but anyway, Maeve is now getting to know him.'

'And Sean? Have you forgiven him yet?'

Michael waited for a reply, listening to the buzzing and clicking on the line.

'Liz, are you there?'

'Yes, I'm here. I might be able to forgive him eventually, but I won't forget what he did.'

'But wasn't he just trying to impress you?'

'Impress me?'

'You set such high standards, sis. It can be hard to live up to them. Maybe he thought he could win you back with money?'

'And when has money ever impressed me?'

'That's because you make loads. Don't be too hard on him. He loves you. He's never been unfaithful to you all these years, has he?'

'Not that I know of,' said Liz. 'Unless you count the booze. I can't compete with that.'

'You won't be reconciling then?'

'Not unless he stops drinking for good and that's as likely as the proverbial pig flying by.'

'Aren't you lonely without him? You were together a heck of a long time.'

'Actually, I'm dating someone new. Well, two people, if I'm honest.'

Michael roared with laughter, and Blessing tapped him on the shoulder, raising her eyebrows in enquiry.

'Two boyfriends? How utterly scandalous. Whatever happened to my staid big sister? I'm shocked, I tell you. Shocked.'

'It's worse than that,' said Liz, a suppressed giggle escaping from her throat. 'They're cousins.'

'Oh my God. Incest? Holy crap.'

'Don't be so ridiculous. Anyway, I'm not serious about either of them. I'm just having fun.'

'Fun? Dating? Cousins? Who are you and what have you done to my sister?'

'You have no idea,' said Liz. 'And I haven't even told you about Nuala yet.'

'I blame myself,' said Michael. 'If I hadn't sold you the house, none of this…'

He tailed off.

'What's up?' said Liz.

'Nothing. I just remembered the name of the man who wanted to buy the house from me for three hundred pounds. Memory is so strange like that.'

'And what did he call himself, the cheeky blaggard?'

'Dermot Gallagher. He said he was a lawyer. Honestly, some people.'

Michael heard what sounded like a gasp.

'Are you okay, sis?' he said.

'I've got to go. Something has come up. I'll ring you soon, I promise.'

'But you haven't spoken to Blessing.'

'I'm sorry. Not now. I'll call soon, I promise.'

The line cut out and Michael scratched his head as he replaced the receiver.

'What happened?' said Blessing. 'Why did she ring off?'

'I'm not sure,' said Michael. 'But I have a feeling we're going to find out.'

Chapter 38

Liz drove with controlled fury, ignoring the speed limit, but not the road signs. She clenched her jaw as her mind whirred, replaying all the conversations she had had with Dermot, the slow seduction, the careful laying of the trap. *How could I have been so stupid? Out of the frying pan and into the fire, that's me.* At first she fought to control the stubborn tears that leaked down her cheeks, but then she let them flow, being determined not to cry when she met Dermot.

She couldn't believe it had been him all along. No wonder the permits were stuck at the starting gate and the bank was hassling her about the loan. Hadn't Dermot been the one to boast of their contacts all over town. She remembered him suggesting Flinty Maguire at the Council. *Were they stalling on instructions from him? Did he want to steal the house from her? It didn't make much sense, but the hairs on her arms were sending her warning signs. Could Dermot really have plotted the whole scenario? Or did he just seize his opportunity when Sean lost all her savings?*

She pulled into a parking space and slammed the door shut, shaking with fury. Then she spotted Dermot coming down the pavement towards her. She took a deep breath and launched herself at him without giving him a chance to greet her.

'Who the hell do you think you are? I thought you were my friend, but all this time you're the one who's been plotting to steal my house. What a fool I was to trust you in the first place. You're just some cheap one-trick lothario, and I'm the idiot who fell for your lies.'

Dermot reeled under her verbal assault. He screwed up his face as he tried to determine why she had attacked him like that.

'What are you talking about?' he said, finally.

Liz shook her head at him.

'As if you didn't know. When George Kennedy died, you rang my brother and tried to buy the house for a pittance. Luckily he decided to come and see the house for himself instead.'

Dermot recovered his voice.

'Your brother? Doesn't he live in Africa? I've never met him. How would I call him? I don't even have his number.'

'Don't play the innocent with me. I wasn't born yesterday. You're a complete bastard and I never want to see or hear from you again.'

'But Liz—'

'Don't Liz me. I've had enough of your blarney to last a lifetime. My brother told me a lawyer called Dermot Gallagher called him and offered him three hundred pounds for Kilanon. Do you know any other lawyers of that name?'

'But it wasn't me. I swear. Don't you see?'

'Oh, I see all right. I see what a fool I've been. No wonder Mr Conran hates you. I bet you swindled him too, didn't you?'

Dermot reddened and stuttered.

'What's he got to do with it?'

'Everything. As soon as I can, I'm finding new lawyers. I can't bear to see your stupid face ever again.'

She turned on her heel and got back into the car, almost reversing into a man walking behind it. Dermot banged on the bonnet trying to make her stay, but to no avail. She sped off down the high street, chuntering to herself and gritting her teeth.

And to think I chose him instead of Sean. *Who's the real eejit here?*

***

When Liz had left, Dermot took a few deep breaths and reviewed their row. *Who had rung Michael Green?* He didn't have the phone number, never mind the balls to offer so little for the house. There was only one person he could think of. He turned and walked back to the office, where he entered Niall's room without knocking. Niall sighed and shut the file he was studying with a theatrical thump.

'Were you born in a fecking barn? How many times do I have to tell you to knock first?'

'Was it you?' said Dermot.

'Was it me what?' said Niall, tensing.

'Did you give my name to Liz Green's brother?'

Niall smirked.

'Well, you didn't expect me to give him my name, did you? I knew I'd have dealings with them over the house. I couldn't let him know it was me who called.'

'You could have used another name. She just found out from her brother that someone called and tried to buy Kilanon on the cheap, and now she thinks it was me. I've lost her.'

'As if you ever had her in the first place. I keep telling you. It's me she prefers. All I have to do is crook my little finger and she'll come running. You're just eye candy, not a serious proposition for a woman like her.'

'But—'

'But what? You loved her? I told you not to be such an amadan. This is purely business. We get the house back and she's history. I can't believe you allowed yourself to get so caught up by her.'

Dermot shook his head.

'I didn't.'

'Well, it sure seems like it. Grow up, man. In a few weeks, you'll have a big pay day, then you can go out and buy yourself a girlfriend.'

Chapter 39

The days following the revelation about Liz's new boyfriend were some of the darkest Sean had ever been through. His suffering had intensified as he had no one in whom to confide. Matt had followed through on his promise and taken Sean's mother on a trip to the Cliffs of Moher. They left in high spirits, giggling like school children at the thought of finding the shed where Liam had been conceived. Maeve's face glowed with love and happiness. Sean, who had hoped for a reconciliation with Liz to fill his days with the same joy, instead found himself struggling against his desire to obliterate his feelings with drink. He even searched the house from top to bottom for alcohol, but Maeve had cleared it all out after the death of Brian O'Connor and not a drop remained.

Sean would have spilled his guts to Mrs O'Reilly but, for some unknown reason, she wouldn't let him in, shaking her head at him when he knocked at the back door. His desperation grew with his loneliness. Just when he had decided to bear the shame of going to a local AA meeting, Mrs O'Reilly wheeled her chair into the kitchen. Her health appeared to have deteriorated an alarming amount. She could hardly sit up straight in her chair.

'Mrs O? You look terrible. Shall I call the doctor?'

'There's no doctor on earth that can help me now,' she said. 'I want you to take me to Gogan's Wood. I haven't been for years, and now the path is adequate for a wheelchair I'd like to breathe in the smell of fresh pine needles before they shut me in my pine coffin with the smell of varnish.'

'Don't be an eejit,' said Sean. 'You'll never die.'

'It's you who's the eejit, remember? I don't know how you managed to lose Liz Green. She loved you more than life itself.'

Sean flushed.

'Can't we go somewhere else?' he said.

'No, and you know why. It's time you made your peace with what happened to your brother.'

'I don't know if I can.'

'Do you want to be a drunk all your life, like your father? You have to put this to rest.'

'Are you sure you're able for it?'

'Are you?'

They set off down the road, narrowly avoiding being run down by speeding local drivers who shouted greetings out of the car windows before accelerating away again.

'We're going to die,' said Sean, sweating.

'That's true,' said Mrs O'Reilly. 'Put your back into it and we'll be able to turn off soon.'

When they reached Gogan's farm, they turned into the newly tarmacked path and set off up the hill. Mrs O'Reilly didn't weigh as much as a wet dog, but Sean found it hard work to get her up the slope. Half way up the hill, they turned into the dark conifer forest out of the sunlight. To Sean it seemed as if the woods were full of menace. He could hardly keep going. As they neared the training ground, Sean felt his ribs constrict around his lungs. Puffing, he stopped and surveyed the trees. The same trees, only taller and wider.

'Why have you stopped?' said Mrs O'Reilly.

'I can't go any further,' said Sean. 'The tarmac has finished. We need to go back.'

'But you must go there without me then. You won't ever stop drinking if you don't make peace with your past. I'll wait here and sniff the trees. You go on ahead, and come back when you're good and ready.'

She pulled up her blanket and crossed her arms. A sure sign the discussion had finished. Sean rolled his eyes.

'Okay. I'll be back soon.'

He set off trudging along the dappled pathway, forcing himself to put one foot before the other. The shadows closed over him and he shivered. His ears were deaf to the singing of the birds and the rustling of the pine needles. He looked back over his shoulder at Mrs O'Reilly in the distance. She made shooing gestures at him like she used to do with the cattle she loaded up for slaughter. *Mrs O would have made a great hospice nurse. 'Off you go now, no loitering.'*

Sean took a deep breath and pressed on, rounding the bend and heading up hill towards the abandoned firing range. The world seemed to close around him as he entered it, a seemingly harmless platform with limestone walls carved out of the hillside. *Had stone been quarried from here in the past?* He approached the wall and ran his hand over it, feeling for imprints of bullets, but the soft rock felt smooth to his touch. *Could it really have been here that they executed his brother?*

The sun had broken through again and a magpie dropped onto the ground beside him with a piece of coloured foil in its beak. One for sorrow. A massive sob heaved its way out of his chest.

'Are you here, Liam?' said Sean. 'It's me, your brother. I miss you. I need your help.'

Only the cawing of the rooks answered him. He sank to his knees desperate for a sign, shaking with pent up emotion. Startled, the magpie flew off, leaving its treasure behind. Sean noticed a piece of paper torn from a magazine underneath it. He picked it up and examined it. His eyes opened wide as he focussed on the words written there – Blood Brothers. For anyone else this was an advertisement for a play, but Sean knew better. Memories of the pact he and Liam had made with the Greens when they were all children flooded back to him. He stood up and brushed the twigs from his knees. The scar on his thumb seemed almost to throb as he shut his eyes and saw them all in a circle holding hands. He could feel his brother Liam's rough palm against his own soft hand. He remembered Michael's white face after Liam cut his thumb too deep. *Had Liam done it on purpose?* He could be malicious. And Liz, stoic, determined not to cry. 'Blood Brothers' he whispered. I still have Liz and Michael. I am not alone. People love me.

He folded the scrap of paper and put it in his wallet with the photograph of Liam. 'I knew you'd hear me,' he said. A feeling of peace enveloped him and carried him above the forest. He floated for a while before coming down and noticing the damp patches on his knees, and the thrush singing in the bushes. He turned around and ran back down the path towards Mrs O'Reilly. As he neared the wheelchair, he noticed her shoulders shaking and realised that she was weeping. Sean had never seen Mrs O'Reilly cry before. Until she had her stroke, everyone had thought she would outlive them all like an immortal battle-axe. He slowed up and kicked some leaves to give her time to recover herself, but she did not show any signs of hiding her tears.

He crouched in front of her and took one of her wrinkled hands, covered in age spots from the years spent outside on the farm.

'I thought I was meant to be the one who cried,' he said.

Mrs O'Reilly took a linen handkerchief, with embroidered forget-me-nots in the corner, out of her pocket and blew her nose into it.

'You don't know what sorrow is,' she said. 'You tried to drown yourself in drink to forget the pain of the past, but I have to deal with my future.'

'What do you mean?' said Sean.

'My sons are dead,' she said. 'And my grandchildren too. I have no one left.'

Sean's jaw dropped open.

'But how—'

'Carbon monoxide poisoning. They rented a house in the Florida Keys and they all went to bed and never woke up.'

'But when did this happen. You haven't said anything to anyone.'

'And what would I say? My life is over now. I'll see them all very soon in heaven, so it's easier to bear. I just don't want you to waste yours, like your father did.'

Sean rubbed his face in his hands.

'I'm so sorry,' he said. 'I don't think I have the right words for such a tragedy.'

'That's why I haven't said anything,' said Mrs O'Reilly. 'I don't want to talk about it. That would make it real.'

She dabbed her eyes with her handkerchief.

'Anyway, that's why I brought you up here. You're not to tell anyone. I'm going to die soon, and I wanted you to know that I've decided to leave the farm to you and Nuala.'

'To us? But—'

Mrs O'Reilly held up her hand.

'Please. It's done. I know you will probably sell it, but maybe Nuala will keep one of the houses. She needs somewhere to bring up the baby.'

'The baby? I'm going to be an uncle? Why didn't someone tell me?'

'Oh, dear. I forgot you didn't know. Well, it's all water under the bridge now. She's helping Liz with her jam business.'

'And where's that?'

'She's using a shed at the back of Kilanon, I think. Maybe you should try to see Liz before you go.'

'I tried that.'

'I know it hurt you, but you owe her an apology, whatever you think about her choices.'

'I'll see.'

'Don't be slow. I'm dying. I'll be gone soon. Now that your mother has finally found happiness, I can leave her at last.'

'I'm not sure I can let Liz go. She is the love of my life.'

'There are other types. It's time to take a new path. You only get one chance to live your life. Look at my sons.' She sighed, a lonely sound. 'You'll stay for the harvesting, will you? I could do with the help.'

'I don't have anywhere better to be. Of course I'll stay.'

'It's getting chilly. Let's go back.'

After wheeling Mrs O'Reilly into her house, and making her a cup of tea, Sean stepped outside and took a deep breath, filling his lungs with cool country air. He climbed over the old water trough and into the field opposite the two houses in the farmyard. Ahead of him, the great oak spread its shade over the lush grass. He made for an almost indiscernible mound at its base. A small metal cross, rusted and battered from cows' hooves kicking it, lay to one side of the mound partially covered by mud. He picked it up and brushed the earth from it, sticking it back into the soil at the foot of the mound. Then he sat back between the exposed roots of the tree and imagined Blue, gambolling in the field with them, great days with Michael exploring and getting into trouble. *Not all my days were bad, but they made the good days even better. I'm on a new road now.*

Chapter 40

Sean jumped out of the cab of the pickup and waved to the man as he drove away. He gazed up the drive at the handsome house and wondered how it came to be abandoned for so long. Too many painful memories Liz had told him. *How had George coped after he lost Lee so young?* His mother had wept for Brian O'Connor, despite his dreadful behaviour. But George had told him he lived for Lee, to see her safe and happy. He had noticed early on that Sean had fallen for Liz, despite their age difference. *If you want to keep a woman who's out of your league, you've got to make her feel loved every day. Why hadn't he taken that advice? Why had he let drink seduce him instead?*

As he reached the house, he spotted two men working on the roof, laughing, and chatting, and flicking their cigarette ends into the air.

'Who are you?' shouted one of them, seeing him approach.

'I'm a friend of Liz's,' he said.

'Another friend? She's no slouch,' said the other.

They both chortled. Seeing Sean wavering in the driveway, one shouted.

'She'll be here soon. Just go around the back.'

Sean gave them a thumbs up and found his way through into the back yard. The long shed on the side opposite the house had a large padlock on its newly painted door. All around the yard, bright red doors and gutters contrasted with the otherwise shabby out-buildings. 'Like lipstick on a pig'. Maybe that's all she could afford though. *And I know why that is.* After ten minutes, Sean's natural curiosity got the better of him and he started to poke around the other sheds in the back yard. He lifted the latch on one of them and peered in.

It was almost pitch dark in the shed, but he could make out the shape of the front grill of some sort of vehicle. He pushed the door open to its full extent and sunlight flooded in. The front half of a Dion Bouton car from about 1910 had been set up on blocks with the hood folded open. Sean's mouth fell open when he took in the beauty of the eight-cylinder engine in Vee configuration. It had been hitched up to a saw, set up on a crude work bench using a pulley. *Thirty-five horse power to chop logs?*

Sean squeezed around the car and behind the work bench. The car still had an intact windscreen and battered green leather seats. Even the klaxon remained clamped to the frame of the windscreen although the rubber bulb had rotted. A dusty wooden steering wheel stuck out of the dashboard. The back half of the car had been detached and there was no sign of it in the shed. *They had probably chucked it out. What a crime!* He ran his hand over the steering wheel and then leaned into the front of the car to get a better look. The keys were still in the ignition. He tried to start the engine, but the battery had died.

He took out his digital camera and snapped several photographs of the car, including its number plate, intending to ask a friend to do a check on it with the RAC.

He stared at it for a moment longer and then he backed out of the shed, pulling the door shut.

'And what were you doing in there?' said a voice.

The tone was humorous, but trepidation seized him as he turned around with his hands up. Liz stood behind him with her hands on her hips. A smile hovered on her lips and he responded with an uncertain grin.

'They told me you were over,' she said.

'I brought Mammy a birthday present.'

'So I heard. Where on earth did you dig him up?'

'He attends my local AA meetings.'

Her eyes widened.

'You're going? Since when?'

'Since I realised what a total eejit I've been. A couple of months now.'

He shrank under her frank scrutiny, as shame overwhelmed him. His ears burned as heat rose up his neck. He looked at the ground and waited for her to say something, but the shrill cries of the fledgling swallows in the eves was the only sound in the yard. He looked up again. She had turned away from him and she had her face in her hands. *Was she crying?* Liz didn't cry. He felt helpless. Sunlight flooded the yard as the clouds blew across the sky leaving a temporary window. Sean took a step forward intending to comfort her. *Would she accept a hug?* He didn't know anymore. Since his walk in the woods with Mrs O, all his certainty had vanished replaced by alien emotions. In the past he would have drowned the invaders with drink. Now he just felt curious and liberated.

'I went to Gogan's wood.'

Liz flinched, but she turned back to face him.

'Was he there?'

'Sort of. Actually, I think he's here,' said Sean, patting his chest. 'He's been with me all along. I just didn't feel it before. The drink numbed me. I s'pose I was afraid of the pain.'

Liz bit her lip.

'And why are you here?'

'I wanted to apologise. It's one of the twelve steps. You put up with me for years, but I didn't deserve your love. I wrecked us. I'm so sorry.

Liz sighed.

'That doesn't change anything,' she said.

'I know it's too late. I saw you with your new boyfriend.'

'But how?'

'I tried to visit you at the Woodstock the other day, but you were there with him.'

'Oh, I see.'

Sean shrugged.

'So can you forgive me?' he said.

'It'll take a while.'

'I can wait.'

Liz sighed.

'Anyway, I broke up with Dermot yesterday.'

'What happened?'

'He imagined he could swindle me out of my house. I'm such a fool. I thought he liked me.'

Sean's heart leapt and ached at the same time.

'I'm sorry. You don't have much luck with boyfriends, do you?'

Liz hit him hard on the chest.

'Ow, what was that for?'

'Don't be such a gobshite. I've got a broken heart.'

But she smiled.

'Anyway, I'm seeing his cousin Niall instead. I don't know why I didn't realise what a con man Dermot was.'

Sean did not want to talk about Liz's new boyfriend. He figured she needed time to give him a chance. He rubbed his chin and grinned at her.

'Have you got a spare car battery somewhere?'

'You don't even have a car. What on earth do you want a battery for?'

'I want to see if we can start the vintage car in the shed.'

'That old thing? Are you mad? It's probably rusted solid.'

'Seriously, it will only take a minute to find out. Where's your sense of adventure?'

Liz rolled her eyes.

'But it's a hire car. I can't take the battery out.'

'Maybe the Doyles can? It can't be that difficult.'

To his relief, he saw her shoulders relax and she smiled at him.

'Okay, but only if it's easy.'

It turned out to be relatively simple, but only because the Doyles had an ancient battery in the Aladdin's Cave of spare parts in the back of their van. They lent it to Liz with good grace, but showed no interest in helping as they were tucking into their packed lunches. Sean fought with the anodised attachments of the battery in the old car before he realised that he only needed to attach the starter wires to the newer one.

'Turn on the ignition,' he said.

'Me? Are you serious?'

'Go on, turn it.'

Liz leaned into the cabin and turned the key. The engine coughed and turned before stopping again. Liz clapped her hands together and then her face fell.

'There's probably no fuel in it,' said Sean. 'Anyway, I only wanted to see if it still worked. Will you show me the house?'

'I can do that.'

Liz headed for the back door and Sean followed her into the house. He listened to her as she talked about her plans for each room, her face animated and beautiful. His heart ached with loss, but he felt grateful for the chance to get to know her all over again. The way she ran her fingers over the door frames, and shut her eyes when she described how the room would look when she finished. Her expression of pride when she showed him the newly plumbed toilet, paid for by the resurrection of her accountancy skills.

'I'm going to move in soon,' she said. 'That way I can start prepping the walls room by room in the evenings.'

'I can help you, if you like.'

'That would be great, if you've got the time.'

'Is there central heating?' said Sean. 'I didn't see any radiators.'

'I haven't bought any yet. I'm trying to find cast iron radiators for sale at an auction so they match the inside of the house.'

'That's a lot of jam'

'I don't have much of a choice.'

Sean sighed.

'I know it's because of me. I'll never forgive myself. Why should you?'

Liz didn't answer.

Chapter 41

Sean walked to Dunbell crossroads at dawn to wait for the bus at the derelict platform where the milk churns used to get picked up by the dairy. A blanket of wavy, pink-tinged mist sat on the rows of wheat, reminding him of a Jacobs' Mikado biscuit, his absolute favourite as a child; not that they had them often, as they were too expensive. The morning dew sat in fat drops on the beech leaves in the hedgerows, spraying him with water as he backed into the ditch to avoid a passing car. The driver lifted a finger off the steering wheel in acknowledgement of him, and Sean forced out a smile and a nod. Freezing liquid crept down the back of his collar and made him shiver.

Then he had a vision of Liam laughing and shaking branches over him while they waited for the school bus all those years ago; his brother before the storm that uprooted all their childhood dreams. *What on earth would Liam make of Matt Harris turning up after all these years?* He had been stunned to find out his biological father was British, or worse, English, all those years ago. It cut down his posturing about the IRA when he thought his mother would reveal his English roots. A lot of good it did him. He still died at their hands. At least his mother had found happiness at last, after all those years at the mercy of Brian O'Connor.

And what about him? He had lost Liz and cold reality had begun to sink in. Life without drink struck him as too real some days, even though he had begun to enjoy waking up without remorse, or the hangovers that got worse every year. Mrs O had reinforced his desire to leave the drinking behind. The fact that he would never see her again in a short while, made him determined his sobriety would be her legacy. And amazingly, he had gone right off drink. He felt revolted by the thought of it. The results of his addiction had been driven home with the force of a thunderbolt when he saw Liz in the arms of another man. A ghastly lesson, and not one he would forget.

A loud blast made him jump, and the CIE bus loomed in the road, leaving no room for a second lane. He dreaded the bus ride to Dublin, but at least he had managed to get a flight back to London, to sort out his affairs. The thought of another sea-crossing on that rust bucket of a ferry made him feel quite ill. He threw his suitcase into the storage bin in the undercarriage of the vehicle, and pulled himself up the steps into its muggy interior.

'Where are you off to?' said the driver.

'Dublin, please,' said Sean. 'Single.'

'Now, did I enquire about your marital status?' said the driver, jocular and friendly, unaware he had driven the stake in Sean's heart deeper.

Sean bit his cheek and waited for the ticket.

'We're almost full,' said the driver. 'But there's a seat down there beside Eamonn Hurley.'

He jerked his head backwards. Sean realised that everyone on the bus must be regulars and know everyone else. Ireland was great like that. He had forgotten how much he missed the easy comradery of strangers that personified the Irish. He had been in Britain so long he had developed a reserved manner, which cloaked him and protected him from explaining himself to anyone. No one judged him here. His accent neutralised any criticism. He wondered why he had been so against coming home for so long. *Demons need to be faced, or they lurk and haunt you and drive you mad.*

Sean made his way down the aisle and sat in the empty seat beside the aforementioned Eamonn Hurley who turned out to be a plump man with a pink shiny face and thinning blond hair. He adjusted his tight tweed suit and nodded an acknowledgement to Sean, before turning his attention back to reading his local newspaper. The bus jerked and shuddered into movement and then chuntered towards Clonmel. Sean dozed in his seat, waking up to find the man looking at him.

'Haven't seen you around before,' said Eamonn. 'What's the story?'

'Oh, you know, just visiting the ould sod,' said Sean.

'I thought I didn't recognise you,' said Eamonn. 'Are you from England?'

'England? No, I'm from Dunbell. But I moved to Britain in the late seventies.'

'Oh. Right. My sister went to Liverpool. She's still there.'

They gazed out of the window as the trees flashed by, replaced by bungalows as they approached the town and then by a large factory behind chain-link fences. Several large billboards advertised the products featuring frothing pint glasses and smiling faces. Sean felt a pang of desire, but brushed it off. He stared straight ahead until they had passed by.

'You won't know the story about the cider factory then?' said Eamonn.

'That's a cider factory? No, I don't think so,' said Sean.

'A local family used to produce good quality jam for sale in restaurants and high-end grocers. About ten years ago, when they noticed how many apples were going to waste every autumn due to having flaws or small bruises, they bought a small press and started to make apple juice, but they couldn't compete with the large manufacturers. Then their son went to Somerset to a concert and drank a load of cider. When he got home, he researched the market and realised that all the cider available in Ireland had to be imported. The family turned their focus to producing cider instead.'

'You're talking about Conran's? I had no idea it was a small family business.'

'It isn't. But that's the whole point.'

'What are you getting at?'

'Conran's is owned by a multinational now. They bought it several years ago.'

'The family sold out?'

'Oh no. They were conned out of it before then.'

Sean swivelled around in his seat.

'You have my full attention,' he said. 'What happened?'

Eamonn turned pinker with pleasure and anticipation.

'The Conran family increased their capacity several times over a period of years and stretched themselves thin on the financial side. They used a firm of lawyers from Kilkenny to monitor and push through all their legal transactions and licensing. The Conrans assumed that the lawyers had everything under control. Phil Conran told me later they had complete confidence in them due to their good contacts with the County Councils and the banks in the area.'

'What happened?' said Sean who had a funny feeling in his gut.

'Well, a multinational company appeared on the scene and made a lowball offer for the operation. The Conran family told them they weren't interested, because they had financing organised. They sent them away with a flea in their ear. What the Conrans didn't realise was that neither the licensing nor the financing was in place. The lawyers had contacts in the council who were bribed to hold off on the award of the licences for increased commercial production. Then the lawyers' contacts in the bank called in the loans. The Conrans were teetering on bankruptcy, and the lawyers offered to take the company off their hands for a miserly sum.'

'What a pack of con men!'

'It gets worse,' said Eamonn. 'The Conrans were forced to sell to the lawyers to save their staff from redundancy. The minute the sale went through, the licenses and loans were released. The lawyers then sold the company to the multinational at a massive profit.'

Eamonn turned to look at Sean.

'What do you think of that?' he said.

'Do you know the name of the firm of lawyers?' said Sean, the words sticking in his throat.

'What's it to you?' said Eamonn, suddenly suspicious.

Sean gripped his forearm hard and looked him straight in the eye.

'This is life and death to me,' he said. 'I must know who they were.'

Eamonn pulled his arm away and rubbed it with a hurt look on his face.

'I didn't intend for you to get riled up,' he said. 'I should never have told you the story. I don't even know if it's true.'

'The name?' said Sean. 'Please.'

'They're called Flaherty, Gallagher and O'Brien, but I heard that O'Brien is the fall guy. He signs all the documents.'

'Where do I find him?'

'He doesn't exist.'

'But who runs the schemes? Is it Dermot Gallagher?'

'Jaysus, no. He's only a patsy too. He just chases women and acts as a go between. The real villain is Niall Flaherty. He uses Dermot's name a lot when he contacts their intended victims. He's all squeaky clean on the surface, but underneath? You have no idea what he's capable of.'

Sean wrenched himself out of his seat.

'I've got to go,' he said.

'But the bus doesn't stop until it reaches the town centre. You've more chance of finding an intercity bus at the station. Come on now. Sit down. We'll be there soon.'

Sean wavered.

'Sit down in the back,' shouted the driver.

He sat down again, but had the tension of a coiled spring. His hand shook with stress.

'I've got to get back to Inistioge,' he muttered.

'But weren't you staying in Dunbell?'

'My girlfriend is staying there. I've got to warn her.'

'Warn her of what?' Then, Eamonn took in Sean's white knuckles and blank face. 'I'm guessing you've heard of these bastards,' he said.

Chapter 42

When Mark Quinn, the loans manager of the AIB did not respond to her cheery greeting, the knot in Liz's stomach tightened making her feel nauseous. He pointed at the chair in front of his desk and she meekly sat down, holding her hands in her lap to stop her fidgeting. The manager shuffled the papers in front of him and took a deep breath.

'I called you in today, Ms Green, because we have a situation.'

'A situation? I don't understand. Haven't you received this month's repayment of my loan?'

'Oh, we got the payment all right. I'm afraid it's worse than that. You don't appear to own your house.'

'But I paid cash for it. The certificate is in my lawyers' safe.'

'Oh, yes, I understand that. Unfortunately, it has come to our notice that the out-buildings are not part of your property. Since they are the subject of the government grant you have applied for, you are highly unlikely to receive it. In fact, I happen to know that they will turn it down.'

He looked smug, and Liz felt sick.

'May I ask you where you obtained this information?'

'I'm not at liberty to disclose our source. Did you know about this issue with your property? It's illegal to lie on your application for a loan.'

'No, I mean yes, but I was told that this is a common occurrence in Ireland, and I have applied to the registry for a certificate of ownership.'

'You'll be waiting a long time for it. You have to live there for fifteen years before you automatically get accepted.'

'But it's mine?'

'Theoretically, yes, but you cannot get a grant without the legal certificate of ownership. The fact is; you borrowed money from the bank under false pretences.'

Liz blinked.

'False pretences? Wait a minute. That's simply not true. The builder told me this would not be a problem, and that a lot of people have this issue.'

'No wonder you're in trouble if you take legal advice from your builder. Some people might have the same issue, but they're not using property they don't own to register for a government grant. Do you possess any collateral for the loan you took out from us?'

'Not apart from my house.'

'That will do for now. I'll make out a loan guarantee form for you to sign. We can give you a month to find the cash to pay us back the entire loan, but after that we will put your property up for sale at auction, and will accept any bid that covers the loan.'

'But I only borrowed thirty thousand pounds. You can't do that.'

'I'm afraid we can. Think yourself lucky we haven't gone to the gardai. Perhaps you should speak to your lawyers next time instead of your builder?'

Liz walked through Irishtown towards the lawyers' office without seeing or hearing anything. She didn't stop at the bridge to gaze into the water, or admire the brightly coloured paintwork on the shopfronts. A man walked straight into her almost knocking her to the ground when she failed to notice him coming. Rubbing her shoulder, she strode on, even as the tears leaked out onto her cheeks. By the time she rang the office doorbell, she had to blow her nose into the grubby tissue she found in her handbag, as her nose ran too. Siobhan's eyes opened wide as she let her in.

'Here to see Mr Gallagher?' she said.

'No, I need Mr Flaherty, please,' said Liz.

Dermot popped his head out of the door at that precise moment, and seeing her distress, wavered half in and half out of his office. Siobhan ignored him.

'He's in there,' she said, pointing at Niall's office.

Liz looked straight past Dermot; her eyes glassy. He sighed and shut his door again.

Niall fought back a smirk as she entered.

'How can I help you, Ms Green?' he said.

Liz bit her lip.

'The bank manager is demanding repayment of my loan. He had threatened to sell my house to cover it. I only borrowed thirty thousand pounds. Can you stop him?'

'Stop him? But you took out the loan knowing full well you didn't own the house.'

'You told me I did.'

'I also told you that you needed to find the certificate of registration for the outbuildings, or at least proof that someone applied for one.'

'But that's like looking for a needle in a haystack. You said so yourself. It could be anywhere. The man in the registry hasn't got back to me yet.'

'How long have they given you to raise the money?'

'A month. But there's nowhere I can go for it.'

Niall turned his back on her to give her time to blow her nose again and wipe her eyes. She saw his shoulders set firm and imagined he had decided on a plan to help her. Instead, he turned back to her and said, 'I could buy it from you if you want. Obviously, I can't pay full price. How about sixty thousand?'

Liz gasped.

'Sixty thousand pounds? But I paid three hundred and fifty for it, including the inheritance tax.'

'It's a lot more than thirty, and if you play your cards right, you could stay there anyway.'

'What do you mean?'

'Don't play the innocent with me. I know you've broken up with my useless lump of a cousin. I like you too, you know. You're just the sort of woman I've been looking for, and I know you fancy me too.'

'Fancy you? I—'

'I don't expect you to decide right away. You have a month after all. Why don't you come to the Hunt Ball with me tomorrow? We can have a nice evening and meet the people who count for high society around here. You can give me a whirl around the dance floor, and, who knows, you might even have a good time.'

'You expect me to go to the ball with you after this? How do I know you didn't plan it?'

'Don't be ridiculous. How could I have planned this? You caused it yourself by lying to the bank. I like you, Liz, and I'm prepared to save the house for you. It's not a cheap gesture.'

Is he gaslighting me? Maybe I've been naïve and fallen into this hole all by myself. Not forgetting Sean's help. But now I'll be almost penniless, and forced to crawl to Bernie, and ask for my job back. So much for my dreams.

'I don't know what to think,' she said. 'To be honest, my world is crashing down all around me.'

'Let me help then. And at least I've been honest with you. Your drunk boyfriend and my useless cousin are hardly worthy of you. I'm a catch, and you get to keep your house.'

'At least think about it?'

***

Dermot waited for Liz to leave the building before he entered Niall's office. His hair stood on end, freed of its normal coating of gel by Dermot running his hands through it again and again. He threw the door open and pointed at his cousin who raised an eyebrow at him.

'Why was she crying?' he said.

'When she came in, or when she left?' said Niall, putting his feet up on the desk.

'Both. What did you say to her?'

'The bank is foreclosing on her loan, due to her not owning the outbuildings at Kilanon. I offered to buy it for sixty thousand pounds.'

'Sixty-thousand? I thought we said one hundred? That's hardly fair—'

'Fair? Have you gone soft in the head? Are you wimping out now?'

Dermot looked away and Niall shook his head.

'Oh my God,' he said. 'You've only gone and fallen in love with her. She's just a spoilt English bitch. We planned this.'

Dermot swallowed.

'No, I haven't. What do you take me for? It's just—
'

'You have. You're such an eejit. I can't believe I'm related to you. You're a slave to your dick. Now get out. I'm busy.'

'That's a bit uncalled for.'

'I meant every word. Feck off.'

Chapter 43

Despite her misery, Liz had to pull out all the stops for the Hunt Ball. It was essential to keep her options open, and whether she liked it or not, Niall represented a chance for redemption. The charming lad in the property registry office at Waterford had not come up with any earlier claims to the out-buildings at Kilanon. But any owner would have been better than none. At least she could make them an offer, or ask them to help her with the loan application. Any deal topped going bankrupt. Being unable to find an owner of the out-buildings represented the worse-case scenario. The government would not give her a grant if she had no proof of ownership, and the bank manager hovered on the brink of foreclosing her loan.

To her surprise, Kathleen Brennan had come up trumps with a gorgeous ice blue gown with violet shimmer running through its shot silk. It had a slight tail, like the designer dresses on Oscar night, and a square cut-out showing off Liz's collarbones. She borrowed a pair of Nuala's heels which made her even taller and more elegant. Her hair had been burnished and coiffed by the local hair dresser, and clipped to one side in another echo of Oscar nights in the thirties. A light shawl of glittering stars and planets in a deep blue sky finished off her outfit. She twirled in front of the mirror at the hair dresser's and tried to manifest a lovely evening. *Cinderella going to the ball with the Frog Prince. What have I done to deserve this?*

Niall drove up to the Woodstock and let out a low whistle when Liz came out to greet him.

'Any man would be proud to have you on his arm,' he said.

She managed a smile, but she did not address a word to him on the journey. He drove with intense concentration and did not look at her again. *Is he ashamed? Unlikely.* Liz tried to concentrate on the evening ahead. She had never been to a hunt ball before, but she remembered the excitement of sitting at the top of the stairs and watching her parents putting their coats on over their outfits, before leaving for the annual Kilkenny Hunt Ball. *Was this the same one? Maybe her parents would be there?* She hadn't factored them in, and had not told them she would be going with Niall. They had inherited a dislike for the lawyers from Mrs O's barbed comments about them. For once Mrs O had not divulged the reasons for her ire, but she didn't hold a grudge for nothing.

Bea Green always wore the same dress when she went to formal occasions, she probably still did, a long green mermaid dress with a ruched tulle top. Her father dressed in his dinner jacket and trousers, bought while at university. He said it would see him out, although it had become noticeably tighter in recent years and he had taken to wearing a cummerbund over the top of the trousers. Liz pulled at her dress, but it fitted perfectly. *Just nerves.*

When they got to the Ball, Liz's legs refused to work as she reached the entrance. She remained stock still as people walked around her, some tutting in indignation at her blocking the way to their first drink of the evening. Finally, Niall took her arm and guided her through the doors. She blinked at the light and noise inside the ballroom. The low murmur of still sober guests and the odd raking laugh or shout of recognition surrounded her. She noticed that Niall greeted people, but not the other way around. No one refused to shake his hand, but they didn't embrace him or give hearty handshakes to him as they did with others. Liz muttered pleasantries and tried to engage, but the lack of warmth made it an uphill battle.

She soon finished her first glass of fizz, which was too sweet for her taste, and she looked around for somewhere to leave her glass. Niall took it from her and placed it on the tray of a waiter walking by. He took her to a table at the side of the hall where three other couples were already seated. They looked up as Niall and Liz arrived and greeted them.

'More cousins,' said Niall. 'Both of my parents came from extended families.'

He did not introduce them individually. Liz felt awkward not knowing anyone's name, but not being that keen on either of the cousins she had already met, meant she restricted her comments to compliments on the dresses of the other women at the table and joining in with the toasts. She ate her way through three courses of lack-lustre food, as having her mouth full gave her an excuse to listen and not talk. The roast pheasant was delicious, but took a lot of chewing. The chat at her table mostly involved horses and Gaelic sport so she hadn't anything to contribute. She laughed at jokes she didn't understand and pretended to have a good time. She could feel her face getting scarlet with alcohol and heat, and wished she could leave, or at least go outside for a moment. Soon after dessert, the music changed from staid to pop and all of the other couples got up to dance. Niall tapped Liz on the arm.

'I've got to go and speak to that fella over there,' he said, pointing vaguely at the other end of the ballroom. 'Get yourself a drink and I'll be back shortly.'

He disappeared into the crowd. The noise of people talking and laughing had swelled to a crescendo as the intake of alcohol had increased. Liz did not hear what he said and assumed he went to the toilet. After about ten minutes, she began to feel embarrassed and deserted at the empty table. She looked around for a friendly face. *Surely I can recognise somebody here?* And then she saw him, at the same moment he found her. The concerned expression turned into a gaze of admiration as he spotted her. He came directly to her table, still dressed in his everyday clothes and greatcoat. Liz noticed a wet stain on his shirt. Warning lights went off in her brain.

'Sean? What on earth? I thought you were on your way to England.'

'So did I. But I met a man on a bus who told me a story, and I had to come and warn you about Niall. You look like a princess by the way.'

'Niall? Don't you mean Dermot? I already told you he tried to swindle me.'

'No, it's Niall. He's the one. He had us all fooled.'

'Are you drunk?' said Liz.

'Drunk? No. I've rushed back from Carlow to warn you.'

'Why do you smell of drink?'

'I don't. Well, I might. I bumped into some guy in the entrance and he spilled a beer down me.'

'And you expect me to believe you?'

'Liz, I—'

'Do you realise I'm about to lose my house because of you. The bank is foreclosing and the only way I can get out of this is cosying up to Niall. Just because you are jealous doesn't give you the right to come in here inventing stuff. You've ruined my life. Are you trying to make things worse? Get out of here. Now.'

'But Liz. The cider factory—'

Just then Niall appeared and Liz stood up, pushing past Sean, and pulling Niall onto the dancefloor. She put her arms on his shoulders and he grabbed her around the waist. Sean stood aghast as Niall and Liz danced together, and then a burly man in a suit tapped him on the shoulder.

'I'm guessing you don't have a ticket, sir,' he said. 'You'll have to leave.'

'But that man is lying to my girl.'

'I'm sorry. We don't do sob stories here, only tickets. And you need to get out before I throw you out.'

Liz watched as Sean left the ballroom with a large man who looked like a bouncer. *Had he really started drinking again? And why was he talking about the cider factory? The smell of drink triggered me before he had a chance to explain himself.* She tried not to cringe as Niall lowered his head to kiss her neck. *What a nightmare!* The music stopped and Niall whispered in her ear.

'You're the most gorgeous woman here by a country mile. I can't wait to make you mine. I'm sorry you were left alone at the table. I've just got to finish my business here and we can go home if you want to.'

What I want is to dance and drink and meet people, but you haven't asked me. He left her at the edge of the ballroom and Liz threaded her way through to a table at the back which had a couple sitting at it. She thought she recognised the man, but his name wouldn't come to her. She smiled brightly as she sat down.

'My feet are killing me,' she said.

'And that's not the only thing if you don't sit somewhere else,' said the man.

His wife laid her hand on his arm.

'Now, dear. It's not her fault. You need to calm down. We were having such a lovely time.'

Too late, Liz recognised Phil Conran, the owner of the jam boilers, who held a grudge against Niall and Dermot. She was about to stand up when she remembered something Sean had said. It triggered a memory.

'Why did you ask me if I wanted an apple press? When we spoke on the phone?'

'What's that got to do with anything?'

Liz moved around the table, and sat closer to the couple, making sure to keep Phil Conran's wife Fiona as a buffer.

'Did you make cider with it?'

Phil Conran's face turned purple with rage.

'As if you didn't know. The cheek of you!'

Liz resisted the temptation to flee.

'Please,' she said. 'I need to know.'

Fiona Conran knitted her eyebrows together.

'Niall Flaherty, and his sidekick cousin, swindled us out of our cider factory.'

'How did they do that?'

'A few years ago, we started selling homemade cider, using windfalls from our orchards. It was an overnight success and we expanded several times. Flaherty and his pal encouraged us to take out loans from the bank, and to apply for government grants. We had built a substantial factory which was state of the art, but after interminable problems getting the permits from the government, we ran out of money. We tried everything we could, but we couldn't save it. Flaherty promised to try and save a few of the badly needed jobs, if we made our shares over to him.'

Liz gasped.

'Oh, my goodness. That's awful.'

'And guess what?' said Phil. 'Suddenly, all the problems evaporated and after a year or so, Conran cider company was sold to the large international food and drink conglomerate. Flaherty made a fortune from the deal.'

Liz almost fainted with horror. Before she could say anything, a man who had been listening on another table, leaned over, and tapped her on the shoulder.

'And they're not the only ones. The bank offered me a mortgage for a house I bought. At the last minute, there was a problem with title. The mortgage was withdrawn and the bank foreclosed on me. Niall Flaherty bought the house at a massive discount from the bank and I lost my deposit.'

Liz felt sick. She took a deep breath.

'What was the name of your bank manager?' she said.

'Mark Quinn, at the AIB.'

'In Irishtown,' said Liz.

'Yes, how did you know?'

'It all sounds horribly familiar,' said Liz.

Fiona's eyes opened wide.

'Not you too?' she said. 'Oh my God, Phil. It's happening again.'

Liz stumbled to her feet.

'I'm so sorry,' she said. 'Thank you for telling me the truth.'

She pulled her shawl around her shoulders and marched towards the entrance. The swell of happy chatter and music behind her seemed to mock her as she struggled to deal with the flood of emotions that beset her. A taxi loitered outside and she flagged it down, hoping she had enough money in her silk purse to pay her way home.

'Get me out of here,' she said.

Niall stood at the entrance watching the taxi pull away. He shrugged and went back indoors.

Chapter 44

Sean shivered as he watched the Nore run under the ten-arch bridge at Inistioge. Water levels had risen after the storm over night, and dark trunks ripped from river banks bounced backwards from the almost submerged arches. He watched small dams form and break as they got caught under the brickwork. The chocolate water boiled and frothed in its hurry to get to the sea. The turmoil matched Sean's emotions as he struggled to arrange his thoughts. His need to see Liz and make her understand about Niall's betrayal, before she made a terrible mistake, conflicted with his inability to remove emotion from his dealings with her.

He kicked the bottom of the wall in his frustration, wishing he could be more articulate. He didn't notice Dermot until he coughed behind him making him start.

'I'm guessing your name is Sean,' he said. 'I'm Dermot, Liz's friend.'

Sean spun around and almost tipped over the low wall into the current in his surprise. Dermot grabbed Sean's shoulder to steady him, and then looked down at his feet, waiting, almost cringing. *Does he imagine I'd hit him? I'd certainly like to, but Liz would be steaming.* Sean nodded.

'I'm Sean. What are you doing here? Haven't you done enough damage?'

Dermot gripped his hand and would not let go.

'I came to see Liz,' he said. 'But I've made a hames of everything, and now Billy Mac says she won't speak to me. She'll speak to you though, won't she?'

Sean shook his head.

'I thought so, but when I tried to warn her about Niall at the Hunt Ball, she sent me away with a flea in my ear. I guess we're both outside looking in, as far as she is concerned.'

'Will you have a drink with me at least? There's something really important I need to give you.'

Sean shrugged.

'I don't drink, but I'll have a coffee. Let's see if Billy Mac will take pity on us.'

The two men slunk into the Woodstock and loitered at the bar. Billy Mac emerged from his office, looked the bedraggled pair up and down and rolled his eyes.

'She's not here,' he said. 'She's gone to pack up at Kilanon with Nuala.'

'Packing? But I thought she loved the house. What's gone wrong?' said Sean.

'I've no idea, but she rang the bank this morning and she hasn't stopped crying since. Do you think they called in the loan? I know she had some problem with the government grant.'

'I've no idea,' said Sean. 'I'll go and see her as soon as Dermot has finished with me. Can you make us a coffee, please?'

'And something to eat?' said Dermot. 'I'm starving.'

Billy Mac sighed, but he didn't refuse. The men sat in the corner of the quiet bar waiting for him to return. Dermot sighed loudly a couple of times, but Sean refused to be the one to break the silence. Billy Mac came back with two milky coffees and some buttered, toasted barm brack.

'Not that yous deserve it,' he said and marched off.

Dermot grinned at Sean who took a large bite of the delicious buttery toast.

'That's gorgeous,' he said, wiping his chin.

'Look,' said Dermot. 'I know Liz still loves you. She told me she doesn't, but it's obvious, even to me.'

Sean sighed.

'It's over. She lost her money because of me, and now it looks like she'll lose her house. I can't make it right.'

'Actually, it's because of me, of us. Niall and I planned this from the beginning. The house belonged to his family before the Kennedys bought it from them. Niall wanted it back, but he wasn't prepared to pay the market price. He saw Liz as an opportunity to get it at a massive discount.'

'But weren't you going out with her?'

'That was part of the plan. To butter her up and blind her to the imminent danger. But I fell in love and almost destroyed Niall's scheme.'

Sean raised an eyebrow.

'Seriously. You fell in love?'

Dermot flushed.

'You, of all people, should know how easy that is. Liz is special.'

'And now we've both screwed up and she's about to become bankrupt as a result.'

'Not necessarily.'

Dermot reached into his pocket and pulled out an envelope. He pushed it across the table to Sean.

'What's this?'

'Something she needs to save the house.'

Sean slipped his finger under the seal and opened the envelope. He withdrew two mottled pieces of paper and skim read them. He looked up and shrugged.

'I've no idea why these are important. I can't make head or tail of them.'

'Liz will know what they are. I guarantee you.'

'But where did you get them?'

'One comes from the office safe, and the other... Well, it's a long story.'

Mystified, Sean put the envelope in his jacket pocket.

'I imagine it is,' he said, turning towards the bar. 'How much do we owe you?'

'I'll get that,' said Dermot.

'No, you're all right. I'll pay.'

The two men stepped outside into gentle sunlight.

'So, you're off to make it right with Liz?' said Dermot. 'I hope she'll take you back. How will you get there?'

'I'll hitch a lift,' said Sean. 'I always find one eventually.'

'Let me take you.'

'No, that's alright.'

'It's the least I can do. My car's over there.'

Dermot pointed at the Range Rover. Sean grinned.

'Nice motor,' he said.

As they walked over to the car, Sean noticed that it was crammed with baggage and miscellaneous belongings.

'Are you going somewhere?' he said, as he got in.

Dermot grimaced as he put the car into gear.

'I've had enough of being Niall's dogsbody. Once I've dropped you at Kilanon, I'm driving direct to Dublin. I've got a new job in a thriving practice up there, and I'll be house sharing with a friend from university. He's newly divorced, so we'll have a hooley together.'

'Sounds like a great idea. I hope it goes well for you.'

'So do I.'

Chapter 45

Dermot dropped Sean off beside the house and drove off before anyone came out to greet the visitor. He waved his hand out of the driver's window as he disappeared down the driveway. Sean waved back and shouted his thanks, watching the Range Rover turn north and head for Dublin. *Will I be making that journey back to the airport for good soon?*

He mounted the steps to the front door which swung open under his hand. The hall had been sanded since he had last visited, and the original wood peeped out of the multiple layers of paint removed from the doors and staircase. A pile of paint dust sat in the middle of the hall, waiting for a dustpan. It struck him that the restoration continued whatever else had happened.

The sound of sobbing led him up the stairs to the main bedroom where Liz sat on the edge of her bed being comforted by Nuala, who jumped up and hugged Sean, before pushing him away again.

'This is all your fault,' she said, and walked out, leaving him helpless in a sea of sobs. Liz raised her head and examined him; her eyes puffy from crying. Her face betrayed her intense annoyance at being found at such a disadvantage. She blew her nose loudly into a tissue and threw it at a paint pot she used as a rubbish container. The tissue bounced off the edge and sat damply on the floor. Sean resisted the temptation to pick it up and put it in the tin.

'Was that Dermot Gallagher?' she said. 'How could you accept a lift from that man. I can't believe you are so insensitive. This is the last straw.'

Sean held up a hand.

'Whoa now. Hold on a minute. We're the cavalry, not the enemy.'

'You two? Laurel and Hardy would be more apt.'

Sean sighed.

'Billy Mac tells me you're packing up. What happened? I thought you were happy here.'

'I'm going to lose the house. The bank is foreclosing on my loan, because I don't own the property.'

'I don't understand. I thought you bought it months ago.'

'I did. But now it seems that the buildings in the back yard don't belong to me, so the government won't give me a grant for my business.'

'And that grant covers the loan?'

Liz nodded.

'What will you do?'

Liz turned away from Sean and he heard her mutter something about Niall.

'Why did you go to the ball with him? Dermot says he's rotten to the core.'

'He offered to buy the house from me to pay off the bank, if I would…'

'If you would what?'

Liz shrugged.

'Can't you guess?'

The blood boiled in Sean's veins and a red mist descended over his vision.

'Did he hurt you? I'll kill him, I swear. The dirty bastard.'

'No, he didn't. Calm down. He didn't touch me. I promise. But—'

'But what?'

'I'm so sorry I didn't listen to you. After you left the ball, I met the Conrans—'

'The cider family?'

'Yes, how did you know?'

Liz raised a hand.

'Wait, tell me later. Anyway, the Conrans told me that Niall had swindled them out of their factory by offering to buy it when the bank foreclosed on their loan.'

'That's what I heard too.'

'Anyway, that's how Niall does it. He has a deal going with Mark Quinn, the loans manager of the AIB. Niall, or Dermot, persuades the victim to apply for a government grant, even though they know of a legal impediment to obtaining the grant. If there isn't an impediment, they get their contact in the council office, a certain Flinty Maguire to block the grant at every turn and find reasons not to approve it. Quinn lends money to clients using a future government grant as surety. When the grant isn't forthcoming, the bank forecloses and Niall cleans up.'

'And his pals get a cut of the profit?'

'I guess so.'

'Dermot gave me something for you. He said it was important,' said Sean, holding out the envelope.

'Knowing him it's probably a valentine card,' said Liz, but she took the envelope and extracted the two documents. She read the first one and her whole demeanour changed in an instant. She put it down on the bed and read the other one. Once. Twice. A rapturous expression lit her features.

'What is it?' said Sean.

'Lee Kennedy applied for the out-buildings twenty years ago. This one's a copy of her application. And this one,' she said, waving it in the air, 'is the confirmation from the registry office of her ownership. Where did Dermot get these?'

'He said Niall had them.'

'That filthy rat. Where has Dermot gone now?'

'Dublin. He's got a new job. He didn't say which company.'

'I can't believe it. This is the key to the government grant. If I show this to the bank, I'll be able to stop the foreclosure. I'll change banks too. I shouldn't have any problem getting a new loan from somewhere else, and there's no way I'm relying on Mark Quinn anymore.'

'Fantastic. I'm so thrilled for you. I—'

A loud shriek came from the hall. Liz and Sean jumped up and ran to the staircase. They looked down into the hall where Nuala leaned on the bannisters, her face pale.

'What on earth?' said Sean.

'I hate to disturb your cosy chat,' said Nuala. 'But my water just broke.'

'Oh my God. She's going to have the baby. Everybody into the car.'

Chapter 46

Mrs O's face crinkled in pleasure as Nuala placed the little girl into her arms. She cooed into its face and sang lullabies in her croaky voice, her lungs creaking with effort.

'Isn't she only gorgeous,' said Maeve. 'I can't believe I'm finally a grandmother. It would only be made better if I knew who the Daddy was.'

'For God's sake, Mammy. Can you leave it out? I'm not telling you, and that's final. Jacinta's got all the parents she needs,' said Nuala. 'And grandparents.'

Matt beamed at her. He had assimilated so quickly into the household that it was hard to remember the cold lonely farmhouse as it had been. He had brought a warmth with him that brightened every place he entered. Sean gave him a hug, feeling the coarse bristles scrape his cheek. He gazed at Jacinta, lying contentedly in Mrs O's arms, and wondered why he had never suggested having babies to Liz. It might not be too late, but first he had to persuade her to forgive him, and that was never going to be an easy task.

She had melted enough to let him come and help her renovate the house at Kilanon. They spent every day scraping and sanding and wallpapering and painting and laughing. Mostly laughing. The sound of Liz laughing filled his heart so full he thought it might explode. He'd forgotten how it sounded when unleashed in the open. It was his fault she'd stopped laughing, stopped smiling even. He didn't know how to redeem himself. He couldn't imagine how he'd filled his years with drink, instead of love with this gorgeous woman.

'Oh, I nearly forgot to tell you,' said Mrs O'Reilly. 'The guards arrested Niall Flaherty yesterday. Apparently, someone sent them proof that he had swindled half the county. He's sewn up like a kipper.'

'How wonderful,' said Liz. 'Serves him right. I hope he gets life.'

'Unlikely,' said Sean. 'I wonder who shopped him.'

'Probably Siobhan, the receptionist. She always looked resentful. Maybe she didn't get a cut of their nefarious earnings,' said Liz.

'I wonder how Dermot is,' said Sean.

'I don't,' said Liz, shutting him down, unfairly he thought. After all, Dermot had given them the key to the castle. He kept his mouth shut though, and went outside to sit at Blue's grave, and told Liam all about Jacinta.

The next day, Sean returned to Kilanon, where Liz slept in the master bedroom, driving Mrs O's old Ford Orion, which needed scrapping, and probably hadn't passed its MOT. He prayed to St Francis to give him a road free of gardai checkpoints, just long enough to earn some money for a second-hand jalopy of some sort. Both he and Liz were studying to get their Irish accountancy registrations, so they could run a consultancy together. They still didn't talk about the future, and he hadn't kissed her yet, despite his deep desire. He felt like a teenager manoeuvring his girlfriend to get his first kiss. She treated him like a brother and never got close except to punch his arm or pat his head depending on circumstance. How he longed to join her in the double bed upstairs and make the feathers fly out of the pillows!

He patted his pocket and felt for his Nokia, the text he had received from Evan contained within. Liz hated to stop in the middle of something, but he itched to tell her the good news. He carried on painting the skirting board, the oily smell of the gloss making him feel light headed, until she bounded down the stairs with their flask.

'How about a quick break on the bench?' she said.

She raced him there, and poured them both a lukewarm tea. They sat in silence contemplating the now baring branches of the orchard. The odd late ripening apple squelched underfoot, all of them holed by ravenous pecks from juvenile birds. Sean noticed her hand resting on the bench beside him. *Was it an invitation?* He took it in his with the caution of stroking a wild cat, and she didn't withdraw it. He rubbed her palm with his thumb. The smell of rotting fruit wafted in the air bringing wasps to forage.

'Would you sell the car?' said Sean.

'And how would I get around if I did?'

'Not that one.'

'The pile of scrap in the shed?'

'That happens to be a rare vintage engine which still runs. My pal, Evan, says he has a buyer for it.'

'Really? How much would he pay?'

'He offered fifty, but I said we'd take seventy-five. We finally settled on sixty-five.'

'And how are sixty-five pounds going to save me?'

Sean grinned.

'Sixty-five thousand.'

Liz turned to him in astonishment.

'What did you say?'

'Thousand. Sixty-five thousand pound.'

He watched as realisation dawned in her eyes. She jumped off the bench and ran around the orchard squealing with delight, her cheeks pink with excitement. On her second circuit, she trod on a rotten apple and skidded to a stop, landing with a thump on her bottom. She sat dazed as Sean approached her and held out his hand.

'I know it's not what I lost, but it should get you back on your feet, and Mrs O'Reilly is leaving me half the farm. It will be mine soon…'

Liz rose to her feet and Sean brushed the leaves from her clothes, trying not to linger on her body. Liz put her hands on her hips.

'I still haven't forgiven you yet,' she said.

'But I hear you're looking for cheap labour,' said Sean, pulling her into his arms. She gave his bicep a squeeze, and leaned in for a kiss.

'You'll do.'

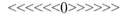

I hope you have enjoyed Fighting Green. Please leave me a review. My other books are available on pjskinner.com

Other books

The Green Family Saga

Rebel Green – Book 1

Relationships fracture when two families find themselves caught up in the Irish Troubles.

The Green family move to Kilkenny from England in 1969, at the beginning of the conflict in Northern Ireland. They rent a farmhouse on the outskirts of town, and make friends with the O'Connor family next door. Not every member of the family adapts easily to their new life, and their differing approaches lead to misunderstandings and friction. Despite this, the bonds between the family members deepen with time.

Perturbed by the worsening violence in the North threatening to invade their lives, the children make a pact never to let the troubles come between them. But promises can be broken, with tragic consequences for everyone.

Africa Green – Book 2

Will a white chimp save its rescuers or get them killed?

Journalist Isabella Green travels to Sierra Leone, a country emerging from civil war, to write an article about a chimp sanctuary. Animals that need saving are her obsession, and she can't resist getting involved with the project, which is on the verge of bankruptcy. She forms a bond with local boy, Ten, and army veteran, Pete, to try and save it. When they rescue a rare white chimp from a village frequented by a dangerous rebel splinter group, the resulting media interest could save the sanctuary.

But the rebel group have not signed the cease fire. They believe the voodoo power of the white chimp protects them from bullets, and they are determined to take it back so they can storm the capital. When Pete and Ten go missing, only Isabella stands in the rebels' way. Her love for the chimps unlocks the fighting spirit within her. Can she save the sanctuary or will she die trying?

The Sam Harris Series
(written as PJ Skinner)

Set in the late 1980's and through the 1990's, the thrilling Sam Harris Adventure series navigates through the career of a female geologist. Themes such as women working in formerly male domains, and what constitutes a normal existence, are developed in the context of Sam's constant ability to find herself in the middle of an adventure or mystery. Sam's home life provides a contrast to her adventures and feeds her need to escape. Her attachment to an unfaithful boyfriend is the thread running through her romantic life, and her attempts to break free of it provide another side to her character.

The first book in the Sam Harris Series sets the scene for the career of an unwilling heroine, whose bravery and resourcefulness are needed to navigate a series of adventures set in remote sites in Africa and South America. Based loosely on the real-life adventures of the author, the settings and characters are given an authenticity that will connect with readers who enjoy adventure fiction and mysteries set in remote settings with realistic scenarios.

Fool's Gold - Book 1

Newly qualified geologist Sam Harris is a woman in a man's world - overlooked, underpaid but resilient and passionate. Desperate for her first job, and nursing a broken heart, she accepts an offer from notorious entrepreneur Mike Morton, to search for gold deposits in the remote rainforests of Sierramar. With the help of nutty local heiress, Gloria Sanchez, she soon settles into life in Calderon, the capital. But when she accidentally uncovers a long-lost clue to a treasure buried deep within the jungle, her journey really begins. Teaming up with geologist Wilson Ortega, historian Alfredo Vargas and the mysterious Don Moises, they venture through the jungle, where she lurches between excitement and insecurity. Yet there is a far graver threat looming; Mike and Gloria discover that one of the members of the expedition is plotting to seize the fortune for himself and is willing to do anything to get it. Can Sam survive and find the treasure or will her first adventure be her last?

Hitler's Finger - Book 2

The second book in the Sam Harris Series sees the return of our heroine Sam Harris to Sierramar to help her friend Gloria track down her boyfriend, the historian, Alfredo Vargas. Geologist Sam Harris loves getting her hands dirty. So, when she learns that her friend Alfredo has gone missing in Sierramar, she gives her personal life some much needed space and hops on the next plane. But she never expected to be following the trail of a devious Nazi plot nearly 50 years after World War II ... Deep in a remote mountain settlement, Sam must uncover the village's dark history. If she fails to reach her friend in time, the Nazi survivors will ensure Alfredo's permanent silence. Can Sam blow the lid on the conspiracy before the Third Reich makes a devastating return?

The background to the book is the presence of Nazi war criminals in South America which was often ignored by locals who had fascist sympathies during World War II. Themes such as tacit acceptance of fascism, and local collaboration with fugitives from justice are examined and developed in the context of Sam's constant ability to find herself in the middle of an adventure or mystery.

The Star of Simbako - Book 3

A fabled diamond, a jealous voodoo priestess, disturbing cultural practices. What could possibly go wrong? The third book in the Sam Harris Series sees Sam Harris on her first contract to West Africa to Simbako, a land of tribal kingdoms and voodoo. Nursing a broken heart, Sam Harris goes to Simbako to work in the diamond fields of Fona. She is soon involved with a cast of characters who are starring in their own soap opera, a dangerous mix of superstition, cultural practices, and ignorance (mostly her own). Add a love triangle and a jealous woman who wants her dead and Sam is in trouble again. Where is the Star of Simbako? Is Sam going to survive the chaos?

This book is based on visits made to the Paramount Chiefdoms of West Africa. Despite being nominally Christian communities, Voodoo practices are still part of daily life out there. This often leads to conflicts of interest. Combine this with the horrific ritual of FGM and it makes for a potent cocktail of conflicting loyalties. Sam is pulled into this life by her friend, Adanna, and soon finds herself involved in goings on that she doesn't understand.

The Pink Elephants - Book 4

Sam gets a call in the middle of the night that takes her to the Masaibu project in Lumbono, Africa. The project is collapsing under the weight of corruption and chicanery engendered by management, both in country and back on the main company board. Sam has to navigate murky waters to get it back on course, not helped by interference from people who want her to fail. When poachers invade the elephant sanctuary next door, her problems multiply. Can Sam protect the elephants and save the project or will she have to choose?

The fourth book in the Sam Harris Series presents Sam with her sternest test yet as she goes to Africa to fix a failing project. The day-to-day problems encountered by Sam in her work are typical of any project manager in the Congo which has been rent apart by warring factions, leaving the local population frightened and rootless. Elephants with pink tusks do exist, but not in the area where the project is based. They are being slaughtered by poachers in Gabon for the Chinese market and will soon be extinct, so I have put the guns in the hands of those responsible for the massacre of these defenceless animals.

The Bonita Protocol - Book 5

An erratic boss. Suspicious results. Stock market shenanigans. Can Sam Harris expose the scam before they silence her? It's 1996. Geologist Sam Harris has been around the block, but she's prone to nostalgia, so she snatches the chance to work in Sierramar, her old stomping ground. But she never expected to be working for a company that is breaking all the rules. When the analysis results from drill samples are suspiciously high, Sam makes a decision that puts her life in peril. Can she blow the lid on the conspiracy before they shut her up for good? The Bonita Protocol sees Sam return to Sierramar and take a job with a junior exploration company in the heady days before the Bre-X crash. I had fun writing my first megalomaniac female boss for this one. I have worked in a few junior companies with dodgy bosses in the past, and my only comment on the sector is buyer beware…

Digging Deeper - Book 6

A feisty geologist working in the diamond fields of West Africa is kidnapped by rebels. Can she survive the ordeal or will this adventure be her last? It's 1998. Geologist Sam Harris is desperate for money so she takes a job in a tinpot mining company working in war-torn Tamazia. But she never expected to be kidnapped by blood thirsty rebels.

Working in Gemsite was never going to be easy with its culture of misogyny and corruption. Her boss, the notorious Adrian Black is engaged in a game of cat and mouse with the government over taxation. Just when Sam makes a breakthrough, the camp is overrun by rebels and Sam is taken captive. Will anyone bother to rescue her, and will she still be alive if they do?

I worked in Tamazia (pseudonym for a real place) for almost a year in different capacities. The first six months I spent in the field are the basis for this book. I don't recommend working in the field in a country at civil war but, as for many of these crazy jobs, I needed the money.

Concrete Jungle - Book 7 (series end)

Armed with an MBA, Sam Harris is storming the City - But has she swapped one jungle for another?

Forging a new career was never going to be easy, and Sam discovers she has not escaped from the culture of misogyny and corruption that blighted her field career.

When her past is revealed, she finally achieves the acceptance she has always craved, but being one of the boys is not the panacea she expected. The death of a new friend presents her with the stark choice of compromising her principals to keep her new position, or exposing the truth behind the façade. Will she finally get what she wants or was it all a mirage?

I did an MBA to improve my career prospects, and much like Sam, found it didn't help much. In the end, it's only your inner belief that counts. What other people say, or think, is their problem. I hope you enjoy this series. I wrote it to rid myself of demons, and it worked.

Box Sets

Sam Harris Adventure Box Set Book 2-4
https://bookgoodies.com/a/B07LH8G6BG
Sam Harris Adventure Box Set Book 5-7
https://bookgoodies.com/a/B09411NQHW
Sam Harris Adventure Box Set Books 2-7
https://bookgoodies.com/a/B0BR8F9NDK

Mortal Mission

written as Pip Skinner

When the science officer for the first mission to Mars dies suddenly, backup Hattie Fredericks gets the coveted place on the crew. But her presence on the

Starship provokes suspicion when it coincides with a series of incidents which threaten to derail the mission. After a near-miss while landing on the planet, the world watches as Hattie and her fellow astronauts struggle to survive. But, worse than the harsh elements on Mars, is their growing realisation that someone, somewhere, is trying to destroy the mission.

When more astronauts die, Hattie doesn't know who to trust. And her only allies are 35 million miles away. As the tension ratchets up, violence and suspicion invade both worlds. If you like science-based sci-fi and a locked-room mystery with a twist, you'll love this book.

You can order any of these books in paperback at your favourite retailer. Please go to the PJSKINNER website for links.

Connect with the Author

About the Author

The author has spent 30 years working as an exploration geologist managing remote sites and doing due diligence of projects in more than thirty countries. During this time, she has been collecting tall tales and real-life experiences which inspired her to write the Sam Harris Adventure Series chronicling the adventures of a female geologist as a pioneer in a hitherto exclusively male world.

PJ has worked in many countries in South America and Africa in remote, strange, and often dangerous places, and loved every minute of it, despite encountering her fair share of misogyny and other perils. She is now writing these fact-based adventure books from the relative safety of London but still travels all over the world collecting data for her writing.

The Sam Harris Adventure Series is for lovers of intelligent adventure thrillers happening just before the time of mobile phones and internet. It has a unique viewpoint provided by Sam, a female interloper in a male world, as she struggles with alien cultures and failed relationships.

PJ's childhood in Ireland inspired her to write Rebel Green, about an English family who move to Ireland during the beginnings of the Troubles. She has written a follow-on in the same Green Family Saga called Africa Green which follows Isabella Green as she goes to Sierra Leone to write an article on a chimpanzee sanctuary. She is now writing a third in the series, Fighting Green, about Liz Green's return to live in Ireland.

She is now mulling a series of Cosy Mysteries, or a book about… You'll have to wait and see.

Follow PJ on Amazon to get informed of her new releases. Please subscribe to the Newsletter for updates and offers

You can also follow the author on Twitter, Instagram, Tiktok, or on Facebook @pjskinnerauthor

Printed in Great Britain
by Amazon

40990191R00172